The christmas Dining Club

OF INTERESTING OCCURRENCES

(12 Tastes of Christmas)

Neil Russell-Jones and Lionel Strub

Fisher King Publishing

To everyone who loves Christmas

Contents

Contents

About the Authors

Neil Russell-Jones is the writer, executive advisor, management consultant and a well-published author with over 15 books: covering management topics, growing food, fiction, history, Sci-fantasy, poetry and he has also written several libretti. He has written many papers on management topics. He is a Non-Executive Director of several not-for-profit organisations covering finance, education and martial arts. He has worked in over 50 countries and his experiences there inspired many of the tales you will read among these pages.

Lionel Strub joined Neil in writing The Dining Club (of Interesting Occurrences). He is the chef/patron of the award-winning Clarendon Inn country pub in the heart of the Yorkshire National Park. Born in France and classically trained Lionel moved to

England thirty years ago.

Lionel has gained many accolades for his cooking including, Professional Chef of the Year, semi-finalist of the National Chef of the Year two years running, Best Rural Pub of the Year and the coveted Outstanding Achievement Award. He is now on the leadership team of the Disciples of Escoffier.

Lionel is author of 'From Alsace to Yorkshire' and has now joined Neil writing this, the second book in The Dining Club of Interesting Occurrences.

Introduction

This book is a collection of short stories. It is based around a group of 12 people who are members of a club that meets approximately once a month for a meal: during each of which a member regales the rest with an extraordinary tale. These 12 people – from many different walks of life – came together as acquaintances or friends of the "Chairman": Professor A. Frank Belvoir, a pathologist. The others are a female Chemical engineer; a female Lawyer; a Ventriloquist/ entertainer/ writer; an Actress; a Nurse; a Banker; a Chief Superintendent; an Architect; a Clergywoman; an Army Officer [ex-SAS] and a Teacher.

Occasionally there might be a guest at any of the meetings, only one at any time, whom one of the members has decided to invite as they also have an extraordinary tale to tell. Thus, on some nights 13 sit down to supper: in which case an extra place is laid for those of a superstitious disposition. The raconteur also decides on the menu – and sends it in advance. They choose the food and drinks on a theme that reflects their tale and is usually linked to the main location of the story. Water is always provided. The member always tells their tale first and then the guest, where one is present, tells theirs.

The members are referred to by the nicknames that the

group has given them:

Chemical engineer	'The Boffin';
Lawyer	'Dryasdust';
Ventriloquist/ entertainer/ writer	'Archie';
Actor	'Janus';
Nurse	'Angel';
Banker	'Marley';
Policeman [CSI]	'Shamus';
Architect	'Eddy';
Clergywoman	'Mary';
Army Officer [SAS]	'Fruity';
Teacher	'Podge'.

The Chairman is known as 'The Professor', and it is in his London town house that they meet. His people – a butler, Groves; a gardener-cum-handyman, Old Jack; and a cook, Mrs Groves - the wife of the butler - prepare and serve the meals. The rules of the club also make provision for the raconteur to bring a chef or cook: for some of the dishes are, to say the least, not the usual fayre you might find in a typical British household; and this assistance is welcomed by Mrs Groves.

Each story has a different setting and a menu that goes with it and in some cases relevant, and in others central, to the tale. The stories are written for enjoyment and have twists and interesting items to hold attention. Some involve deaths or attempted deaths; others crimes, some are humorous, ghost stories or mysteries. The stories do not necessarily have to have involved the member who tells the tale directly or even indirectly; although in many cases this is so.

This book contains 12 stories which were told during meetings of our club over the Christmas period, and across a number of years. They do not reflect the song 'The 12 days of Christmas' but instead reflect some key days/festivals/ historic events which broadly occur during that festive period. The first story is told on the first Sunday in Advent and they continue until 6th January – Epiphany – the day after 12th night.

The exact start and finish of the 12 days of Christmas is unclear and hotly disputed. Some say it starts on Christmas Day, the 25th December: some say the day after Boxing Day/Feast of St Stephen - and so there is controversy as to when 12th night occurs.

The key thing is the word 'eve' – which has become translated as night - but means the evening before (in this case the evening before the 12th day). The twelfth eve is thus the 5th – so the 12th day is the 6th.

The club takes 12th night or 'eve' as the 5th January - the day before Epiphany – when, by tradition the Wise Men arrived and, also traditionally in some countries e.g. Spain, children only then receive presents. Thus the 12th day of Christmas is the 6th of January.

This controversy does not affect the stories.

Each story not only has a location/culinary theme, as usual, but also has a specific spice/herb theme – hence the '12 tastes of Christmas.'

As before Lionel has created unique recipes to reflect the festive settings.

In this volume – each story has a Christmas or winter related poem to accompany it. Each member was asked to craft a poem – if they felt able. The majority did – some were not accepted, others produced several, so we have a blend of poems covering winter and the festive period.

A Star

The star foretold the coming of the Baby Jesus so what better poem to start with: and the Professor read it out.

A Star hangs on the Christmas tree
To symbolise the babe who there was born
With ox and ass surrounding him
Upon that blessed ancient Christmas morn
There in that stable, cold, windswept, forlorn.

The Lights hang on the Christmas tree
Reminding us of shining Beth'lem ray
That led the shepherds to his crib
In time to see him there on Christmas day
The Wise Men were still plodding on their way.

The Baubles on the Christmas tree
Remind us of the message that He brought
Of peace and joy and happiness
Across the world in evr'y deed and thought
The Wise Men journeying that wisdom sought.

The Lament on the Christmas tree
Reminds us of the Virgin's later tears
When she sat weeping by a tree

Though that was not for many, many years
She wept to see our hope cut down by spears.

The Tinsel on the Christmas tree
Reflects the shining, starry midnight sky
With angels winging from the dark
And singing sweetly, gladly from on high
The wind blew through the stable with a sigh.

The Presents by the Christmas tree
They follow the tradition of the Kings
Of gifts they brought to that small babe
The Christmas choir evr'y Yuletide sings
And we repeat the song that each bell rings.

And over all the Christmas Tree
Reminds us of that peaceful joyous birth
In that poor stable long ago
With shepherds kneeling on the strawy earth
Which we recall with jollity and mirth.

And high above the star shines bright
A symbol of that special heavenly night
When angels sent that special call
To bring the shepherds to that stall
To worship in that wonderous, graceful light

Story and Culinary Themes

12 tastes/days of Christmas – not as per the song

Spices/herbs	Event	Date/key feature
Cinnamon	1st Sunday in Advent	Prophets' candle 1
Nutmeg	2nd Sunday in Advent	Bethlehem candle 2
Ginger	3rd Sunday in Advent	Shepherd's candle 3
Cloves	Shortest day/Winter Solstice	21 - 12
Mace	Christmas Eve	24 - 12
Sage & Onion	Christmas Day	25 - 12
Frankincense	Boxing Day	
	(St Stephen's Day)	26 - 12
Thyme and Parsley	Little New Year's Eve	30 - 12
Coriander	Sylvester Abend	
	(New Year's Eve)	31 - 12
Cardamon	New Year's Day	1 - 1
Star Anise	Perihelion	4 - 1
Paprika	Epiphany	6 - 1

1st   candle symbolising Hope

2nd   candle symbolising Faith

3rd   candle symbolising Joy

4th   candle lit on Christmas Day symbolising Peace - a fifth candle is also usually lit in the middle of the Advent wreath to symbolise the arrival of the Baby Jesus.

The first Sunday in Advent

The First Advent Candle

This is the candle, the first that we light
The candle for what you say?
The candle for that first Advent night
When night was turned into day.

It is the first of four we light
They stand for peace, love, hope and joy.
To shine out clear and shine out bright
To herald the birth of a boy.

The first reminds us to think of peace
That the Christ-child's birth will bring.
All wrapped in blankets or inside a fleece
of whose coming the Angels sing.

Its colour is a purple hue
A symbol of waiting, restraint.
For a prophecy that was brought to you
Of the birth of a heavenly Saint.

It goes on a wreath – full five in all
That will hang from the church's rafter.
As we wait for the birth in that lonely stall
And the promise of heaven thereafter.

We shall light the rest as the weeks go by
In order, one by one.
Till all five are lit and the flames fly high
For the Advent season's begun.

The Fountain of Artemis

As we entered, we could see that the room was festooned with Christmas decorations, but no tree as yet, and there was an odd-looking juxtaposition of the festive hangings and oddments with occasional Greek artefacts.* There was, inter alia, a statue of Zeus hurling a thunderbolt, one of Athene and a representation of the Acropolis in what looked like icing sugar. All quite small – and I remembered that, when I had been to Athens and seen the Zeus statue in the museum, it had actually been disappointingly small in real life as well.

We were offered a glass of wine, Groves murmuring that it was a white wine from one of the Greek islands, although I didn't catch the name – but it was dry, nice and chilled and very pleasant.

When we were all assembled, and before we sat down to dine, the Professor stood by a wreath suspended from the roof in the corner of the room, on which we could see five candles.

'This wreath and these five candles represent the candles of Advent – as is traditional: although few actually light the candles in their homes now. I thought, however, it would be a nice tradition for our little group. As I am sure you know, a candle is lit on each Sunday in Advent, progressively and the fifth one finally on Christmas Day itself. Across the years, as I hope that we shall continue to meet during the festive season, this is something I will do each year. Given that we only meet approximately monthly during each of our meetings, although we have tended to meet twice during this very special and festive season, the candles that are lit and to be lit will, of course, vary.'

He said, and lit the first one.

He then spoke again with a degree of solemnity - as was befitting – but not too much.

'This is the First Candle of Advent. It is known as the 'Prophets' Candle' as well as 'The Candle of Hope'. It is named in anticipation of the birth of a Messiah and/or Redeemer – i.e. Hope.' It burned whilst we ate and during the tale.

We started with a selection of Greek mezes, followed by a chicken soup with hint of cinnamon – highly unusual, but in keeping with the taste of Christmas along with broad bean guacamole served with haloumi & sweetcorn fritters. For the main course – Spanakopita - Spinach pie – which was new to us all. This was followed by almond & cinnamon short bread with honey roasted figs.

We were offered coffee afterwards, with or without cinnamon, depending on taste, which is a very acquired taste, as I mentioned to Groves when he offered it to me and I declined. Truly this had been a real culinary adventure. We looked forward to the tale.

We had finished eating and Groves had served a glass of a pudding wine for those who wished it, and then Mary stood to tell us her tale.

'This tale is from when I was on a cruise in the Greek Islands. A 'culture vulture' cruise where there was a professor of something or other to do with Greek history and the Ancient Mediterranean, who would tell us the history of each island and/or famous site which we were visiting. It was very interesting. We went in winter as it is less crowded then: and also a good deal cheaper which, when you are de facto a pensioner – and not in receipt of a particularly good pension at that - is an important consideration. The academics are free from lectures for the Christmas holidays and this is a good way of supplementing their income – and an opportunity for them to show off a little!

We had visited a few islands, which had had one or two interesting items worth seeing such as a very nice temple to Artemis and an amphitheatre, which appeared to be in the middle of the Mediterranean with no real purpose – but in very good condition. We sat on the stone benches and someone declaimed a part of Homer, I think it was, all 'wine dark seas and so on' I suppose although it was in Attic Greek of course, and I must say that the acoustics were spot on. It had been built into a hill or mountainside and felt very real, not to say uncomfortable, sitting on cold stone: I suspect that piles were a common feature of Greek life if you went to see plays unless you had a cushion. It is interesting how all those years ago the Greeks got that engineering aspect right.

Then the Professor had told us the amphitheatre was, in fact, a 19th century folly, built by the owner of the island; and that he would sometimes invite friends to stay and bring players from a Greek theatre company to re-enact Greek tragedies. The last one had been a play about Troy and Hecuba the wife of Priam, King of Troy, who after its fall was enslaved by Odysseus. That explained why it was there in the middle of nowhere.

One thing I recalled from my study of Greek plays – Sophocles, Euripedes and Homer etc is that there is not a lot of joy and mirth. The Iliad starts with tragedy of Eris sowing discord at the wedding feast of Thetis and Peleus, runs through the Judgement of Paris, due to the cowardice of Zeus, which incurs him the enmity of Hera and Athena, which leads to the sacrifice of Agamemnon's daughter, the destruction of Troy, the death of Patroclus and Achilles – Greek heroes - then of Hector, Paris and the rest of the Trojans, the assassination of Agamemnon by his wife, her death by her son etc and leads into the Odyssey. So dark!

We returned to the boat and had our evening meal. I sat on the deck, out of the wind, for it was a little cold being early December, and remembered that it was Sunday. The first Sunday in Advent. One or two others were also enjoying the evening light and joined me. There were two Americans from the north west – Montana I seem to recall; two Scandinavians from Finland, with more vowels than consonants in their names; another English person who was an ex-international consultant; and a Welsh couple on their honeymoon (I assumed their second from their age and some comments they made par passu); as well as two Germans from the Rhineland. I mentioned the date and we had a short discussion about it and what it had meant in the past to them. The Germans and Americans had especially strong memories from their churches, but the over-riding memory was that, after children had grown up and nativity plays were less common for us to attend, it almost always passed by unnoticed in the run up to Christmas itself. I went to the galley and asked for a night light. I brought it back and lit it to serve as our Advent candle. It burned softly, guttering in the breeze – the gentle Zephyr of Greek tales.

We finished our wine, and then the steward had come round and taken orders for, and served, a warm drink against the wind which was just becoming a little fresher and we wrapped our jumpers around our shoulders, and then we turned in, for we had been told to get a good night's sleep. The next day was a very interesting trip, we had been informed by the Greek Professor, but it involved a good climb, not too arduous, but not so easy. As most, if not all, of the people on the cruise were well past their first flush of youth this was sage advice!

As I was making my way back to my cabin, I heard two voices. They were American and I realised it was that odd couple. She was a woman of very matronly proportions indeed, reminding me of the lady in the Marx Brothers' films who was often the butt of Groucho's rudeness and he a small, slight wisp of a man. She was giving him a very hard time and I recalled that this had been the same since the cruise started. Many of the people on the cruise were American and the rest were mainly British. It is a US/UK thing I suppose to go on culture cruises. There was also a smattering of Scandinavians and the odd German or two, and a large French extended family.

The American woman was talking to her husband: at least so I assumed, that is what he was. And it would be more accurate to state that she was talking AT him, in a very condescending and nasty manner. Berating him for being so useless and poor and how that, without her money, he would have starved. I also recalled that whenever we had seen them, she would be eating, and I also recalled she made steady inroads into the buffet each evening. He merely picked at a meagre helping on his plate. She was dressed in expensive looking, but ill-fitting clothes. They had to be, I thought, due to her size; and covered in jewellery. I don't know why people like that, who are grossly overweight, think that lots of diamonds and gold etcetera make them look thinner and prettier. They don't, of course, they just draw attention to their size. Her fingers were fleshy and bulged over her many rings which looked painfully tight on her hands. He was dressed in well-cut, but shabby clothes which had clearly seen much better days. I assumed that she had come into money somewhere along the line of their married relationship, whilst he had probably lost his money or his job. Very sad, and they were avoided by most of the rest of the passengers, after the first day, due both to her behaviour towards him and generally as a glutton. Poor little man I thought, he needs to get away.'

Mary took a sip of water, wiped her lips delicately on a napkin, and then carried on.

'Her berating could be still be heard as I walked back to my cabin.

"You rely on my money, you useless little worm. Without me you would starve, unless you learn to eat grass!"

He murmured something indistinct – some sort of "Yes dear." I suppose. Poor little man I thought again. Then her voice lifted up once more in an unpleasant shrill tone.

"Yes. Unless you can eat grass, you will starve without me. Now come let us retire, I am hungry, and we have a steep climb tomorrow."

I closed my cabin door and thankfully, as the door and walls were made of robust steel, I could no longer hear her mithering. I slept well and arose next morning for breakfast.

The breakfast was a buffet style as usual, and in deference to the UK/US clientele it always offered many aspects of what we would call an English breakfast - that is eggs, bacon and sausages - as well as many local Greek delicacies, which were worth trying as a nice change and, after all that is one of the things about travel – to try new foods and experiences. At home I rarely have a full English – except occasionally at weekends, or if we have guests.

So. After breakfast we assembled on the deck for our trip. We were docked at a very nice little Greek harbour where the white marble of the buildings sparkled against the wine dark sea. See my Homeric allusion there?' she added as an aside

'We were told once again, as we had been told at dinner the night before, that walking boots were essential for this climb but, as all appeared to be wearing them, we were, we thought, set to go. Then the Professor noticed that the little wispy husband was not wearing boots, but instead a pair of broken-down slip-on shoes.

"I am afraid that they will not be adequate. You will get no grip from those shoes."

"Well, my friend. These are all I have I am afraid." And he shrugged his shoulders. His wife said nothing but looked insufferably smug.

Then one of the French extended family said "Monsieur, you look about the same size as me in shoe terms. I have a spare set which you can borrow. Come with me. Immediatement, s'il vous plait. And he quickly, before the little man's wife could say anything, took the little man away. They came back a few minutes later with him wearing a decent set of boots.

"So…" said our guide "..now we are ready let us go. Ase mas tote" he added in Greek

We disembarked and assembled at the foot of a white path that we could see would wind up and across the hill. It looked like a good climb and, due to the criss-crossing around the hill, I thought it would be quite a long one.

As of he had read my thoughts the guide said

"Do not worry. We have arranged for a stop half way up at, what would you call it, ah yes, a 'way station', for a quick lunch and a good drink."

"We will take it in easy stages." Added our Professor of Ancient Greek History.

On the way up, which we took at an easy ambling pace, the Professor told us about the history of the island. His voice, although not strident, was very clear and we could all hear him.

"It is believed that this island was sacred to Artemis -the goddess of the hunt. She was Apollo's sister and the favourite goddess of the Greek rural poor as she looked after animals. She was said to dance in the hills and on this island with wood nymphs. She is also associated with springs, wells and running waters – often attended by Naiads - the water nymphs - and in fact at the top we shall see a fountain that is sacred to her.

We walked up and around and across the hill. It was very pleasant and, as it was December not too hot. I thought I would not like to climb up this hill in summer!

We reached the way station and there was our faithful steward from the ship: with a very appetising spread of mezes, Greek wine and water. There were plenty of stone benches on which to sit, so we sat there nibbling at various pieces of interesting food and generally chatting. The children of the French family sat on the benches with their legs swinging gently eating their food. It reminded me of mine when they were that sort of age. I could see that the big lady was tucking into the food with gusto, whilst her husband was merely picking at his food. She was giving him a hard time again.

"You really embarrassed me with your sad shoes, but of course, you have no money so you could not buy any new ones. Well, you should have saved from your allowance."

He said something back indistinct – probably "But my allowance isn't enough." Or something similar – for she got really angry and laid into him again.

"Well maybe when you learn to eat grass, you can also develop hooves and run free in the hills and pastures with no need for shoes."

She really was objectionable.

Apart from that it was a pleasant meal. I got to chatting to the Finns who remarked that that lady was a pig and quite horrid. This was my view, but I thought it unChristian to say so, so I merely nodded. The American couple joined in saying

"Yeah. She really is abhorrent. We know of people like that back in the States. I am ashamed to say that she is American. Would that we were in the Homeric age where Gods and Goddesses listened to mortals and would exact retribution on people like that."

I shrugged my shoulders and said "auto einai I moria" - that is fate!

The Greek Professor was sitting near us and having heard added "oi theoi ta blepoun ola!"

We all looked blank and he added "The Gods see all!" and then he crossed himself in the Orthodox way with finger and thumb together.

Clearly hedging his bets, I thought.

We had finished our meal and the guide said "Well. Ready for the final ascent?"

We all nodded.

He set off again at an easy pace, which we found easy to cope with. After about an hour or so easy going we reached the summit.

The guide said "Look left first."

We did, and could see how far we had come. It looked a lot further than it felt I am glad to say.

"Now look ahead."

We did and there was a small stone fountain, with a marble pedestal and a dish on top – he explained that there was a bubbling spring at the top, under the fountain and we could see the water flowing over the dish and running away over the far lip of the hill.

"This is the fountain of Artemis. Sacred Goddess of Hunt, animals, water and chastity. In the Iliad Agamemnon offended her by killing one of her sacred stags, and thus she commanded Boreas, the wind God not to blow; and marooned the Greeks so they could not sail to Troy. As expiation she demanded a sacrifice. And not just any sacrifice – but his daughter. He tricked his wife Clytemnestra into bringing his and her daughter to Aulis where the becalmed fleet was, by telling her that Iphigenia was to wed Achilles. But then he killed her. The wind then blew – but Clytemnestra became his enemy and killed him when he returned to Mycenae! It was a tough old world then!"

I had always thought that.

"Now." Said our Greek Professor "This fountain, sacred to Artemis, is said to grant wishes to those in utter dire need who drink from it. Just a myth of course, but it is good for tourism. I am not aware of anyone who has had a wish granted – but perhaps they were not in dire straits enough."

We all laughed at that and I noticed that the little wispy man sidled over to the fountain and took a long drink.

We enjoyed the view and then after a while we started down the path. After about half an hour or so I noticed that the large lady and her husband were not with us and drew it to the attention of our guide. He suggested we stopped at the way station and that some of us went back up to find them, as it turned cold of an evening in the hills, and they would suffer if they stayed and perhaps they had got lost. I could not bring myself to worry about her to be honest, but I felt for that little chap so I volunteered to accompany him back up. It wasn't too far and I like to think I am fit. The Finns came too.

We crested the hills and walked across to the fountain. What we saw will stay with me until the end of my days as an inexplicable thing. There was a goat, eating grass and running and gambolling free, and a fat pig snuffling around for things to eat. Lying next to the fountain were the boots that the French family had lent to the little man. There was a pile of what looked like rags and they were a few clothes, ripped and torn and of no value, but on top were a few gold rings.

We stood open mouthed and then the goat ran down the hill and disappeared. The pig had what looked like a gold band on one of its trotters and it too ran down the hill.

We looked at each other and agreed with the Greek Professor that the interpretation we had all subconsciously put on this was impossible and that it was clear that they had decided to leave the cruise for whatever reason.

We picked up the boots and walked down in silence, returning the boots to the kind French family. I can say that I had a very large whisky that evening.'

The Professor extinguished the candle and we all left: deep in thought.

The Fountain of Artemis

menu

Broad Bean Guacamole

Flat Bread

Haloumi and Sweetcorn Fritter

Chicken and Cinnamon Soup

Spinakopita - Spinach Pie

Almond & Cinnamon Short Bread
with Honey Roasted Figs

Flat bread

Prep time:	10 minutes
Cooking time:	4 minutes
Method:	easy
Serves:	12

Ingredients

- 500 gr self raising flour
- 500 gr wholemeal flour
- 100 ml rapeseed oil
- 50 gr butter - optional
- 2 teaspoons salt

Method

Using a medium bowl

- add flour, salt, 2 tbs oil & 150 ml warm water
- mix until dough is soft but not sticky
- knead for 3 minutes
- leave to rest for 20 minutes
- divide into 6 equal amount and roll each out into a thin 20cm circle
- using a non-stick pan on a medium heat drizzle a little amount of oil into it
- cook the flat bread for one minute on each side
- leave to cool

Chef's tip: If the dough is sticky add flour & add water if too dry. You can brush the flat bread with a bit of butter to give extra flavour and shine.

Broad bean guacamole

Prep time	20 minutes
Cooking time	N/A
Serves	12
Method	easy

Ingredients

- 500 gr broad beans shelled - fresh or frozen
- 2 avocados
- juice of 1 lemon
- 3 tablespoons Olive oil
- 3 garlic cloves chopped finely
- salt & pepper – to taste
- smoked paprika – to taste

Method

Using a mortar & pestle

- peel and mash the broad beans
- add avocado and keep mashing
- add salt, pepper to taste
- add a sprinkle of smoked paprika
- add lemon juice & olive oil
- mix well
- serve at room temperature

Haloumi & sweetcorn fritter

This will go well with the broad bean guacamole

Preparation time	20 minutes
Cooking time	4 minutes

Serves   12

Method   easy

Ingredients

- 600 gr sweetcorn - tinned or frozen
- 3 eggs
- 100 gr plain flour
- 1 teaspoon baking powder
- 4 spring onions finely chopped
- 1 teaspoon cinnamon
- 150 gr halloumi cut into small cubes
- fresh coriander
- oil

Method

In a food processor:

- put in half the sweetcorn, eggs, flour, baking powder, salt & cinnamon
- blitz until smooth
- transfer to a medium bowl
- add the remaining sweetcorn, spring onions, halloumi & coriander
- mix well
- season to taste
- using a non-stick frying pan:
- add oil
- add a good spoonful of the mixture and leave to cook for 1 minutes each side or golden brown
- repeat the process until all cooked

Chicken & cinnamon soup

Preparation time	25 minutes
Cooking time	1 hour
Serves	12
Method	easy

Ingredients

- 12 chicken thighs
- 2 litres of chicken stock
- 2 onions chopped
- 4 garlic cloves
- 1 chilli - medium heat
- 1 tablespoon cinnamon
- 4 tomatoes
- 500 gr potatoes diced into small cubes
- fresh coriander
- roasted peanuts
- sultanas

Method

- place the chicken thighs in an oven tray
- season to taste
- sprinkle cinnamon
- add onions, chilli, tomatoes & potatoes
- cook for 1 hour in the oven 180*C (Gas mark 4)
- remove the bones from the thighs
- in a large saucepan
- add the chicken stock

- add the chicken, tomatoes, potatoes & onions
- stir well and bring to the boil
- simmer for 1 hour
- season to taste
- sprinkle coriander, peanuts & sultanas
- serve hot

Spanakopita - Spinach pie

Preparation time	30 minutes
Cooking time	30 minutes
Serves	12
Method	easy

Ingredients

- 1 kilo spinach
- 1 leek chopped
- 5 spring onions
- 100 ml olive oil
- 4 garlic cloves crushed
- 300 gr feta cheese
- cinnamon
- nutmeg
- 1 pack of filo pastry
- salt & pepper

Method

In a large pan:

- add olive oil, garlic, leek & spring onions
- cook gently for 5 minutes

- add the spinach, salt & pepper
- cook for a further 2 minutes
- add cinnamon, nutmeg & feta cheese
- cook for 2 more minutes
- leave to cool

Using a shallow tart mould

- line the filo overlapping the mould
- 4 sheets of filo for the bottom
- place the spinach mixture into the mould
- add a further 4 sheets of filo for the top
- brush the top with olive oil
- bake for 30 minutes at 180*C – Gas Mark 4
- leave to cool before lifting out of the mould

Chef's tip: for a vegan dish use non-dairy cheese.

Almond and cinnamon short bread with honey roasted figs

Preparation time	30 minutes
Cooking time	15 minutes
Serves	12
Method:	easy

Ingredients

- 12 fresh figs
- honey
- 200 gr flaked almonds
- 500 gr unsalted butter 'soft'
- 150 gr icing sugar

- cinnamon
- 4 egg yolks
- 3 tablespoons of vanilla essence
- 500 gr self raising flour

Method

Using a frying pan at medium heat:

- toast the almonds until brown
- leave to cool
- pre heat the oven to 180*C (Gas Mark 4)

Using a roasting tin:

- place the figs in it and drizzle honey over them
- cook in the oven for 15 minutes
- leave to cool
- using a medium bowl:
- add the butter, icing sugar
- mix well
- add egg yolks, vanilla essence, cinnamon
- mix well again
- add the almonds
- add the flour until it forms a dough
- leave to rest for 30 minutes room temperature
- roll the dough to 1 cm thick

Using a pastry cutter:

- cut 12 large round shapes for the shortbread
- bake for 15 minutes at 180*C – Gas Mark 4
- leave to cool

- place the shortbread on a plate add a fig on top with juice
- optional cream

The Second Sunday in Advent

The Second Advent Candle

This is the second candle of light
To join the first on the crown.
The Bethlehem candle, named for the mite
Who was born in that Judean town.

There are now two candles which we can see
Shining out in the night.
The second brings hope for you and me
With its flame that shimmers so bright.

Its colour is blue, but the flame is white
As it glows out all around.
Symbolising the hope which that rare night
Brought to all where're they were found.

We are half way now to the Virgin birth
As the Advent Season moves on.
And the song of the Angels covers the earth
Even after the candles have gone.

The green hued wreath is two fifths alight
With a brace of Sundays to go.
'Til that Holy, Sacred, special night
When the word was made 'just so'.

A Question of Cheese

It was a typical December rainy day as we arrived at the Professor's house and, as we entered, we were given a plateful of crumbly cheese with biscuits, and a glass of very nice white wine, to take to our seats. Groves said "This is a French wine, in fact from Alsace, a very nice Riesling - which goes very well with the cheese."

The cheese was delicious and Groves informed us that it was a Múnsterkaas, a speciality of Alsace-Lorraine and I confess that few, if any of us, had heard of it – never mind tasted it – but it was, nevertheless, excellent.

Then, the Professor arose and went over to the Advent wreath with the five candles on it. It was in a different location from last year I noticed, now nearer the front of the room. The first candle was burning as he lit the second one.

'This is the second candle – known as the Bethlehem candle – that is the candle of Faith.'

So now the two candles burned brightly in that dim corner of the room.

We were then served a solidly French meal consisting of a very nice wild boar terrine to start with, followed by a main course of Chou croute which is, as Groves also pointed out, the Alsace-Lorraine version of sauerkraut, but with a difference as it is served with sausages or other meats along with large dishes of potatoes and a walnut rye loaf. This was accompanied by a different wine, also from Alsace – a Sylvaner – which I recalled my wine society had described as vivacious and spontaneous with the personification of spring – who writes this stuff?!

We finished our main course which was followed by a delicious pudding of Tarte au Mirabelles and, for those who still had room, a small minority I felt, as I gently touched my stomach, a further helping of cheese, served with Schnapps – which latter I gratefully received – also an Alsatian marc.

We could see that we had a guest, and those who had managed to chat to him had understood, from his accent, that he was French. Dry-As-Dust stood up and introduced the guest.

'This is an old friend of mine. I got to know him through a few business projects on which he was good enough to engage our firm and I, as a French speaker, was despatched to our French office to oversee it. I shall not tell you his name. I will leave it to him to tell the tale and give such details as are pertinent. I believe it is a most interesting story for us here tonight.'

At this the guest arose, fiddled with his tie, tugged at his shirt collar nervously as though he was unused to wearing such 'formal' attire, coughed a little and then, sipping a little of the excellent schnapps, started to tell his tale.

'Bonsoir tout le monde: Good evening, everyone. I am

French, as you may have noticed, in fact from Alsace-Lorraine, and although the difference may seem slight to you British – for us it is of vital importance. As vital, peut-etre, as the difference between English, Welsh, Scots, and Northern Irish. We are tucked away in the middle-east part of France and our two provinces, sisters as someone once described them, have see-sawed back and forth between both France and our historical enemy – Germany. Now we are once again wholly within the French embrace, and all is well and peaceful. Eh Bien. Forgive me, my English is not too strong so, if I lapse into the French occasionally, bear with me s'il vous plait, please.

We have a rich and varied history and you have probably seen the films from the early 20th Century of the girls in local garb with the very grand, that is to say large and distinctive, headwear and very full dresses. We incorporate the Moselle region – known to you I am sure - and famous for wines if nothing else! It is today known as 'Bas- Rhine' which I am absolutely sure means nothing to you.'

There was a general nodding of heads here – but whether agreeing, disagreeing or just being generally agreeable was impossible to tell. The superb wines and the very agreeable schnapps had mellowed everyone.

'I understand from my good friend here, and Dry-as-Dust gave a slight incline of the head, that you enjoy interesting tales, with all sorts of topics, locales and out-turns, Hein? I have a tale to tell you tonight which I think you will find interesting. However, I need to take you back to a television interview given on mainstream French TV a few years ago.'

He paused and sipped a little of his wine and nibbled a morsel of cheese. Then he took a deep breath and carried on.

'Imagine a television studio in France. A man is being interviewed. You can see from his persona that he is very relaxed. The interviewer asks him to tell his story.

He says "I'm very lucky. I have just sold my chain of stores to a very large conglomerate. It has made me some money – but I have worked hard for it."

The interviewer is wearing a very sharp suit and has flashing white teeth and looks like a TV 'personality' but not a star. The interviewee looks very comfortable and very relaxed wearing a well-worn, but exquisitely cut, suit of tweed. As he crosses his legs, we can see that he is wearing very good shoes. He has a beautifully tailored shirt, with discrete, but expensive looking cufflinks and, were it not for the large diamond ring on one of his fingers, you would have thought he was a member of the old British landed aristocracy, apart from that and his accent of course.

The interviewer picks up on this and asks "Tell me, monsieur, from where did you get those wonderful clothes?"

"Ah well now. They are in fact mainly from England.

The suit I had made a few years' ago in Saville Row, London; the shoes are from Shipton and Heneage, from whom I order my slippers and a few other items. Please understand, mon ami, I am normally for la Belle France in everything – and especially Alsace over étrangers – but not in clothes in this case! For well-fitting, hard-wearing clothes you cannot beat English tailoring. And I mean English – not Scottish. I also have my shoes especially made, as I have unusually shaped feet and, at my age, comfort as well as style – le chic – comme on dit - is important to me."

"And your clothes, so exquisitely cut!"

"Ah oui – encore – made especially for me in England. Mon tailleur est riche!" and he shrugged his shoulders – but he didn't say 'Bouf!'

"So please tell the viewers how you got to where you are today – what is your history, please – S'il vous plait."

"Mais oui – bien sur! I shall do so – but in a roundabout way. I have a story I wish to share – un raconte - if you like – it has a bearing on this."

He crossed his legs, steepled his fingers and closed his eyes – casting his mind back it seemed, then began to speak in a very mellifluous voice.

It was a cold, in fact very cold, winter's day. In the churchyard of a small Alsatian village the Sacristan was going about his duties – that is he was digging a grave. It was hard work, as the ground was frozen, and he had only an old spade with a poor blade, worn down by use. He was about half way down when the priest, Father Antoine, came out to see how he was getting on and pass the time of day. A friendly, well-loved man: who in turn loved his flock and those who worked for him.

"Bonjour M Le Père. How can I help you?" said the Sacristan as he paused from his difficult labour, easing and stretching his back, resting on the spade.

"Rien mon ami – comment ca va? – I was just interested to see how you are getting on with this poor soul's grave."

"Eh bien mon Pere – ca va bien – mais c'est difficile par ce que la terre est tres froid et si dur!"

"Yes I know – in the bleak midwinter the ground is hard as iron and difficult to dig. It will lie all the more heavily on her poor corpse: but we have to hold the ceremony - malhereusement. She was a stalwart of Mother Church. Madame Maxine had a robust personality as well as, hem, a matronly figure. So sad that she passed away at such a relatively young age." And the priest crossed himself and continued "Her family is devastated."

"It is not to be wondered at. They were a close-knit group, and trace their ancestry back for many generations in our lovely Alsatian village. Many sons they gave in the Great War against the Boche. In both wars!" And he spat on the ground.

"Now, now, no need for that – both wars are many years in the past and, whilst devastating, are long over and we now march forward with Germany to a better future."

The sacristan said nothing.

"But mon ami," rejoined the priest "we can both also trace our family back many years. Our church records are detailed and we both have family connections back well into the 17th Century – even if my line comes to an end with me. My oath of celibacy you understand. A sole son of a sole son but I had to respond to my calling."

The Sacristan took the priest's hand and kissed it. "Mon pere – vous et un Divin!"

"Far from it mon ami. I am no Saint. But come: my housekeeper has good chou-croute cooking: so let us share a glass of schnapps on this cold, cold day and then eat."

The priest then coughed heavily into a handkerchief, concealing the material with his hand but not quick enough and thus could not hide from the Sacristan that it was a scarlet splattered cough.

"Father. You are unwell." The priest made a remonstrance. The Sacristan held up his hand. "No, Father. I saw. You should go into the warmth and I will arrange for the Medcin to visit."

"Merci mon ami – tu as raison - mais je pense que… non a ce moment…" and he left the sentence hanging and went back into his house and then into the kitchen, where there was a good fire burning in the grate.

The Sacristan sighed, rapidly finished the grave as the lower down he went, the easier the earth was to remove; put his spade in the tool shed, wiped his hands clean on the towel he carried for this purpose: and then followed the priest inside. He checked that the fire was still alight and burning merrily and then started to make some coffee. He glanced across and saw that the priest was shivering badly so the Sacristan fetched a blanket and gently wrapped the priest in it, and sat him down in front of the fire. He carefully moved the chair closer to the fire to increase the warmth for the priest. He picked up the WWI bayonet, from the Priest's grandfather a veteran of, inter alia, Verdun, and poked the fire to stimulate the flames, with some vigour: as he was still thinking of the evil of the Boche; throwing a couple more logs onto it which crackled and hissed as the moisture was expunged.

"Merci mon ami, mais j'ai besoin de fait fiere. I must be strong. Demain l'Archveque nous visitera."

"Que'st que c'est? What is that? The Archbishop is visiting us tomorrow! – but why?" and the Sacristan crossed himself in reaction.

"Je ne sais pas - I do not know yet. But it is un peu etrange, a little strange." And he coughed a little more, but not as badly as previously.

The Sacristan poured out some coffee for both of

them and they drank their coffee in silence until the housekeeper came in to make the father his evening meal. The Sacristan got up, took both cups back to the sink, motioned her towards him and in hushed tones told her about the coughing. The housekeeper clucked her tongue saying "Aah you must fetch the medcin. Whilst you do that, I will make a good potage and make sure the good father eats it: with some good bread and maybe some of this chou croute which I made earlier, perhaps with a slice of Gendarme – or land jager as you and he call it. He must eat: to keep up his strength. I will see if I cannot tempt him with a little Mont-Blanc.

Before you go to the Medcin, do you bring me some of that excellent fromage which you make – the Munster kaase aussi-tot." And she poured them both a glass of good Alsatian beer and the Priest a small glass of schnapps.

They drank the beer slowly and then she gave the Sacristan a glass of schnapps too. "You will need this – Il fait froid á ce moment – very cold indeed." The Sacristan was, of course, fully aware of this - as he had been digging in the open air: but she meant well, he knew, and he took the schnapps gratefully.

The Sacristan put on his hat, coat and a long, old and frayed, but still warm, scarf and went out to fetch the medcin, for there was not a telephone in the village except at his house and that at the gendarmerie.

As he walked, he could see his breath in the air and, in the moonlight, the frost was glistening on the roads, paths and leafless trees. The rime-frost crackled underfoot. Shrugging his shoulders more closely into his coat, and wrapping the scarf around his mouth and nose, he strode manfully on to the Medcin's house which, as (bad) luck would have it, was on the opposite side of the village from the Priest's house and the Church. Although the village was quite small in population terms – it reflected its typical mediaeval village history – as the population expanded, having followed along the road and, thus, it was strung out along that very road, which was more of a broad lane really, in a long river-like or ribbon shape.

It was a good four kilometres to the doctor's house and he was quite warm when he arrived. He had walked rapidly, for his concern for the good father was deep but, although he wasn't out of breath, but he could feel it in his legs as he rang the bell, caught his breath, and waited for someone to answer it. He leant a little on the doorpost and rested.

This was long before the advent of mobile phones you understand. After only a few moments, however, a maid answered the door and, recognising him: for everyone knew the Sacristan, asked him into the warmth. Gratefully he crossed the lintel explaining to her why he was here. She bit her lip a little and immediately ushered him onto a room, which was the Doctors study, where there was a bit of bright fire burning. He was sitting reading, with a large pipe in his mouth – ironically called in English I believe a Churchwarden - enraptured by the book. The maid announced him and the doctor removed the pipe from his mouth, closed the book, placed it on the table next to a glass of red wine, and asked the Sacristan to sit down gesturing with the stem of the pipe towards a chair.

"Eh bien mon ami! What brings you out on such a cold evening – qu'est-ce que je peux fait pour toi? What can I do for you? S'asseoir." He used the familiar 'tu' form for, although a good man, he was still a doctor and the Sacristan was a rude mechanical, a casual labourer and not at all his equal, incidentally a difference long ago lost in your English language, and a good thing too in my opinion, but he had said it in a friendly enough manner, smiling.

"Non merci monsieur Le Medcin. C'est assez urgent. It is urgent. M Le Prete est malade, tres mauvais, very unwell." And he explained about the coughing, shivering and blood on the handkerchief.

The doctor's face became very grave and he quickly stood up, knocked his pipe out on the ashtray, picked up his black bag and motioned for the Sacristan to follow him out through the back door and to his car, picking up his hat and coat on the way as well, as a pair of driving gloves.

The Sacristan was very glad to be asked to accompany the doctor back in his car: for the night had turned raw, the first few flakes of snow were beginning to drift slowly down, looking like large white ghostly moths in the headlights, and it would have been a very miserable walk back. They were swirling slowly and lazily down. Big flakes, as if it meant to do a good job. On the way to the car, one landed on his sleeve and he gazed intently at it noticing, as if for the first time, the hexagonal symmetry. He stared at it until, ephemeral, it melted: then shaking himself out of his reverie he got

into the car. He mentioned this to the doctor who said by the by.

"Yes. Each snowflake has the same beautiful hexagonal symmetry and every single snowflake is different, unique."

"Pourquoi?"

"Je ne sais pas – mais Le Bon Dieu connait."

"Yes I suppose so. The Good Lord knows all. And he shrugged his shoulders "Beouf!"

The doctor softly hummed an old French carol 'Il est ne le Devin Enfant' until they reached the Priest's house: which did not take long in a car as opposed to the four kilometre walk the Sacristan had had to make. In fact, the car's heater hadn't even got warm before they pulled into the driveway. The Sacristan thanked the doctor for the ride back and led him into the Priest's house.

The housekeeper was there silently kneading dough for tomorrow's bread. She smiled sadly at the doctor who nodded his head saying "Madame."

The Priest was sitting in his favourite chair by the fire, the remains of his supper still on the table beside him, with a half-drunk glass of schnapps in his hand. He was staring intently into the flames, clearly thinking.

The doctor went across, took his hand and said "How are you? Comment ca va?"

The Priest replied "Bien merci, M Le Medcin." He was clearly not being truthful for as he said it, he burst into a fit if extended coughing and a few flakes of blood spattered the handkerchief he was holding and had raised up to his mouth. The doctor felt his pulse, popped a thermometer into his mouth, and in due course examined it. He placed his hands on the Priest's chest ad could clearly feel something disturbing there, for his face was grave as he turned round to his bag.

"M Le Medcin?" said the housekeeper – but he merely shook his head gently. He turned back to Father Antoine. "Father, why didn't you come and see me, or call me sooner?" and he shook his head at this lack of action. "Rest now." And he placed the blanket over the good priest's shoulders and he and the housekeeper helped him into his bed, she bringing a warm hot water bottle, for his feet, which she had prepared whilst the doctor was examining him.

They came back to the Sacristan who was waiting

anxiously by the fire.

"Is the boiler well set to provide central heating?"

"Mai oui, certainnement M Le Medcin."

"Bien, bien. Good, good. He needs rest and warmth."

"But, but, he will be alright won't he?" asked the Sacristan, now very anxious.

"What is wrong with him?" asked the housekeeper

"I am afraid that the good father is unwell. Very unwell indeed."

The housekeeper looked at the doctor's face and stiffed her knuckles into her mouth. The Sacristan said "Mon Dieu. M L'Archveque arrivera demain!"

"What!" said the doctor "The Archbishop is coming here tomorrow – why? He is the new incumbent and, as I understand not very well liked so far." He thought for a moment. "Eh bien. With a little sleep he should be fine to talk to the Archbishop tomorrow. But no more than that. I have given him a sedative for tonight. I shall come back tomorrow as well to check up on him."

"But he will be alright, n'est-ce pas?" asked the sacristan

The doctor merely patted his shoulder gently and closed his bag. The housekeeper was biting her knuckles to hold back the tears. Then she pulled herself together and offered the doctor a glass of schnapps for the cold – which he accepted gratefully. He drank it and placed the glass on the table, picking up his bag.

"Make sure he eats. Some of your excellent cheese too M Le Sacristan. It is full of protein."

And he left them and left behind an atmosphere of deep sadness, sorrow, gloom and not a little foreboding.

The housekeeper and the Sacristan ate their supper largely in that gloomy silence, with a large schnapps both to help with the shock and to come to terms with what the doctor had implied but left unsaid. Then she went home and the Sacristan went to his little room at the back of the house, behind the boiler shed.

The next day dawned crisp, cold and with a few centimetres of snow covering everywhere. It looked beautiful – a real wintry scene in the run-up to Christmas, which of course does not have the same intensity in France, as in the UK where it is a key festival, although given the German influence in Alsace-Lorraine it is more Christmassy than other parts of France – more like you would understand, expect and enjoy here. But it was the Second Sunday in Advent and that is celebrated in France.

The Sacristan was busy that morning making his cheese when a large car pulled up and two young priests sprang out, one opening the door for an older man, pompous looking man who was clearly the Archbishop. The parish priest came out, did a reverence, then burst into a fit of coughing, just as the Archbishop was about to offer him his ring to kiss. The Archbishop withdrew his hand, unkissed, and looked at the priest disdainfully, but one of the younger priests came over and asked him if he was alright. "Bien sur. S'il vous plait – entrez." He replied and opened his front door. The Sacristan was not invited in. Well, he thought - the Archbishop is far too grand and I am far too humble for him to talk to me. And he shrugged his shoulders and strolled off whistling to dig another grave – for that was his job. When he had finished, he was walking back when the door of the house opened and the priest came out – using a walking stick or cane. The Sacristan remembered that in his youth the father had been a master of La Cane Francais – a martial art using a stick. What a change he thought sadly.

He was followed by the two young priests. He was looking pale. One of the priests started the car and the other opened the rear car door. As the Archbishop came out the Priest motioned towards the Sacristan saying "Notre Sacristan." But the Archbishop ignored him and merely got into the car. The young priest closed the door and, as he walked past the Sacristan and Father Antoine, made a small shrug of his shoulders saying "Desole messieurs." And smiled. He then got into the front passenger seat and the car pulled off – a little too fast.

"Such rudeness from a supposed man of god is truly appalling." said Father Antoine and burst into another fit of coughing.

That afternoon was the funeral of the lately departed Madam Maxine. It was intensely cold with a bitter wind adding considerable wind chill to the already freezing air. The priest held the service and the committal: but everybody could see that he was suffering badly. When the funeral was over and after the Pomp Funebres, the undertakers had whipped up the horses and driven the hearse away the Sacristan quickly filled in the grave and then guided the priest gently into the warmth of the kitchen. The housekeeper gave them both a glass of warming schnapps and then placed a bowl of the now famous the world over, but then simply quotidian to the villagers, country vegetable soup with a few slices of the bread she had baked that morning. She put a good helping of the Sacristan's cheese on the plate.

"Your cheese has received many accolades from those visitors to our good father with whom I have shared it. You should sell it at the monthly third Saturday market in the square in the town. My daughter sells her surplus produce there and can give you a lift on the way. The Sacristan absent-mindedly, for he was thinking and worrying about the priest said "Merci beaucoup. Je le pensera – I shall think about it."

A few days after, quite late in the evening, the Sacristan was awoken from a light doze in front of his fire by an urgent knocking at his door. It was the housekeeper. "Vite,

vite M Le Pret est tres malade. Nous avons besoin de le Medcin."

"What's that – we need the doctor?"

"Oui oui! Vite vite"

The Sacristan ran across the road too Rene's farm and asked to borrow his brand new bicycle explaining why.

"Bien sur mon ami." Rene replied "Voila!" and he took him to the shed and pressed it into his hands.

He rode to the doctors in a fury, much faster than normal, and the doctor wasted no time and bundled the Sacristan into his car. "Leave the bicycle here now. Rene can recover it later."

He drove furiously to the church and screeched to a halt in the road.

"Wait here!" he said as he went in: but only a few moments later he came to the door beckoning for the Sacristan to enter. The doctor sat him and the housekeeper down in the kitchen, but they both knew before he spoke what he was going to say.

"Il est mort! Le bon dieu repose son ame!"

The housekeeper wailed and clutched a handkerchief to her face and the Sacristan crossed himself. All three had tears pouring down their cheeks.

"There was nothing that I could do. He was already dead. No blame on you madame. I will go home and I will tell the coroner - he will know what to do."

"But what do we do now?" said the Sacristan it is Sunday tomorrow and we must have divine service tomorrow and we have no Priest." And he threw his arms up into the air and then clasped them across his knees and rocked back and forth.

"I will telephone the bishop. He will do what is necessary." And he squeezed them both on the shoulders in a gesture of companionable solidarity, picked up his, unopened and indeed unnecessary as it had turned out bag, and slowly and sadly went out.

They sat there in silence for some time quite numb: then the housekeeper pulled herself together, stood up and poured them both a good glass of Alsatian wine.

"Votre Santé Pére!" and then they went sadly to bed.

Next day a young priest appeared at the church very early in the morning, knocking on the Sacristan's door. It was one of those who had come to Bishop, the one who had apologised for the Archbishop's rudeness.

"Bonjour Monsieur Le Pret." said the Sacristan "How may I help you?"

"Bonjour. Merci monsieur. I have been sent here by Monsieur l'Eveque for divine service. I am temporary until M L'Archveque chooses the new incumbent."

"S'il vous plait." and the Sacristan lead him into the Church, unlocking it: as he kept the keys and one of his roles was to lock it and unlock it each day. "Sadly, the days when we could leave it unlocked are long since gone. Malheureusement." And he shrugged his shoulders

The word had got round the village and, even for such a devout group, the church was full to overflowing: for Father Antoine had been the incumbent for many years and generations had never known anybody else. The new priest was very pleasant and in sympathy with the village's loss. He personally spoke to all the congregation as they left. A few days later he also conducted the funeral service and committal. The Bishop, but not the Archbishop, also attended and gave comfort to the flock as well, for he had been in his office for many years and knew and loved Father Antoine.

The Sacristan had dug the grave with tears flowing down his cheeks throughout: notwithstanding the coldness which caused ice crystals to form from time to time on his face. He kept at it – digging it in one spell – perspiring profusely but at the same time exorcising his grief demons.

The Priest took it upon himself to walk around the village and get to know the congregation. Well, they all thought, he is a nice young man, even if not local, and he will fit in nicely. After a month or so at Mass the Priest announced that the Archbishop had chosen a replacement priest and that he would be arriving in due course. This caused a flurry of talk. Who would it be? Why not the nice young priest we have already? But when they asked the priest why he wasn't to be the permanent replacement he merely smiled, shrugged his shoulders and said "It will be as the spirit moves M L'Archveque."

This disappointed the village as they had come to like and respect the young priest as he was a genuine shepherd caring for his flock. They, of course, did not think that the new priest would not be the same, but still...

Who will we get? Was the question on everybody's lips, and was the talk of the square, the zinc bar and in the houses when the women met.

Later in the week a car arrived at the church and a priest got out. No-one who saw him recognised him, which was not surprising. Except for the Sacristan. It was the other priest who had accompanied the Archbishop - but of course he knew nothing of him.

"Ah well. On verra!"

It soon became apparent however, that the new incumbent was nothing like Father Antoine nor even the temporary young priest whom he had replaced. Quite quickly he introduced changes. Too many. Too soon after the death of Father Antoine when the village was still mourning the loss of such a long-standing priest. One of the villagers was in the market square of the market town, having given a lift to the Sacristan and his cheese and having helped him set up his stall, he looked up and saw the local priest, whom he knew a little, strolling by. He went over and after a few pleasantries asked him about the new priest that they had. Did he know him? What was his background? And so on. The new priest had not spoken to many of the villagers and so they still knew little about him.

The priest, Father Raoul looked a little embarrassed and then answered softly. "Father Jacques. Why yes. He was at the seminary when I was instructing there. He is the, ahem, nephew of the Archbishop. In confidence I may say he was not well liked at the seminary. Too arrogant and full of himself: especially for a Man of God – say it as I shouldn't." and he crossed himself hastily.

"In what way Pere?"

"I cannot really say – but I wish you 'bon chance avec lui!' I think that you will need it." and he took his leave and went back to his church to prepare.

He returned to the Sacristan, who by now had sold all of his cheese, which was gaining quite a reputation and people had queued up to buy it.

"Eh bien mon ami – c'est deja tout vendee? Fantastique!"

"Yes, my friend all is sold – and so quicky. I have been lucky."

"No no – it is not good luck – it is good cheese."

And they returned to his car and drove back to village. The Sacristan offered money for petrol, but his friend would not hear of it. "I was going there anyway and it gives me great pleasure to help you and to have company on the trip." And he told the Sacristan what he had learned of Father Jacques.

He dropped the Sacristan off at the church – where they could see that the priest was waiting for him.

"Bon chance mon ami." he said as the Sacristan got out and he handed him his bag of provisions. "He looks in a difficult mood."

The Sacristan walked up to the Priest, smiled and said

"Bonsoir M le Pret. Comment puis-je vous aider?"

"I have been waiting for you." said Father Jacques, not pleasantly.

"I am sorry to have kept you waiting Father, but it is Saturday, my day off, and I have been to the market."

"No matter." And he waved his hand diffidently. "I have been pondering on your duties and tasks and I have drawn up a new list with priorities and a schedule of days and timings and what I expect from you by when. Voici! Here!" and he handed the Sacristan a sheaf of papers with handwritten notes, numbers and lines on them.

"Mais Mon Pere – je ne peux pas utiliser cette document."

"Pourqui non?" he replied testily

"Parce-que – je ne peux pas lire."

"What! You cannot read?"

"But you can write?

"Non – nor write either. Desolee!"

"Quoi! Well, I have never heard of such a thing!" and he walked into his house muttering. The Sacristan was very upset and went to his room and sat moodily in front of the fire, wondering and worrying.

By strange chance the very next day the Archbishop arrived, unannounced, to visit his 'nephew' and was told about the Sacristan's illiteracy.

"Well, my son, this will not do. Mother Church cannot have a Sacristan who can neither read nor write. I will be a laughing stock. He must go!"

"Bien sur M L'Archveque." And he poured them both a schnapps.

Next morning Father Jacques summoned the Sacristan into his study and made him stand on the carpet – as if he was a schoolboy getting a dressing down from the headmaster. He explained, not too kindly, that due to his lack of reading and writing he could not continue to be employed as a Sacristan and he must leave. He allowed him a few days to find somewhere else as he would have to move out of his rooms to make way for a new Sacristan once appointed. He offered no condolences whatsoever, and merely turned back to his books.

The Sacristan was devastated, he had been there for 26 years, since he was 14, and it was the only thing he had ever done. He turned on his heel silently and went into the kitchen where the housekeeper was preparing the evening meal. She had heard, and anyway the Priest had already told her, but she was just as upset as the Sacristan. She sat him down and poured him a large Schnapps.

They sat in silence until he said to the housekeeper "What am I going to do? I have always worked here and I have no other skills! And soon I will have nowhere to live!" He sat there disconsolately.

"There, there, mon petit choux.." the housekeeper said "..ne t'on fais pas. Do not fret. I have been thinking about this already. My house has a two room annex where my bellemere used to live, my mother in law, before she died God rest her soul." and she crossed herself "You can stay there."

Merci, Merci beaucoup. Tu es gentille – so kind" he gasped - then "But I cannot pay rent. I have no job."

"Do not worry. I shall not require payment, don't be silly, we have been friends for many years."

He gasped again, shuddered once more and took a large gulp of the schnapps.

But what should I do? I have no job?" he said clearly too distraught to think about the future rationally.

"I have also thought about that mon pauvre garcon. We have an unused shed which you can use to make your most excellent cheese, which you can then sell in the market and earn money. It is really very good cheese and we French and even more we Alsatians love notre fromages."

He is quite overwhelmed by her kindness and still numbed by the magnitude of it all.

She leans a little closer, but not too close, and says in a whisper "For your ears only mon ami. I too am leaving. I do not like our new priest and I cannot work for such an arrogant and callous man even if he is, or purports to be, a man of God. Come now: it will all look very different in the morning." and she gave him a bowl of soup and some bread. "Take this to your rooms, light the fire, eat and get some rest. He took her hand and kissed it tenderly saying "You are so kind Madame, Merci, merci beaucoup!"

Next day the housekeeper's husband and one of her sons took the Sacristan in his very old Renault to show him the room and the shed. He was overwhelmed by their generosity.

"I have some savings, albeit they are meagre, but I will pay you something now."

"Ce n'est pas necessaire mon ami. Nous n'avons pas besoin."

"Tu es gentil."

"Now my wife has already found another position, so she will be earning more than at the Priest's and not only that but my cousin has some dairy cows and is very keen to work with you on your cheese. Your cheese is excellent, as we know. Also, by an amazing coincidence I found these in one of our old barns. I know that you have been making small amounts of cheese already but these will, I feel, enable you to increase production hugely. Come."

And he showed him some cheese making equipment that had clearly been there for some time, but well wrapped and not damaged by time.

"Let us drive into town and buy a few things to clean and sterilise them and I think you will find they are trés utilisable, very usable."

"Thank you but please: I insist on paying for the fuel."

"Comme tu veux." and he shrugged his shoulders in a typical French style.

"So.." he said to himself "the priest loses a sacristan and a housekeeper in one week. Domage pour lui. Tant pis!" and he took the Sacristan into town.

And the sacristan started producing cheese and selling it. His Munster Gerome also called Múnsterkaas, proved to be extremely popular as had already been demonstrated when he sold it in the market. He was soon making it in industrial quantities: but always to a very high standard. Before long he had a shop in the local town selling it and other local produce as well. He asked the housekeeper's son to be his assistant and took her husband and his cousin in as partners.

One thing led to another and slowly and carefully it expanded to the point where he had several shops, a mail order business and they had bought a few dairy farms to ensure good supply of the right milk. It was a huge success. Then, after some years, the housekeeper's husband had a heart attack and decided he wanted to retire from the venture. At that point he decided to sell up completely.

And here I am and I still can't read and write.

"Ma foie! - My goodness." said the interviewer "and to think you did all that without being able to read and write. It's incredible – c'est incroyable, and just think where you would be if you had not been illiterate."

"I would be digging graves in the churchyard in the village."

A Question of Cheese

menu

Terrine de sanglier - Wild Boar Terrine

Pain seigle aux noix - Walnut Rye
Bread

Choucroute

Sauerkraut

Tarte aux Mirabelle - Plum Tart

Tarte aux Myrtille - Blueberry Pie

Munster Cheese

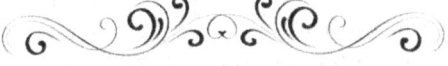

Terrine de sanglier - Wild boar terrine

Preparation time	45 minutes
Cooking time	90 minutes
Serves	12
Method	easy

Ingredients

- 1 kilo fatty belly pork
- 1 kilo wild boar (can be substituted with pheasant, partridge or rabbit)
- 1 large onion chopped
- 4 garlic cloves crushed
- 200 ml white wine
- black pepper
- salt
- 2 tablespoons Dijon mustard

Method

- dice the belly pork into 1cm cubes
- dice the wild boar into 1 cm cubes
- place in a large bowl
- add salt, pepper, onion & garlic
- mix well
- place the white wine in a jug
- add mustard
- mix well
- pour over the meat
- mix well and leave to marinate for at least 4 hours -

ideally overnight
- strain the meat
- mince through a mincer
- mix the meat well
- season to taste
- put the mixture into an oven proof dish
- place in the oven and cook for 90 minutes at 180*c
- leave overnight to rest

Pain seigle aux noix - Walnut rye bread

Preparation time	20 minutes
Cooking time	40 minutes
Serves	12
Method	Intermediate

Chef's tip: Can also be used for cheese course too.

Ingredients

- 1 kilo bread flour
- 200 gr rye flour
- 2 tablespoons salt
- 1 teaspoon nutmeg
- 1 teaspoon sugar
- 250 gr crushed walnuts
- 2 tablespoons dry yeast
- 700 ml lukewarm water

Method

Using a large mixing bowl

- add both flours, the nutmeg, salt & walnuts

- in a small jug
- add the dry yeast, sugar & lukewarm water
- mix well and leave for 10 minutes
- mix the wet mix into the dry mix
- the dough should be sticky but not too wet
- if too wet add flour - if too dry add water
- knead well for about 5 minutes
- leave to rest for about an hour or until it doubles in size
- knock back the dough and shape ready to bake
- leave to rest for another hour
- bake in a preheated oven at 220*c - gas mark 6, for 40 minutes
- leave to cool before serving

Choucroute

Preparation time	20 minutes
Cooking time	90 minutes
Serves	12
Method	easy

Ingredients

- 4 onions sliced
- 400 ml white wine
- 400 ml lager
- 50 ml white wine vinegar
- bay leaf
- thyme
- tablespoon black peppercorn

- 8 garlic cloves whole
- 6 potatoes peeled and halved
- 2 large cabbages sliced thinly or 1.50 kilo sauerkraut
- 2 smoked ham hocks
- 12 smoked sausages
- 1 kilo smoked cured bacon

Method

To cure the cabbage

- put the cabbage in a plastic tub
- add salt and vinegar
- mix well
- leave to marinade for 48 hours
- rinse thoroughly

Note if using shop bought sauerkraut you can go straight to the method below.

Using a large saucepan

- place the garlic, onion, thyme & bay leaf with a drizzle of oil
- cook gently for 5 minutes
- add the cabbage
- add the meat
- pour the wine, vinegar & lager
- place the potatoes on top
- cover and simmer for 90 minutes
- remove the meat & the potatoes
- slice the meat

- place the cabbage in a dish with the potatoes & meat on top
- serve hot

Chef's tip: avoid stirring as everything should cook as it is placed in the pan. Add water if you are running short of liquid.

Tarte aux Mirabelle - Plum tart

Preparation time:	30 minutes
Cooking time;	25 minutes
Serves:	12
Method:	easy

Ingredients

For the pastry

- See 'tarte aux myrtilles' below

Ingredients

- 800 gr sweet or shortcrust pastry
- 1.5 kilo Mirabelle /plum
- 150 gr sugar

Method

Line 2 medium tart moulds

- pre heat oven to 180*c – gas mark 4
- place plums half side down
- fill the mould well

- sprinkle sugar
- bake for 25 minutes
- serve hot or cold

Tarte aux myrtille – Blueberry pie

This is a very popular dessert in Alsace as blueberries grow in abundance in our forest.

Preparation time:	30 minutes
Cooking time:	25 minutes
Serves:	12
Method:	easy

Ingredients

- 1 kilo fresh blueberry
- 800 gr sweet or shortcrust pastry
- 3 eggs
- 250 ml double cream
- nutmeg
- 100 gr sugar

For the pastry

- 600 gr plain flour
- 300 gr unsalted butter
- 200 gr sugar
- 4 eggs yolk
- 100 gr almond powder
- pinch of salt

Method

Pastry

In a medium bowl

- add the flour, butter, almond, nutmeg and salt
- rub into crumb or use a blender
- add egg yolk and 100 ml water
- mix into a soft dough
- preheat oven to 180*c – gas mark 4
- leave to rest for an hour
- roll out 4 large circles - around 20cm diameter
- place onto 2 pie moulds
- add the blueberries
- in a medium bowl
- mix 3 eggs, sugar and cream
- pour onto the blueberries
- add the top pastry neatly and press sides well
- bake for 35/40 minutes 180*c – gas mark 4

Munster & pain aux noix

See bread recipe above.

The Third Sunday in Advent

The Third Advent Candle

This is the third of our candles we light
It is known as the Candle of Joy.
It is lit to remind us of that sacred night
When the shepherds adored a young boy.

There are now three candles standing tall
In our holly wreathed Christmas crown.
The lights shine out in church and hall
As the Advent season counts down.

It is the colour of musky rose
Reflecting a glimmering dawn.
When the Christchild came to take our woes
In a stable, bare, forlorn.

The shepherds came, left flocks in fold
They knelt on the strawy byre.
On a night so dark, so sere, so cold
But the candles provide us with fire.

There is just one candle left to light
On our wreath where it hangs in the aisle.
When the choir will fill the empty night
With the songs that will make us all smile.

The Trojan Horse

As we filed in, past the Christmas tree, we could see that the table was laid out with a very interesting assortment of dishes. Including humous, with pitta bread, a spicy lamb and rice dish, and a fascinating dish of fish with ginger – very redolent of the eastern Mediterranean. There were puddings of the sweet sticky kind so loved on that area, as well as several types of fruit including fresh oranges and grapes; as well as figs and dates. On a small table to the side stood the drinks: there was a Lebanese red wine, Turkish beer, an Israeli white wine, fruit juices – including freshly pressed orange juice - and, of course, water.

Before we started to try the fabulous dishes the Professor ceremoniously lit the third candle on the Advent Wreath. The other two were already alight, but we could see that they were new ones to replace those lit in previous meetings. He spoke as he lit the candle.

'This is the third Advent Candle. It is called the Shepherd's Candle and obviously commemorates those poor shepherds who left their flocks that Christmas Night and journeyed into the stable at Bethlehem. That was, not by tradition the third Sunday, of course, it was Christmas Eve: as it is pretty difficult to celebrate a birth before the birth actually takes place, but this is the traditional name of the candle. It symbolises Joy and is a rosy-red colour – said to reflect the glimmering dawn. It is also known as the Gaudete candle – Latin for rejoice. For those interested, in the Orthodox Church the wreath has six different coloured candles celebrating six Sundays covering the Advent and Christmas period, and starting earlier in Mid-November. A green candle, symbolizing faith, is lit first, usually the second or third Sunday in November; the second is a blue candle, symbolizing hope; the third is a gold candle, symbolizing love; the fourth is a white candle, symbolizing peace; the fifth is a purple candle, symbolizing repentance; the final candle is red, symbolizing communion. I have to say I rather like that, but we are sticking with the Protestant tradition as usual.'

He sat down, and we started in on the tasty looking dishes. The fish in ginger was absolutely fabulous.

I also very much liked the white Israeli wine: Israel of course having thousands of years of wine producing history although, as Groves pointed out, the grapes used are very much the modern varietals now.

After the meal Groves came round and offered all several different types of gin – with appropriate mixers. That was odd, I thought, what has that got to do with the Mediterranean food we had had, but I shrugged metaphorically and accepted an interesting looking gin with botanicals both in it and in the mixer.

Then the Boffin stood up and, raising his glass of gin, said "Cheers". We all replied in kind.

'This story is from my family history on my mother's side. I am not sure if I quite believe it or at least everything – but it is a good tale. There is a long tradition of sea-faring and Royal Navy service in my family going back several generations. I am afraid that I rather broke that tradition by becoming a chemical engineer! This story has been handed down from grand-parent or parent to grand-child or child for some years – no doubt embellished with each new telling – but largely, I believe the same germ of the story.

It is set in the Mediterranean, and the action takes place largely in the eastern end near what is now Turkey and Greece and the Lebanon shores – where the old Phoenicians used to live many years ago and from where the Carthaginians set out to found their Carthage – which is the Anglicised version of 'Qart hadast' which just means 'new city' in Punic. Those of you who studied the Aeneid by Virgil, in Latin studies, will recall that, having fled the fall and sack of Troy, Aeneas visits it, and has a dalliance with the queen, Dido, whose brother was called Pygmalion, before leaving to found another new city in Italy on the banks of the Tiber which would eventually become Rome.

Seafaring has always been a major aspect of the shore-based civilisations: with the curious exception of Troy which, although right on the coast, and generating its wealth by offering a sheltered haven and port at the watery crossroads between the Med and the Black Sea – the pontus Negra, sometimes thalassa mavrus or pontus euxine, never developed a navy. That would, of course, prove to be a major omission when the Trojan War came along and they had no fleet with which to harry and harass the Greek landings. But that is another tale for another day, but the locale and the ghost of the story is germane to my tale.

The tale is set at a time when ruffians and pirates were rife across the Med. The Barbary pirates, or Barbary Corsairs, were pirates, often Muslims, but not always, who operated from the Northern Africa ports such as Algiers, Tunis, and Tripoli, but also out of ports in the eastern Mediterranean as well. The North African littoral was also known in Europe as the Barbary Coast, in reference to the North African Arab tribe – the Berbers.

Typically, they would base themselves in what we would now call a 'broken or failed' state or port and then build up operations, from where they would raid. They became a considerable nuisance in the 16th and 17th centuries and continued to attack shipping up into the 19th century until they were suppressed by several naval countries - the British, along with the Portuguese, French and US.

From their bases they would raid over surprising distances – on occasion even raiding the UK – for plunder and slaves. They often pretended that they were doing it in the name of Islam – but really - they were just slavers and pirates stealing Christians, but sometimes others too, for the slave markets. Some countries tried to snuff them out – but they would resurface in another place.

The nascent USA in particular suffered badly as, being a confederation with no ability to raise taxes in its early days, it had no navy to protect its ships. The pirates tended not to attack ships from countries with powerful navies such as the French and British – but not always. When the USA adopted a constitution in 1789 it could then tax and spend and it developed a navy to try to deal with the pirates. It then built 6 ships and declared war on the Pasha of Tripoli. It beat the ruler of that state by a joint combined naval assault and a landing by marines who freed US prisoners. It was then embroiled in several other wars and skirmishes until the 19th century when the pirates were largely destroyed as a force by the British Royal Navy, working with Dutch and US fleets. They still continued their raiding and slaving activities sporadically, however, until the capture of Algeria by the French in 1830 which destroyed their power base for good.

One of my ancestors was a merchant captain and had suffered raids on his ships. He resolved to do something about it, and in particular the pirate who had attacked his ships several times. He was called the Red Bey as he had, allegedly a red beard, although the rumours were that it was dyed to make him seem 'more Muslim'. Bey also being an Arab title, usually the governor of a province in the Ottoman Empire – but he wasn't a governor – just a thug of a pirate. My ancestor, therefore, assembled a small fleet of war ships, which rendezvoused at Minorca, manned by well-seasoned sailors from the UK, France, the USA and various other countries, and sailed out to attack the known base in the Eastern Mediterranean, where the Red Bey had, unusually, based himself.

It was, according to intelligence reports from other ships' captains to which he had spoken in the harbour at Minorca, based on the coast of what is now present-day Turkey across the sea from Greece. Close, I imagine, to where the hill of Hissarlik which contained the ruins of Troy was later on 'discovered' by Schliemann. Minorca, for those of you who do not know it, is the second largest island in the Balearics, after Majorca (their names coming from Spanish and meaning, more or less, large and small) and used to be the major base of the Royal Navy in the Mediterranean. It is a natural deep harbour and is the second largest in the world, after Pearl Harbour in Hawaii – of which you have all heard - I am sure. They are both calderas of ancient volcanos.'

He raised his glass again and said 'Now you see, we are drinking gin. It is now a little-known fact that before the acquisition of the West Indies, and the discovery of rum, gin was the drink of choice for the Royal Navy. And, given that Minorca was the main Royal Navy base, it is not surprising that a bustling economy grew up there to serve the Royal Navy's and in particular the sailors' needs. We won't go into all the things that were supplied to sailors, but gin became a major product. A trip around the harbour, even nowadays, will show you many, many small individual gin factories dotted around the harbour, all making many-flavoured gin. This was long before the invention of quinine water which was horrible – but it was found that mixing it with gin made it much more palatable and therefore an effective anti-malarial drink and thus it became associated with India – tiffin on the verandah and so on - and became a staple of British drinks.'

He raised his glass again

"Cheers and chin-chin." and we again responded in kind.

'So, to carry on. My ancestor, we shall call him William, spent some time on Minorca with both he, and his crew, gathering intelligence on the Red Bey. Much of it was hearsay or conjecture, but some of it came from ships' captains and crew, that had had fairly recent encounters with him and his ships, but had survived to live the tale. One of the things that the crew, who spoke an amazing array of languages amongst them, picked up – by listening to other seamen, but pretending not to understand what they were saying - was that sometimes the Red Bey sent spies into

Minorca, in disguise as merchants or travellers, sometimes as Muslim pilgrims etc, to gather his own intelligence on ship movements. William noted that and wondered firstly how to identify these spies and then secondly how to make use of them.

The captain of one of the other ships in William's fleet was an America called Captain Johnny, who had been involved in attacks on corsairs before. He hailed from Boston, a well-known seafaring town on the eastern seaboard and one of the original 13 colonies, named after a town in Lincolnshire. He had useful experience and William often consulted him about the best way ahead. He cautioned against precipitous action until the number of ships and guns that were with the Red Bey was known. He explained that each ship was captained by its own ruffian who sailed individually, but who would choose with whom to sail in pirate groups depending on their own foibles and whims, and, perhaps more importantly, the potential opportunities offered by the 'leader' for plunder, booty, slaves etc.

They spent some days in Minorca, gathering intelligence and ensuring that the ships were well loaded: especially with water, food, powder and shot. William laid much emphasis on fresh fruit and vegetables to fight against scurvy – the scourge of sailing then. His father was a physician and had shared this information with him.

One day, just after breakfast, William was approached by a well-to-do looking merchant, or so he supposed him to be when he looked at him.

"Good Morrow. Am I correct in supposing that you Captain William are, the leader of the war ship fleet in harbour here today?"

His English was quite good, but with just a slight accent and the odd grammatical error. Dutch possibly William thought.

He answered.

"Yes, you are correct. How may I help you?"

"Well, may I join you in a pipe?" and he took a wooden pipe out of his pocket.

"Please feel free, but I do not smoke."

"In that case I shall not either." And he replaced the pipe and smiled.

"Now, you asked me what you could do for me; well, my name is Hubertus Van der Valk. I am Dutch merchant. I am carrying good cargo of manufactured goods as well as few other things, to the Eastern Mediterranean. We will trade them there for wood, spices, herbs, other tings for which there is a ready market in Northern Europe. I was wondering if I could hire your fleet to escort me. There are also two or three other carracks or caravels who wish to make same voyage. Would that be possible? The Barbary Pirates, and the Red Bey in particular, an evil man who shows no quarter and offers no mercy, are known to be active in that locale."

William closed his eyes and thought for a few moments. He then opened them, looked at the Dutch merchant and said

"Well, Herr Van der Valk, that is indeed an interesting proposition. Let me talk to my fellow ships' captains and I shall give you a response. Where can I find you?"

The merchant pointed to a fine looking ship and said "That is my barque there. At night you can find me usually between 5 and 6 of an evening at the 'mano azul' that is the Blue Hand Tavern, where I meet with my fellow merchants and others to chat and gossip and to plan, sometimes to trade and deal over a glass of gin or wine. I look forward to seeing you again. Danku Vell."

And he gave a short bow from the waist down and turned and left.

William thought to himself. Well - this could be useful. Not only might I make a little money from seeking out the pirates, these ships might also provide bait to entice this Pirate King out from his fastness.'

Here the Boffin paused, took a sip of his drink, and then carried on saying.

'William was, allegedly, a very wealthy merchant indeed and could well have afforded to finance the fleet himself. Of course, in fact that had been his plan all along, as he very much wanted to rid the Med of this infestation and, thus, make his ships safer and so increase his profits by increasing his trade and also reducing his losses. I should also add that the wealth, alas, did not descend to my part of the family, more is the pity.' And he made a moue with his face.

'So, William called his captains together and explained the Dutchman's proposition. He explained that Van Der Valk had had delivered to him a note saying that the merchants will be heading for Cairo and then Beirut and latterly Cyprus, still then within the Ottoman empire, which would take them close to where the Red Bey was said to have his base. They agreed that it was a good idea and so William went to seek out Van Der Valk and took Captain Johnny with him.

They met the other merchants and their captains and talked over where they were going and what they were going to do. Captain Johnny noticed a swarthy looking seaman, with an earring in one ear, seemingly not taking any notice, but clearly listening intently to the conversation. He said nothing but looked slightly askew, away from him, seeming not to notice, but took good notice of his appearance so he could describe him fully later on.

During a break in the conversation, he bent close to William and apprised him of his suspicions, at the same time pointing something out which is well away from the character so as to allay the Seaman's suspicions in turn.

William gazed out of the window saying in a low voice with his face turned away from the Seaman, for you never know who can lip read

"Good, good, we could make use of him I think in the future – as long as we manage him, and what we tell him, properly."

They talked for a little while longer to finalise the details, payments etc and then bought a round of drinks for the merchants and their captains, chatted a little of inconsequentialities, and then left the Mano Azul and went back to their ship.

Later on in the week, and as expected, the swarthy sailor tried to sign on with Captain Johnny: and, as they had previously agreed – they took him on. He claimed to be from Spain – but they did not believe him, but said nothing.

They set off and sailed across to Cairo, then up to Lebanon, then on to Cyprus. This brought them close to what is now the Turkish shoreline – but there was no sign of the pirates. They escorted the ships into Cyprus and the merchants transacted their business. William's fleet had also brought goods for trade and they progressively sold these as they hopped from port to port across the Mediterranean.

William then called his captains together and the discussed what to do: they thought that they should try to find him or else the venture had been largely in vain.

The merchants had by now transacted all of their business and were ready to leave. William discussed this with the merchants and they asked hm to escort them back to Minorca – just in case. He agreed subject the proviso that they sail near to the Red Bey's fastness and try to draw him out. Not too happily, but happy to have his fleet as escort, they agreed.

The fleet sailed north from Cyprus and towards the rumoured location of the Red Bey's fort. They rounded a cape one morning and there it was, lying and gleaming white in the sun. It was fairly near to where we now Troy was situate, but of course, although familiar with Homer's The Iliad, they did not know that

The pirates had been there sometime, and had built a formidable fortress, based loosely on a Crusader Castle, right next to the shore with a protected harbour, and had extended the walls to include it inside.

William realised that even by bombarding the walls, his cannon, though good against wooden ships, would have little, if any, effect on the strong walls, no doubt also packed with earth to absorb the force from cannon balls. Any sustained broadsides, therefore, would just be a waste of powder and shot. Nevertheless, to show willing he instructed the ships to let off a few shots every now and then, aimed at the battlements and the gates – just to keep their heads down.

They anchored in the bay, opposite a large beach, and not too far out from the fortress.

William and Captain Johnny stood looking at the fortress from the fo'c'sle.

"We are lucky that as we are in the Mediterranean there are no tides: so we can anchor and, absent any unforeseen storms, which can, I believe, come up without warning hereabouts, not worry about waves. That is what did for Julius Caesar, you know, on his first invasion of Britain in 55BC."

"How so, my friend?" said Captain Johnny

"Well, he being from Italy in the Mediterranean, where there are no tides, had no idea what a tide was, and pulled his ships onto the beach and left them there. The tide, however, came in and wrecked them!"

"Strange are the ways of the seas!"

William carried on, looking at the castle through his spyglass.

"Well, we cannot bombard this fort and the Red Bey into submission, that is clear: and that will not free the slaves in any case – they would slaughter them if they felt they were going to be stormed. We must, therefore, try a more subtle approach. I have, luckily, had a plan stewing in my mind for a while, in case of this eventuality. It is not guaranteed to be successful, but then – we have little choice in my view. This headland being near where Troy was situate, according to legend – and having studied the Iliad - it inspired me to think of this plan."

William asked Hubertus to join him on his ship for a glass of Madeira, some cheese and ships biscuits.

"Now then my friend. You have offered me payment in gold, but I am going to ask you instead for a part of your cargo. The wood, or some of it. I need enough to do this."

And he outlined his plan to Hubertus and Captain Johnny. He ended by saying "Now do you arrange for the wood, but not a word to anyone else about what I am going to do. You understand? In good time I shall explain to the rest of the fleet."

The Dutch merchant slapped his knee with his hand and said.

"Ja, Ja! Dat is een goed plan - that is a good plan - mijn Kaptiein!" and he rushed off to consult with the other merchants to ensure that an adequate amount of wood is made available.

William then called all the ships' carpenters together and asked them to build a wooden horse. "Just like the Greeks did at Troy." he explained. He then called his and Captain Johnny's crew over to his ship, and explained the plan.

"We are going to construct a wooden horse, just like the Greeks did at Troy, and then leave this horse outside the fortress, with a few pieces of gold and treasure draped over and partially inside it. We hope that the pirates will take it into their castle fastness. Then, at midnight, a few selected men who have been ensconced inside, will creep out and open the gates so that the main force can rush the castle and take it."

The swarthy sailor was one of the crew to whom he explained the plan. Captain Johnny had been tasked with following, or rather, observing him, subtly and seeing what he did. The guards had also been given instructions not to stop anybody who jumped overboard - or at least to make a show of stopping them - but not too much.

So, the scene was set. The wood had been delivered to the carpenters, who had landed around the other side of the dune, away from the fortress where no-one could see them – the location unknown to any of the crewmen - and had been constructing the wooden horse. The carpenters had been working steadily on the construction and it was nearly, but not quite completed. They were very good carpenters and woodworkers, and it hadn't taken very long to build. They had made the seams 'watertight', using pitch and tar, so nothing of the interior could be seen.

The ships were still firing random broadsides at the castle fortress just to keep the corsairs awake and on their toes: as well as lulling them into a false sense of security – inasmuch as they think an assault will come soon.

As expected, the swarthy sailor leapt overboard around midnight and swam powerfully to the beach. The guards fired a few musket balls at him or rather randomly into the sea, but making a good noise and the flashes could be seen from the castle. They were taking good care, as they had been ordered, not to hit him. He then ran up to the castle shouting in Arabic, and waving his arms - he clearly had a password of some sort as he wasn't shot out of hand.

We can presume that he was ushered into the presence of the Red Bey who had sent him on his mission and the conversation would have gone something like this:

"Salaam aleikum Your Excellency."

"Aleikum salaam – kaif halek?"

"I am well your magnificence – and I have such news for you."

"Well – speak by the Prophet - peace be upon him. Speak!"

"I have heard the plans of the Feringees. They plan to build a wooden horse and leave it outside the fort, draped in treasure, in the hope that you will take it into the fortress. They will pretend to sail away, defeated, and offering this horse with gold, silver, and treasure: to placate you and hope you will cease your attacks on their ships. Then at night, a few men, hidden inside will creep out and throw open the doors and let the main force in to storm the fortress."

The Red Bey stroked his beard saying

"Hahaha! You have done well, Ali, my friend. I did well when I sent you to spy on these Frankic and Anglic dogs. How do you know that this is truth?"

"I pretended that I had no other tongues other than the language of the Prophet – peace be upon him - and Spanish - so played dumb when they were discussing their plans in English. But, more than this - the Anglic leader – actually told all of his crew what he planned. Others translated it for me - he had no idea that I was a spy. Naturally I agreed that it was a clever plan."

"Yes – they have realised that although their fleet is as strong as ours, if not a little stronger in some aspects, they cannot assault us here; and we have many, many weeks' worth of provisions and access to good water, as well as to the hinterland where camel trains with food pass from time to time, thus a siege is not practicable."

The Red Bey strode up and down thinking and then turned and said:

"Does this Englishman think we are ignorant – we Arabs? Kul Wahad! Does he think we are illiterate? Does he not know that it was our Arabic scholars in Andalusia that resurrected the ancient learning from Greece and Egypt; and that we are familiar with the old Greek tales? Even without your knowledge, gained at great personal danger to you, my friend, I would have known this tale and his attempt to trick us."

He strode up and down a little more, thinking, and then called his lieutenants together. He quickly outlined the news and then said.

"Now – gather ye wood and oil, in secret so that they cannot see you from their ships, and pile it just inside the main entrance. We shall trick the English with a trick of our own." And he laughed out loud at his cleverness.

Next morning, just before dawn, Captain William's men rolled the horse around the headland and left it outside the castle walls. They then scuttled quickly back to their jolly boats and rowed back to the ship. The fleet then fired off a few desultory shots and then sailed away, seeming in dejected defeat, as per the plan.

One of the other fleet captains said

"William, we all know that the spy escaped with the news of what we are doing. How then will this trick work?"

"Have faith David, have faith. Things are not always as they seem."

Some way away, out of sight of the fortress, the fleet struck anchor and then launched a small jolly boat in which were William and Captain Johnny and a few picked men. They quietly climbed up the very large grassy sand dune, which they had seen and then scouted over the past few days, and which gave them a view, through telescopes, of the castle and the shore where the horse was standing. They could see the odd jewel gleaming and glinting in the early morning sun, which was rising in the east behind, as planned, them so that it didn't reflect off their lenses.

They heard the wailing of the Muezzin as he called 'The Faithful' to morning prayers and then after a while, the gates opened slightly, and a few men came out cautiously well-armed with cutlasses and pistols, cocked and ready.

"A sorry looing bunch of Ruffians they are at that." said Captain Johnny.

"Yes." Agreed William.

Then David, the Captain who had queried the trick last night, and whom William had asked to accompany them for he was an old friend, asked

"William, I did a quick headcount this morning. All our men are present and accounted for, apart from the traitor spy. So, who is in the horse?"

"Wait and see, my friend, wait and see." said William and lifted his spyglass again.

The corsairs crept towards the horse and then searched for any sign of anyone else, with one eye on the gold and jewels: but they were on pain of death not to touch them. When they were satisfied, they despatched one man back to the castle, William could see it was the swarthy so-called Spanish sailor, to summon the Red Bey.

Then the gate opened fully and the Red Bey came out along with the entire pirate crew. They were all carrying wood, which they proceeded to pile under and around the horse, and pitchers or amphorae of oil, which they poured and threw over the horse.

"Oh my Lord!" said David "They are going to set fire to it!"

"Oh yes, I do hope so said William." And he and Captain Johnny looked very pleased with themselves

"But, but the men…" said David and then he saw it "Ohh!"

"Now watch and see, oh ye of little faith."

They could not, of course hear what anyone was saying, but we can presume it was something like this

The Red Bey approached the horse carrying a burning brand.

"Now then Feringhee dogs. Can you hear me in there? We know you are there – we have not been fooled by the smatterings of treasure or drops of gold scattered across this horse. We are not so easily fooled. Are you comfortable in your wooden prison? Well, you are about to get more uncomfortable! As you know, the Mediterranean is hot – now you will see just how hot it can get."

And William and his men watched as he thrust the burning brand into the wood. The pirates broke open several bottles of grog or wine or brought pitchers of beer and started drinking, and dancing round and singing coarse insulting songs we may suppose. They fired their pistols into the air and occasionally at the horse.

And, as they watched, and as the flames got hotter and hotter, licking greedily at the oil drenched wood it happened.

The horse exploded and bullets and bits of metal, as well as many splinters of wood flew out extremely fast in all directions as the gun powder which had been secreted inside the horse, along with sealed metal tubes containing musket balls, reached ignition point.

All the pirates were either killed or badly wounded.

William gave the signal to the fleet and it sailed back to the castle, collecting him and his men on the way and they landed, finished off any pirates left alive, and then burnt the castle, having looted it of the many chests of treasure, gold and other items as well as freeing the slaves.

Curiously the Red Bey was not quite dead, nor was the spy - these they crucified to the gates as a stark warning to other pirates.'

"What an excellent tale." Said Archie "and so clever too, to use a trick within a trick."

"I love it." said Dry-as-Dust. "It is always good to see evil get its come-uppance."

"But supposing it hadn't worked?" asked Angel.

"Then they would have thought of something else I am sure." The Boffin replied "But it did work: as it was designed to appeal to the Red Bey's sense of importance in his own cleverness, by playing on an old trick, with a twist. Cheers – more gin me hearties."

And we all replied.

The Trojan Horse

menu

Turkish Bread

Hummus

Seabass with Ginger, Coriander, Chilli & Lime

Baked Spicy Potatoes

Cucumber Salad

Chilled Rice Pudding With Honeyed Figs

Turkish Bread

Preparation time:	10 minutes
Cooking time:	4 minutes
Serves:	12
Method:	easy

Ingredients

- 1 kilo bread flour
- 300 ml warm milk
- 300 ml warm water
- 2 tsp salt
- 4 tbs dry yeast
- chilli flakes optional

Method

- whisk flour with salt and yeast
- add warm water and milk and knead just until the liquids are absorbed
- add olive oil and knead until smooth dough forms (around 10 minutes)
- form the dough into a ball, cover with vegetable oil and set aside in warm place for 1 hour or until doubled in size
- when the dough has finished rising, cut it into 12 equal sized pieces and roll each piece into a ball
- roll out each flatbread and place on a pan preheated

to medium-high heat
- cook for 5 to 6 minutes (2 ½ to 3 minutes on each side)
- serve hot or cold

Hummus

Preparation time:	10 minutes
Cooking time:	N/A
Serves	12
Method:	easy

Ingredients

- 800 gr chickpeas
- 160 ml olive oil
- fresh coriander
- 4 garlic cloves crushed
- 2 lemon juice
- 6 tbs tahini

Method

- Rinse the chickpeas well

Using a food blender - add into the blender

- chickpeas, coriander, olive oil
- blitz until smooth
- add garlic lemon juice, tahini 30 ml of water
- blitz again until smooth
- add water and olive oil if not smooth enough

Seabass with ginger, coriander, chilli & lime

Ingredients

- 12 large seabass fillets
- 3 limes sliced
- 15 gr fresh ginger peeled & chopped
- 3 fresh red chillies chopped – heat to taste
- bunch of fresh coriander chopped
- 4 spring onions sliced
- 6 tbs olive oil
- 6 tbs fish sauce
- 4 tbs dark soya sauce
- 4 sticks of lemon grass sliced
- 1 tsp sugar

Method

- Pre heat oven to 170*C

Using a large shallow oven tray

- drizzle the olive oil
- place the seabass in the tray, skin up
- place the sliced lime over the top of the seabass

Using a medium bowl add

- chilli, ginger, fish sauce, soya sauce, lemon grass, sugar, spring onions
- mix well
- add half the coriander into the mix
- pour the mix over the seabass

- cook for 15 minutes
- add the remaining coriander once cooked

Baked spicy potatoes

Preparation time:	20 minutes
Cooking time:	30/40 minutes
Serves:	12
Method:	easy

Ingredients

- 12 medium potatoes peeled
- 6 tbs olive oil
- 1 tsp black pepper
- 1 tsp chopped fresh thyme
- 1 tsp fresh mint
- 1 tsp ground chilli
- 1 tsp smoked paprika

Method

- Pre heat the oven to 190*C (Gas mark 5)

Using a large saucepan

- add the potatoes & a pinch of salt
- cover with hot water
- bring to the boil
- simmer for 2 minutes
- drain well

Using a small bowl

- add the olive oil, chilli, mint, smoked paprika, black pepper
- pour the mixture over the potatoes
- add a pinch of salt
- cook for 30/40 minutes, or until golden brown

Cucumber salad

Prep time:	15 minutes
Cooking time:	N/A
Serves:	12
Method:	easy

Ingredients

- 6 medium cucumbers sliced
- 1 tsp salt
- 1 tbs black pepper
- 1 tbs parsley chopped
- 6 tbs vinegar
- 150 ml olive oil
- 100 ml double cream

Method

Using a large bowl

- place the sliced cucumber into a large bowl
- add salt
- mix well
- leave to rest 30 minutes
- rinse well

Using a medium bowl

- add oil, vinegar, parsley, black pepper, cream
- mix well
- pour over the cucumber
- serve cold

Chilled rice pudding with honeyed figs

Prep time:	20 minutes
Cooking time:	20 minutes
Serves:	12
Method:	easy

Ingredients

- 6 tbs honey
- 12 fresh figs
- 3 oranges, zested and juiced
- 1 juice of a medium lemon
- 3 litres of whole milk
- 1 kilo arborio rice
- 400 gr brown sugar
- 1 cinnamon stick
- 2 vanilla pods; split and seeds scraped out

Method

Figs

place the figs onto a baking tray

drizzle them with the honey

bake for 15 minutes 180*c (gas mark 4)

leave to cool

Rice pudding

Using a large saucepan

- add the milk, sugar, vanilla, cinnamon, orange zest
- add the rice
- simmer gently for 12-15 minutes
- check the rice is tender
- stir regularly
- add the orange juice

Move the rice into a flat dish and place in the fridge over night.

- Dish out the rice in individual bowls, placing a fig and honey on top of the rice

Shortest day/Winter Solstice

Winter solstice
An owl swoops down, a vole is gone
And winter's grip goes on and on.
It takes it back into its nest
The winter's hard - it does its best.

A fox has come out from its den
To brave the freezing winter cold.
It wanders round the woods and then
It sniffs the air: sheep in the fold.

So silently it pads around,
Its paws a soft, faint crunching sound,
Within the snow that lies so deep,
It draws close to the sleeping sheep.

While sheep may doze the dog's sharp nose,
Can smell the fox a-prowling,
It lifts its head and licks its lips,
and sets up quite a howling.

The fox quite startled lopes away,
Its belly cold and empty,
To search for prey: not far away,
There's mice and rats a-plenty.

Migrating birds have flown away,
The butterflies are sleeping.
All triggered by the shortening day,
As winter comes a-creeping.

The leaves have fallen from the trees,
The trunks stand dark and lonely.
No wasps, no flies, no buzzing bees,
Just carrion crows only.

The day is at its shortest now,
The night will grow no longer.
The sun returns increasingly,
It's warming rays grows stronger.

And how do we prepare good cheer,
To celebrate mid-season?
We quaff good mugs of foaming beer,
And drink to rhyme and reason.

The wassail cup is passed around,
Whilst songs are sung together.
We raise our happy heartfelt sound,
And never mind the weather.

Draw round the fire and tell a tale,
Of heroes long ago.
Pass round the cheese, top up your ale,
And pay no heed to snow.

The boar's head is then brought in hot,
Bedecked with Rosemary and bay.
Be thankful for the things we've got,
Upon this cold midwinter's day.

A Miracle

As we walked into our usual room, the fire was flickering in the grate and the Christmas tree was standing proud and tall in the corner – its blue and gold decorations shining out, the lament also catching the light and twinkling. It was a cold day, so we were glad of the fire, and it was the 21st December – the Winter Solstice – that is the shortest day and the longest night. A night for celebration probably since mankind first set foot on the planet. Indeed, the early Christians had appropriated this night as the day for Christmas – to wipe away the memories of the old pagan festivals traditionally held on that day. It occurs when the pole is furthest away from the sun – also known as the Hibernal solstice, from Latin, and from where both hibernation and the Roman name for Ireland – Hibernia - come. It occurs twice a year – once in the northern hemisphere and once in the southern hemisphere – 6 months apart. The opposite solstice – Summer - is the shortest night and the longest day.

The Winter Solstice has been significant time in many cultures, with festivals held to commemorate the symbolic 'death' of the sun and its subsequent 'rebirth' as days wax longer. Stonehenge in Salisbury plain and Newgrange in Ireland are aligned with the solstices and are thought to be ancient monuments to this and centres of rituals and celebrations. At this time dwellings and other places would be garlanded with much greenery and also with – that most hated of pagan plants to the early Christian Church – mistletoe: the oak tree parasite which was cut, traditionally, by druids with a golden sickle.

The room was similarly garlanded with fresh greenery and dried autumnal fruits and nuts, and pine cones etc making it all look very welcoming and warm. Groves was there in his usual place and we were offered Irish stout or a shot of Irish Whiskey as we entered. There was a limited range of stouts (ie two): but several bottles of Whiskey – from both Northern and Southern Ireland. I myself only drink Irish stout when in Ireland (Dublin or Cork) as I do not think it travels well – but it is of course a very popular drink in the UK – one of the brands even sponsors the Six Nations rugby. I was, however, partial to Irish Whiskey – no matter which part of the island it came from. It has a very nice smooth finish I felt as it is double distilled. These drinks were, we felt, a considerably good clue as to the tale we would hear tonight. Interestingly – there was also Italian wine on offer – so a dual location I presumed.

We took our seats and Groves proceeded to serve the meal. For a first course we had a broth – from Ireland with Irish bread. The main course was a proper Irish stew and potatoes in garlic and herbs – very traditional Irish, followed by an Italian pudding tiramisu – very rich – how intriguing I thought. Then there was a selection of both Irish and Italian cheeses, with Parmesan flavoured biscuits which deepened the mystery for us.

With the cheese was also a strong Italian red – and further measures of Whiskey were available. I tried Slane which was new to me.

As we sipped our post-prandial drinks Janus stood up. He hadn't told a tale for some time so we were intrigued to hear what he had to say. He was an accomplished actor so we had high expectations of his tale.

He raised his glass and said 'Slainte' which we knew was cheers in Irish and then 'Salut'. So Italian as well as expected from the menu.

He started to speak, pacing back and forth as he did so – unusually for our little group - who normally stood in their place, or sometimes even sat.

'Imagine, if you will, an old Irish man - we'll call him Podrig – pronounced, apparently as we might say porridge – who lives on his own but is very self-sufficient in a little Irish village near the north south border. He has a daily wash in cold water, for he doesn't waste good money on heating it very much – he does however take a hot bath once a week – whether he needs it or not!'

That got a laugh

'It was early November – and it was a particularly cold month too that year, and snow had fallen unusually early.

On this day Podrig decided to walk into the village, buy some bread from the village baker, and go home and make breakfast in his bothy. It was a beautiful crisp winter's day and he had decided to have toast and marmite. He went into the baker's, which was very warm from the ovens, exchanged some platitudinous banter with the assistant who served him and bought a fresh farmhouse loaf. He then returned to his humble abode, with his loaf in a paper bag clutched tightly in his hand, opened the door, and placed the loaf on the table carefully. He went to his cutlery drawer, quite poorly supplied in fact, and took out his carving knife. He sharpened it on his steel and stoked up the fire, for it was quite cold inside. He sat down at his small kitchen table of rough-hewn, but strong wood, and began to slice the thick farmhouse loaf carefully. He held up the resulting slice of bread up, whilst he inserted a toasting fork into it carefully.

He pulled his chair up to the small fire and started toasting the bread. The fire was however, quite weak so it took some while to toast it on both sides. Whilst he toasted the bread he was humming an old Irish folk tune – let's say it was 'Whiskey in the Jar' popularised in the UK by T'in Lizzy: an Irish group with members from both north and south, who reportedly only got a contract as the record company thought that they had written the song themselves.

When the toast was done, he started buttering the bread with good Irish full fat butter but, as the butter ran down the knife and onto his hand, he dropped both the knife and, in his surprise the toast, which he was holding in his other hand whilst buttering it. To his amazement it dropped buttered side up. Now, we all know that life being what it is when this type of event occurs it always – without exception - drops buttered side down, and what is more always in the dirtiest, dustiest part of the kitchen and picks up all sorts of detritus – thus normally rendering the bread unfit for human consumption.

Quickly he hurried down to the local bar where he orders a whiskey to steady his nerves and told everybody what had happened. Most simply do not believe him, but the barman said "You must tell Father Rafferty about this and get it declared a miracle."

"Really?" he replied

"Yes. Quick go now. He is just back from his parish rounds."

So he downed his whiskey and walked round to the Fathers house. There he told him what had happened. The Father made him swear by Mary Mother of God that this is the truth and then said "Sure, Podrig, and I can't proclaim a miracle. It is not in my gift. We need to see the Bishop."

This unsettled Podrig as he has never met a Bishop, but the Father reassured him that he is a decent man and, in any case, he will accompany him, as he was due to meet with him to discuss the next year's services etc.

"I will make an appointment to see him. In the meantime, get you back home and preserve this miraculous piece of toast."

So Podrig went back to his bothy and placed the piece of toast on a cheese plater, with the cover on it, then put it in the cellar, where it was cold: even colder than the rest of his bothy. It was by now snowing so he stoked up the fire, poured himself another whiskey, slowly sipped and then and fell asleep. He then had a dream where his toast had been declared a miracle, he was 'The most famousest man in the village!' and tourists and pilgrims flocked from across Ireland and beyond to see his modest house where this miracle took place.

He was awoken by a knocking at the door and a voice calling "Podrig, Podrig! Are you there My Son?"

It was Father Rafferty with news that he had made an appointment for them both to see the Bishop on Friday 22st December - which happened also to be the shortest day/ longest night: the winter solstice.

"How will we get there, and where is he, Father?"

"Do not worry: Jimmy Murphy will take us in his lorry and he will wait for us. He is going into town to deliver some of his produce then, lucky for us. Get you to bed and sleep well Podrig."

So that night Podrig went to bed, feeling full of hope for the forthcoming visit.

The days seemed both to drag and also fly by and eventually the day of the solstice, Friday 21st December, dawned crisp and clear. The snow was sparkling in the weak winter's sun as he walked to the Priest's house full of optimism and also a little apprehensive at meeting so august a person as a Bishop!

Father Rafferty was waiting for him, and as they chatted Jimmy Murphy in his lorry pulled up. They squeezed into the front seat, Podrig sitting in the middle, and they set off. It was a very old lorry, a jalopy you could say in fact, and as the roads in that part of Ireland were not quite the M1, so it was a bone-shaking ride. But they got there despite that: and despite there being virtually no brakes to speak of. Luckily the roads were virtually deserted and the snow had been moved off them.

Jimmy dropped them off in the middle of the town and went off to sell his produce, having agreed to collect them in the same spot later on.

Podrig followed Father Rafferty as he led him across the square and to the Bishop's house. The house was not especially imposing, but definitely more grand than any of the homes in the village. The Priest knocked on the door, and a lady, who Podrig assumed was the housekeeper, answered it. She was clearly expecting them as she motioned them into a parlour where there a bit of bright fire burning, and asked them to take a seat while they waited.

She brought them some tea after a few minutes saying. "Sure, His Reverence will not be long. Will you be having yourselves some tea now?"

They sat in the comfortable parlour having tea and then, after a short while, a severe looking man came in in a black suit wearing a dog collar. But then he smiled at Podrig, nodded at Father Rafferty, and said

"Welcome my son. Please tell me what this is about?"

So Podrig told him about buying the bread, toasting it on his little fire and then buttering it and then "And then Your Reverence, the miracle occurred – it landed butter side up."

"Well now, and you have already discussed this with the Good Father here?"

"Yes, Your Reverence."

"Well, I must think on it. We don't get miracles every day and I am unsure as to the exact protocol – but I imagine it is not a swift process. It would be good to have a miracle locally, however. Now, do you go back to your village and I will call Father Rafferty in a day or so. I wish you both a Merry Christmas." And he poured them each a glass of Whiskey.

"Slainte"

"Slainte."

They arose, drained their glasses and Podrig said

"Thank you, Your Reverence."

The housekeeper showed them out and they walked back

to the square where Jimmy had dropped them and after a few minutes his lorry came around the corner with many rattles and slewed to a stop, and they got in.

They were both silent on the way back -deep in thought - and Jimmy, who was not a talkative man at the best of times unless he had had a few whiskeys, also kept his peace. He dropped them off at Father Rafferty's house and the Father said a few kindly words to Podrig and then wished him good evening.

A couple of days later Father Rafferty came to see Podrig again with a response from the Bishop.

"He says that this is beyond his purview and we need to see the Archbishop. He has spoken to him but he is a very busy man and we will not be able to go until after Christmas. We shall go by train."

"B-b-but Father – I have no money for such a trip." Exclaimed Podrig

"Do not worry my son - the Church has some funds put aside for the incidental expenses incurred in such an interesting occurrence as this. I will get the tickets."

A few days later Father Rafferty came round to see Podrig and explained that he had bought tickets for March. "That is the earliest that the Bishop can fit us in."

"That is a long way away, Father. I am not sure that I can wait that long."

"Well, you must Podrig, we have to. It will come around

soon."

So, Christmas and New Year came and went, Winter turned into Spring and then as the day approached Podrig became agitated, especially when Father Rafferty came to remind him.

"We shall go tomorrow. Be ready."

That night Podrig could hardly sleep. In the space of a few months he, who had hardly ever been out of the village, had met a Bishop and was now going to meet an Archbishop. Unbelievable: however, he eventually dropped off to sleep and next day presented himself outside Father Rafferty's house at the appointed time. Jimmy was there again to take them to the station.

They boarded the train and Podrig was fascinated as he had only rarely caught a train. It was one of the old types with manually operated doors. Known as 'slam doors' – now progressively phased out and replaced with automatic ones. The carriage was completely full with no empty seats at all. As they approached the end of their journey the train came to a slow halt, outside the terminus, as they do sometimes, awaiting its place in the queue on the platforms. One of their fellow passengers, who had been asleep for the whole journey suddenly woke up, saw that the train had stopped; hurriedly jumped up and, grabbing the door handle, opened the door and stepped out, before anyone could say anything. There was a cry of anguish and then silence. Then, after what seemed like an age, but was only a few seconds, a hand appeared and grabbed the edge of the train, then another and he pulled himself up and got back into the carriage. He was dishevelled and looked very sheepish and said

"You must think I am an idiot!"

But all were too polite, and shocked to say anything. Then he walked across to the other side - and did exactly the same thing. Just at that point the train moved off so they could not see what happened, but reported it to the Guard and the Station Master.

Father Rafferty and Podrig approached the Archbishop's Palace - the former with anticipation - the latter with with trepidation. They were shown into a sitting room and Father Rafferty told him the story. The Archbishop had, of course already heard the gist from the Bishop but wanted both to hear the details and question Podrig.

He questioned Podrig a little and then said, rather portentiously.

"This is not something on which I, a mere Archbishop, can pronounce. You will need to go further up the ecumenical hierarchy. You need to see Cardinal Mazzini."

Podrig looked very disappointed but the Archbishop ignored him and said

"He is in Rome, in the Vatican with His Holiness just now. I will find out when he will be back and arrange for you to see him. You will have to go to Dublin though."

And he dismissed them after giving them his ring to kiss.

They trudged disconsolately back to the station, their walk made more miserable by the spring rain that had started to fall, although they were wearing coats as it was only March after all.   They went to see the Station Master and asked after the passenger who 'fell out'.

"Oh. He is alright – he landed in some hay and then picked himself up and walked to the station."

Then Father Rafferty and Podrig went to the platform and boarded their train back.

"Dublin, Dublin. It is a while since I went there Podrig. It is a City, very different from our little village."

"I have never been Father."

"No. I know. Luckily it is not too far away from us and will not be too difficult to get there."

"But when will that be Father?"

"I know not My Son." In his own time the Good Lord will let us know I am sure: or at least the Archbishop will. Funny I have never heard of an Archbishop describing himself as 'merely an Archbishop'- curious."

Their trip home was a lot less eventful than the outward bound trip and they arrived back that evening. Podrig went straight to bed, very disappointed.

It was indeed a long time in coming and it was not until August that they were allowed to meet with the Cardinal.

Spring had given way to Summer – the fields were full with corn, potatoes were being harvested, strawberries on Podrig's bush were in profusion and apples were beginning to ripen.

The Bishop had been told of the Archbishop's referral to Cardinal Mazzini and had placed his driver at Father Rafferty and Podrig's disposal, which as the Father said, was very kind, much kinder than the Archbishop had been. He collected them and drove them to Dublin, where the Cardinal was staying in an hotel.

They were taken to his suite by an hotel porter and ushered in by the Cardinal himself.

"Benvenuto! Welcome!"

He was very friendly and after giving his ring for them to kiss, shook their hands.

"Bene, Bene. How are you, Father? It has been some while since we met – when you were just Joe Rafferty and training to hoping to be a priest and I was one of your instructors. How have you fared in this iniquitous world – questo mondo terribile?"

"Thank you, Your Eminence. Grazie Mille. Tutto bene. I am well – it is good to see you again. And now you are very senior in our ecumenical hierarchy."

"And you My Son.." he said turning to Podrig "… how goes the world with you?" Podrig, however was so overcome that he could only stammer and gulp.

"No matter. Come, please tell me about this miracle – questo miraculo, per favore."

And his smile did a lot to put Podrig at his ease.

They again told the story and he listened attentively, steepling his fingers and looking at each one as they told bits of the story and the 'journey' they had already been on. He then asked a few perfunctory questions and said. "Come let us pray together." and he indicated a prie-dieu he had set up. They kneeled down and the Cardinal prayed for guidance. Then they knelt in silence. Eventually the Cardinal arose, which was a good thing for Podrig as his knees were aching, bade them arise and said

"Mi dispiace, I am sorry to disappoint you, yet again, but I am only a temporary Cardinal in Ireland and I cannot pronounce on this. I think that you will need to go to Roma and ask His Holiness for a decision. It is a long way I know: but you can look on it as a pilgrimage as well. I shall be returning to Roma later on in the year and will be able to present you to His Holiness. That will help, I am sure. Bene, bene. Chow."

And he ushered them out, kindly.

They were driven back by the Bishop's driver and sat again in silence for some time. Eventually Father Rafferty broke the silence.

"Sure, Podrig, this is turning into an epic tale of tales. It will be a miracle in of itself if we ever get this event declared a miracle!"

"Yes Father – but Rome! How?"

"We shall see, My son."

And they went back to their respective homes.

Now it turned out that Father Rafferty, a good-natured soul, had made known Podrig's adventure and quest for the miracle and the villagers, and even others further afield in local villagers and the market town, had responded magnificently by having a collection to buy a ticket for Podrig to go to Rome. For they were all good Catholics and seeing the Pope was the apotheosis for them.

And so it was, by an amazing coincidence, that the visit was planned to coincide with the Winter Solstice.

"Curious..." thought Podrig "… a whole year has gone by since my miraculous event! And now I am going to see His holiness in the Vatican – in Rome."

So the day dawned when he and Father Rafferty made the trip to Dublin, again in the Bishop's car, and boarded a flight to Rome – the Eternal City. Podrig had never flown before and Father Rafferty had only made a couple of flights so it was very much a big adventure for them. The aeroplane was full with many others making a pilgrimage to Rome so they were in good company. The flight was uneventful and they touched down in Rome and made their way to the guest house near the Vatican which had been boked for them. A modest place, but adequate. That evening they dined in a little restaurant around the corner from their guest house and had what now seems commonplace to us – Spaghetti Bolognese – but to Podrig was the most different and foreign food he had ever experienced. They had a glass of rich Italian red wine to wash it down, again something out of the norm for Podrig, and then retired, for they were tired and tomorrow would be a day for sight-seeing before their big day, coinciding with the Winter Solstice, not that the Roman Catholic Church celebrates the day – but it was nevertheless the shortest day.

The Vatican – or more properly The Vatican City State - is an independent fiefdom, wholly within the City of Rome. From here in the past previous Popes had exercised power as 'Princes' and held sway over large swathes of Italy, since incorporated into the State of Italy during the 19th Century. It is a little over 100 acres and contains, inter alia, the largest Catholic Church - St Peter's Basilica - and the very famous Sistine Chapel containing Michelangelo's famous art. Podrig, under Father Rafferty's guidance wandered around the outside of the Vatican City. They strolled along the banks of the Tiber – the famous river of Roman legends and then wandered around, with Father Rafferty telling Podrig some of the history of Rome and the Popes.

"It goes back over 2,000 years Podrig – from the earliest days of its founding, shrouded in legend and myth, through the Roman Empire – which as we know invaded England

and Wales and parts of Scotland, but never captured Ireland; and through to Emperor Constantine's conversion to Christianity, and the end of persecution of Christians by the pagan Romans; and then to when Rome became the centre of our faith. Not all Popes were good, and not all clever. But for good or evil they were in charge."

Podrig had nothing to say to that.

They had lunch in a pizzeria – again something strange for Podrig, wandered around a little more and then after an early supper, went back to their guest house for an early bed.

Next day they met with the cardinal who told them that he had obtained an audience with His Holiness.

"This is approximately how it works. Once the ceremony begins, His Holiness will greet in the visiting groups in all their languages. Then He will lead the audience through Bible readings and parables, teachings etc: mainly in Italian. He will then lead all attending in a recitation of the Lord's Prayer – Pater Noster. This is in in Latin – but it is printed on the back of the Papal Audience Ticket. Next, He gives his Apostolic Blessing to the crowd, and after this, those near His Holiness can approach to ask that He bless them or their religious articles such as rosary beads. I have agreed that at that point you can ask about your miracle. He will then withdraw, and I shall accompany him, to consider it. He will no doubt mediate and pray for guidance. Then He will tell me His decision and I will convey it to you. If it becomes a miracle there will be other things to do – but we shall worry about that later. Ready?

"Yes father."

"Bene. Let us go to get near the front of the queue."

So, they joined the queue several hours in advance and, partly as they had a Cardinal with them, were able to get to the front. Podrig marvelled at the costumes of the Swiss Guards – which were utterly alien to this poor Irishman – although one aspect was vaguely reminiscent of the Irish kilt. The Pope went through the ritual and then Father Rafferty explained the background to His holiness, again, as the Cardinal had already imparted the information to Him. They then withdrew.

The Pope and the Cardinal then went inside and The Pope said

"Come, let us pray for guidance."

They both went down on their knees and bent their knees, clasping their hands together.

The Cardinal waited until the Pope stood up before he too rose.

"Well, My Son. I have prayed for guidance regarding this miracle of the toast landing buttered side up. It is clear that we cannot have every Tom, Dick and Podrig claiming miracles everywhere. Tell him he buttered it on the wrong side!"

Slainte!!

A Miracle

menu

Irish Parsnip Soup

Soda Bread

Irish Stew

Expresso Martini Tiramisu

Parmesan Cheese Biscuits

Irish parsnip soup

Prep time	20 minutes
Cooking time:	30 minutes
Serves:	12
Method:	easy

Ingredients

- 150 gr butter
- 3 tbs oil
- 5 cloves
- 1 kilo parsnips peeled and cut into cubes
- 3 apples peeled and cut into cubes
- 3 onions peeled and diced
- 4 tsp of garam masala powder
- 1 tsp hot curry powder
- 1tsp cumin seed
- 1 litre chicken stock 'optional for vegetarian base soup'
- salt & pepper

Method

Using a large saucepan

- add the butter & oil
- add the onions and cook for 5 minutes
- add the garam masala, curry powder, cloves & cumin
- cook for a further 2 minutes
- add the parnsips & apples

- cook for a further 2 minutes
- pour the chicken stock & 500ml water
- stir well
- simmer for 30 minutes
- blend the soup well
- season to taste

Chef's tip: You can substitute hot curry powder for mild curry powder

Soda bread

Prep time:	15 minutes
Cooking time:	30 minutes
Serves:	12
Method:	easy

Ingredients

- 300 gr wholemeal flour
- 300 gr plain flour
- 1 tsp salt
- 1 tsp bicarbonate of soda
- 600 ml buttermilk

Method

- Preheat the oven to 200°C

Using a large mixing bowl

- pour all the flour, bicarbonate of soda & salt
- mix well

- pour the buttermilk and mix to a soft dough
- turn onto a lightly floured surface
- shape into a round shape
- pressed the dough lightly to flatten the shape
- place onto a floured baking tray
- cut a cross on the top of the dough
- bake for about 30 minutes
- the loaf should sound hollow when tapped

Chef's tip: If the dough is too wet add flour and if it's too dry add a little water.

Proper Irish Stew

Prep time:	20 minutes
Cooking time:	2 hours
Serves:	12
Method:	easy

Ingredients

- 100 ml oil
- 500 gr bacon cut into cubes
- 3 kilos lamb's shoulder cut into cubes '4cm cube'
- salt & black pepper
- 6 garlic cloves chopped
- 2 large onions diced
- 2 large swedes peeled and chopped
- 300 gr carrots peeled and cut into cubes
- 3 large potatoes peeled and cut into cubes
- 6 cloves

- 2 litre beef stock or 2 litre of water & 4 beef cubes
- 1 pint of irish stout

Method

Using a large saucepan

- pour in the oil
- add the bacon, onions, carrots, swede,
- season to taste
- add the beef stock
- add the meat
- add the stout
- mix well
- simmer for an hour
- add the potatoes
- simmer for a further hour
- season to taste
- serve

Chef's tip: Make sure you have plenty of liquid whilst the stew cooks: add a bit of water if it gets too dry.

Espresso Martini tiramisu

Prep time:	30 minutes
Cooking time:	N/A
Serves:	12
Method:	medium

To be made the night before

Ingredients

- 400 ml strong black coffee
- 2 tsp brown sugar
- 4 tbsp vodka
- 4 tbsp Kahlua
- 500 gr mascarpone
- 600 ml double cream
- 3 tbsp icing sugar
- 1 tbsp vanilla extract
- 2 tbsp instant espresso coffee powder
- 300 gr sponge fingers
- 50 gr dark chocolate

For dusting

- cocoa powder

Method

Step 1

- Mix the black coffee, brown sugar, vodka and 3
  tbsp of the Kahlúa in a shallow bowl. Mix the
  mascarpone in a separate bowl for 2 minutes to break
  it up, then beat in the double cream, icing sugar and
  vanilla with electric beaters until it forms soft peaks.
  Spoon out 1/3 of the cream into another bowl. Mix
  the coffee powder with the rest of the Kahlúa and stir
  in to make a coffee cream;

Step 2

- Dip the sponge fingers briefly into the vodka-coffee
  mixture, then put a single layer of the fingers in the

base of a large serving dish;

Step 3

- Spoon over 1/2 of the plain cream, then finely grate over a generous layer of dark chocolate. Layer on more soaked sponge fingers, and spoon over the coffee cream then another layer of grated chocolate. Add another layer of fingers then finish with the rest of the plain cream. Chill until ready to serve, but for at least 4 hours. Dust with cocoa powder to finish.

Chef's tip: If you don't have any Kahlua 'coffee liqueur' use Tia Maria or similar

Parmesan biscuits for cheese

Prep time:	5 minutes
Cooking time:	10 minutes
Serves:	12
Method:	easy

Ingredients

- 500 gr strong flour
- 250 gr unsalted butter softened
- 200 gr parmesan grated
- 1 tsp smoked paprika

Method

- pre heat oven to 180*c

Using a large mixing bowl

- pour the flour, paprika & parmesan
- add the butter
- rub into a dough
- roll out on a floured surface around 1 cm thick
- cut into chosen size
- bake for 10 minutes
- leave to cool

Christmas Eve

Christmas Eve

Here we are in late December,
We've said goodbye to old November,
We await that magic night,
When Christmas Eve hoves into sight.
We picture now the snowy scene,
Our house bedecked with living green,
The eve is mother to the day,
As Mary was so far away.

And anyone can light a candle,
Let it glow and shine out bright.
Yes. Anyone can light a candle,
To remember that Christmas night.

On Christmas Eve the bells will ring,
and we will gather round to sing,
Christmas songs around the yule,
Whether you are King or Fool.
Noble, Squire, Prince or Knave,
Upright Yeoman, Warrior brave,
Bishop, Deacon, Vicar, Priest,
All enjoy the Saviour's Feast.

So. Everyone should light a candle,
and raise a glass of wine.
Yes. Let's all light a candle,
and drink to thee and thine.

So push the Advent doors ajar,

And look to see what's there,
Three Wise men coming from afar,
With gifts enough to spare.
Christmas cheer in homes and halls,
Drive the winter's dark away.
The Christmas Eve which we all love,
This special festive day.

So. Let's keep lighting candles,
While we anticipate,
The Christmas that is coming,
That fine mid-winter's date.

And let us remember that first Christmas Eve,
When first was revealed the things we believe,
So long ago so far away,
In Bethlehem that Christmas Day.
With angels singing songs so loud,
Old Joseph standing there so proud,
Young Mary overwhelmed by all,
Who bore the child at her Lord's call.

No-one lit the candles,
Not in that stable bare.
No. No-one lit the candles,
To shine on the babe so fair.

There were no bells on that first night,
No Christmas trees festooned in light,
Not in a palace grand nor hall,
But just a baby in a stall.
With ass and oxen on the straw,

The shepherds standing by the door.
Or so the tale was handed down,
Of Christmas night in Bethlehem town.
And so, we wait and by-your-leave,
We shall see in this Christmas Eve.

So. Let's keep lighting candles,
Upon these Christmas nights.
Yes. Let's keep lighting candles,
The real Christmas lights.

(thanks to Jon Anderson for inspiration)

Security

It was Christmas Eve. That magical night for children when they are, on the one hand, so keen to go to bed - knowing that the morning will bring Christmas Day and presents – but on the other they are too overwrought and excited actually to go to sleep. I remembered that, when my children were young, over the Christmas period I read the Christmas Mystery to them each night, with each chapter representing a day on the Advent calendar. They would listen with rapt attention and join in with the cries of Elijah, one of the main characters in the book as they journeyed down to Bethlehem and back across time, as he rapped his staff on the ground saying: "To Bethlehem, To Bethlehem!" Happy days. And, of course, we read 'T'was The Night Before Christmas' by Clement-Moore Clark – I knew that poem off by heart so often had I read it. Now all grown up and soon to be reading it to their children, my grandchildren.

When we had realised that our December Dining Club evening would fall on Christmas Eve, we had unanimously agreed that it should go ahead on that special evening. The room was decorated in its usual tasteful manner – this year in subtle blends of reds, greens and gold: with the splendidly large Christmas Tree, as usual, being the focal point of the room, next to the blazing log fire at one end of our usual room.

As we filed in Groves was on hand as usual to offer exciting, and in this case particularly exotic, drinks.

There was beer – nothing exotic about that of course - East African: a Nile special which was like a cross between Guinness and mild; but I also noticed that Tusker, a lager type beer and especially good, when served cold in the East African heat, but from S Africa, was also on offer, which was preferred by some. There were also several cocktails using the East African liqueur – made from the fruits of the Amarula tree. I remembered, from my time in East Africa, that this was the yellow fruit of a tree that was especially enjoyed by elephants. They can smell them from miles away and head towards the trees. It gets them drunk – which is a thing to think about and even more bizarre to behold! It is only found in sub-equatorial Africa and has resisted attempts to cultivate it elsewhere.

In fact, when I was out there, we organised a trip to a small game park or reserve near the coast and, during the night, I was staying in a caravan of sorts, sharing with a colleague, when, suddenly, the caravan started rocking quite severely and woke us both up. This continued for a few minutes then ceased. Once it had stopped, I opened the door and looked out, but could see nothing. We went back to bed, but I slept fitfully as I recall – but my colleague on the opposite bunk fell into a deep snoring sleep which was irritating to say the least! A few years later, he and I were on a golf tour, and staying at the house of another of our colleagues and we were billeted together – and his snoring was even worse. He was lucky to survive the night! He was a small chap – not more than 5' 4" but oh – the noise!!

In the morning I recounted the event to the camp manager – stressing that it didn't feel dangerous – just a little odd.

"Aah " he said "That is Lonesome George."

"Lonesome George?"

"Yes. He is an elephant, ageing now, and he wanders around these parts. Harmless. Elephants are, however, partial to the Amarula fruit, it gets them drunk, and your caravan was parked just near to one of these trees. He was helping himself to the fruit no doubt and your caravan was just in the way."

A bit like Denmark when Nazi Germany invaded Norway I thought – but I said nothing.

My colleague said "Well - what can you say!"

So, then Groves offered the cocktails – there was "East African B52" – which, he informed us was 1/3 Amarula, 1/3 Kahlua and 1/3 Grand Marnier. It reminded me of the US Group whose female singers had the B-52 haircuts – a conscious throwback to the 50's or 60's; and also one which rejoiced in the marvellous name of "Zing Amarula Mint Music Muddle". I felt I had to try it just for the name.

This was, it seemed to me, the East African version of a Mint Julep – neither of which I had ever had. It contained Amarula, naturally, mint leaves, sugar and water – with plenty of ice. I have to confess it was not to my taste, and I grabbed another beer to wash it down. But you have to try these things.

Then we turned to the food.

To start we had a small plate of sambaza fish, which is deep fried and served with fresh lemon wedges. At the side was Ugali – which is a flat bread – used for scooping up food and sauces.

The main course was Tilapia - which was a delicious grilled fish – accompanied with a vegetable dish which was, according to Groves, made out of mashed cassava leaves, also known as manioc leaves and known as Isombe, with onions and peppers used in the preparation and aubergines cooked in a sauce flavoured with peanut butter and palm oil. It was also accompanied with okra. The whole thing was a gourmet's delight. Delicious.

Mace is a spice that comes from the outer coating of the nutmeg seed. Latin name (I looked it up) Myristica fragrans and it is an evergreen tree that was originally indigenous to Indonesia, known as the Spice Islands. It was brought by Arab traders (it is believed) to Zanzibar (now a part of Tanzania after it was 'forcibly', but "bloodlessly", merged with Tanganyika – known as the 'bloodless coup') and in turn it was known as the Spice Island, but Mace is nowadays available from many sources. I recalled from my time on Tanzania that the visit to Zanzibar was thoroughly enjoyable and was well worth the effort – full of history and with those amazing carved 'Arab' wooden doors or gates – often worth more than the rest of the building! On a more sombre note, Zanzibar was also the centre of the slave trade to the east. The port on the east coast of Africa, nearest Zanzibar, is known as Bagamayo - which means 'lay down my heart and weep' in Swahili – the language of Eastern Africa that is a blend of Arabic and Bantu - as it was where slaves were brought by Arabs to be taken across to Zanzibar and thence to Arabia and the rest of the Middle East. I visited the museum and saw the shackles and chains and pictures and I remembered the guide telling us that, although some slaves ran away, they were commonly killed by lions and/ or hyenas and few escaped.

Given its Latin name – I wondered if mace was related to myrrh and perhaps it was this that the Wise Men brought rather than pure myrrh? Perhaps a more useful gift, which could be used for flavouring the often very poor food available then, rather than Myrrh which was more commonly used in embalming corpses. We shall never know probably.

After, the meal we were offered an Amarula Dom Pedro

– as a combination pudding/pudding cocktail consisting of Amarula Cream Liqueur blended with double cream and Vanilla ice cream and some chocolate. It was intensely indulgent and I felt a bit porky afterwards – but my goodness it was nice.

Then the Professor stood up.

'I am reminded of a story from East Africa. I was out there on a safari and, as part of it, we were offered the opportunity to scale Mount Kilimanjaro. This is, as you probably know, the highest mountain in Africa, and it sits right on the equator.   When the first Victorian travellers came back to the UK with tales of a massive mountain straddling the equator and covered in snow: the armchair savants, of whom there were many, scoffed and said this could not be. But, of course, they were unaware of how much temperature falls as you rise. Anyway, I and a couple of other travellers decided that as we were unlikely to have the opportunity again, we would climb Kilimanjaro. It stands 19,500 feet high – so not a small hill!! It was a very professional climb and we were advised to take a good number of things with us including:

- A -20 Degree Sleeping Bag
- Sleeping Pad
- Trekking Poles
- Insulated Trekking Gloves, Pants, and Winter Jacket
- Hiking Boots

- 70 Litre Main Rucksack
- 30-40 Litre Day Pack

There are several routes you can take – each lasting between 6 to 8 days. The Marangu Route—sometimes referred to as the Coca-Cola Route—is the oldest path to Mt. Kilimanjaro's top and is a six-day roundtrip trek and you sleep the night in designated dormitory huts – it is about 50 miles in total.

The Machame route is called the Whiskey Route, as it is a step-up in difficulty from the Coca-Cola Route and is the more popular way to reach the mountain peak, for a more rugged experience, but it takes seven days just to reach the summit. There ae other, more difficult, routes too.

We opted for the quickest route, with a guide, and even so as we approached the summit we were feeling very sick and throwing up from the altitude. We were determined to make it, however, and so we struggled on. To our amazement, and I still cannot believe it now, we met a little Chinese man sitting at the top, drinking tea, who had climbed up on his own, carrying a bicycle – yes a bicycle - and was intending to cycle back down. And he did. Incredible – made us feel like total wimps. And now I hand over to Archie.'

Then Archie got up, and we knew who was telling us the tale. I recalled his last tale which he told using a ventriloquist's dummy – and how funny had that been. He did not have the dummy, however, so I thought he was just going to tell the tale straight; but then he said:

'Please come with me.'

And we followed him into another room, into which we had never been before. In it were several rows of chairs in front of a Punch and Judy stall. That was more like it.

We sat down in anticipation and he disappeared behind the striped canopy.

The curtains opened and an elephant's head appeared and spoke in a deep, but nasal (or trunky) voice

"My name is Tembo. I am an elephant and we live across much of Africa, but I am from East Africa. I live in a large herd and we wander around the lands across the years following food and water. We are known for our great strength and stamina."

The puppet was then joined by the head of a lion which spoke in a very rich tenor.

"My name is Simba. I am a lion and I live in Africa too. Generally, we do not eat elephants as they are a bit large for us. We do like antelopes though. We are known for our great strength and we live and hunt in packs – but it is the lionesses that do most of the hunting - I just help myself to the lion's share."

That got a laugh – and then it gave out a sort of cross between a roar and a laugh. Tembo replied with a trumpet like noise, and disappeared. Then the head of another cat appeared, spotty this time, and it said in a soft voice.

"My name is Chui and I am a leopard – we are not as large as lions – but we are more cunning." And it gave out a sound more like a very loud purr and disappeared.

Tembo reappeared

"Now you are wondering why we are here – well, I will tell you."

And the elephant ducked down and appeared with a set of large glasses perched on its trunk saying. "As you know we elephants never forget – that is because we write everything down!" and a piece of paper appeared in front of it and it bent its head forward slightly as if reading it.

"We animals were here long before man evolved into the many different races and nations that now exist and we have observed your antics with great amusement and sometimes great fear."

The Leopard reappeared

"As we observe we also listen and we heard this story one day whilst we were travelling south in search of water in the country you call Zambia. We animals do not, of course know borders – it is all our land. Note that we were not travelling together – just that it had been a bad year for rains that particular year – they were late – although they did arrive eventually - and we had to go far and away in our search. We just happened to be in proximity serendipitously

– but too near each other – for obvious reasons. Three man-beings were sitting around a campfire in the bush. We were all standing silently in the shadows that evening and could hear every word that they uttered, for sound travels far in the bush at night, crystal clear."

Tembo took up the story

"This is what we heard – the first man-being had a South African accent, the second man-being had a Scots accent, and the third man-being was accent less – effectively English."

The room darkened and the light shimmered faintly as if t'were a campfire glow.

"It is night now let's have a beer. It is Tusker, from ma own country."

"Och mon, that I will and right gladly!"

"Thank you very much Marius. Ahh it is nice and cold – not like the beer in the UK, which is often served warm: useful in winter – but not now that summers are much hotter. This is a running joke in the Asterix in Britain book which you have all read - I am sure?"

"Na man na!"

"So. It is Christmas Eve. What a strange place to be spending it – far away from family.

Still - Merry Christmas! Cheers"

"Geseënde Kersfees! - Goeie gesondheid!"

"Nollag Shona! Slainte"

And they drank each other's health.

Then another head appeared – a snake.

"Jambo! Habari gana. My name isss Nyoka. I move in the sshadowss and also watch what iss going on. But I jusst want to ssay 'Afya njema!' Good health to you all." Then it disappeared.

A strange interjection I thought.

"So Mac, what are you doing now? You used to work in a bank did you not?"

"Och ja mun, what is going on with you?"

"Weell, I'll tell you. We had a wee bit of bother and the bank went broke. We were only a small one, essentially a branch that was missed out in the great nationalisation fiasco, and became a separate bank with a few small branches, serving an up-country town and its hinterland – sort of nondescript Scotch border country. I was asked to run it by the owners, a mixture of locals and a Middle Eastern investment company. They had some concerns about some of the loans. The first thing I did was to analyse the loan book to understand it. That is the spread of loans, the sums involved, the security and the cashflow. I identified some suspect individuals – including one who had gone bankrupt before, and now claimed to be solvent again."

"Ach mun – the leopard cannot change its spots!"

At this point the leopard shouted

"That was uncalled for! I like my spots and would not

change them for all the Amarula in Tanzania!"

"You could not reach the fruits unless they had fallen down!" said Tembo

The lion popped up saying "A windfall that would be – your plan would bear fruit." Then disappeared.

Then a new fawny-brown head appeared – a giraffe.

"My name is Twiga. I, however, can reach those fruits – in fact I can reach most things with my long legs and my 6 foot long neck. Interestingly though despite that I have the same number of bones as Tembo, Chui, Simba and you man-beings - 7. They are slightly larger though! My tongue also adds another foot or so – so I don't have to have the low-hanging fruit."

Tembo carried on narrating the story, adopting the Scots accent.

"Weell coincidentally this chap who had gone bankrupt said he had come into a windfall – this was how he was solvent. But I checked his account and it was, in fact, all ok. So I progressively trawled through the rest."

"What did he catch?" asked Chui popping up again with an English accent now. "For, of course, we Leopards often take fish from lakes and rivers."

Tembo ignored this and carried on with the story.

"So, I reviewed the larger accounts: ranking them by size and looking at how the account had performed over its history. Those with unco bad performance I placed for deeper review, those with good records I left, as there was no need to review them."

"Well Mac, what did you do to those that were suspect?"

"Well, I thoroughly investigated them and marked them all up for action. This ranged from immediate recall of the loan and the realisation of security held; through setting up a plan for accelerated repayments and or further security; for discussion with the customer; and down to more frequent, but light touch monitoring depending on the perceived risk and amounts. The larger the amount the greater the review and frequency."

Simba interjected "Presumably those accounts that you left were the good customers, mine Vriend?"

"Aye. Although they were also the larger amounts by some way – especially one that was quite large. But this one had been a customer for many years and, what is more we were more than covered with the security over its land, buildings, fixtures, fittings and stock ye ken?"

"No actually – what does that mean exactly old chap?"

"Wee-ll as a bank we often take security over items belonging to borrowers when we lend – like a mortgage on a house. This is to ensure that, if anything goes wrong, the bank's interest (metaphorically as well as actually) is protected."

As the story went on the animal puppets gradually, and imperceptibly became the characters, Tembo the

Scotsman, Chui the Englishman and Simba the South African. Very clever I thought.

Then another head popped up – a monkey and in a wheezy voice said

"My name is Nyami – I am a baboon and live on the plains too - but I am also called Mzee – old man – or eldest - for I have lived a long time and seen many things. I have seen many dawns and many departures – more even than our pachydermic friend here. My people saw the Mzunga – the white man - come and we have seen them go from most of Africa. With their guns and dogs they hunted many of my animal friends so that few are now left. Especially that so symbolic friend – the Kifaru – now hunted by Chinese for their horns in the mistaken belief that when powdered it is a medicine. It is sad." The puppet gave out a sigh and a sob. And having lectured us he disappeared.

"So Mac – what else did you do?"

"Well, I visited many of the customers to check on them, to make sure their businesses were thriving etc. This involved up-country trips: for which we had to take our own food and often camp out as there was nowhere to stay. I do not know how well you know Tanzania – but it is four times the size of the UK and there are few useable roads to speak of, more dirt tracks really. When the rains come even these are washed away – as are the bridges."

The leopard and lion nodded their heads in understanding.

"So, I spent a lot of time travelling around checking up on companies, checking the security and making sure it as up-stamped etc."

"Up-stamped mon - What does that mean?"

"Och it is a peculiarity of the local law. Each time you take security or you advance a sum you have to make sure that the security is registered locally at the Government Office – like Companies House I suppose. There is a charge for it: of course. Well then – I came back to our Head Office, to take stock of where we were. By the way put your glasses out – here is a wee dram for us all."

Here a zebra's head appeared. "I am Nyeusi-Nyupe." And he held up a piece of paper. "It is written here in black and white. We animals cannot understand why man-beings are always drinking odd drinks. We animals just drink water – maji - and it does us very well."

Tembo replied in the Scottish accent "But this is water – Uisge Beatha -the water of life!"

Chui adding "akva-vit."

"Sliante!"

"Cheers!"

"Gesondheid!"

Then he made as if to carry on with his tale whilst the zebra shook his head and disappeared, but then Chui said

"I'll tell you what – as it's Christmas Eve - let's have a Christmas song."

"Och Ja. – but which to sing. We have different traditions"

"Well – yes but we all know Silent Night don't we?"

"Stille nacht? Ja!"

"Well, then let us sing it – together."

But just then several more animal heads appeared and spoke

"Jambo – I am Nguruwe. Can you see my curly tusks and snout?"

"Duma is my name – I am very fast – and a tip: don't play me at cards!" said a spotty cat

A large greyish brown head said "Kiboko – that's me a horse from the river! And this is my friend." Indicating a large grey head with a horn "Kifari."

And last a long brown snouty head with teeth – "Myy Naame is Mamba. I nevver met a maan-being I diidn't liiike. Or any otherr aniimal forr that matter, my monochromatic friend." And he gazed at the zebra.

Then all the heads started (or so it seemed) singing 'Silent Night' – both in English and in German I suppose – but it could have been Dutch. Furthermore – whilst it could have been a cacophony – it seemed to work – strangely enough. They sang just one verse and the chorus and then the heads disappeared leaving the three main protagonists. 'I wonder how he did that' I thought. Then, in the half light, I saw the shape of Groves just coming out silently from behind the puppet box. 'Aha!' I thought but I said nothing. And he served us all with a drink. I took a tusker beer. We were now all enraptured as to what the story held.

"Now och – where was I? och yes – I was heading back to the HO. Well, I felt that I had done a grand job. Reduced our exposure, confirmed our security on several dodgy loans and I was just about to file my report when one of the staff came up to me saying "Might I have a word, baas?" I had tried to stop them using this term but old habits die hard. They also called me Mr Ian too.

"Of course, Freeman (for that was his name) what can I do for you?

"It is about Impexco."

"Oh – what is it?" for it was one of our long-standing clients.

"It has missed a repayment and there is no money in the account."

"No. but it has been functioning well for years – hasn't it?"

"Yes and no. There have been glitches - but it has never missed two payments."

"Two?!? You said one just now."

"Well, yes – technically it is one but with no money on the account and the next one due at close of business today – in 5 minutes – that makes it two!"

I thought about it. this was an import and export

business that we knew well. I had reviewed it and seen that we had security that covered our loan three to four times – so from that point of view we were covered if push came to shove! Furthermore, its office was on the main road between two large buildings – and the staff walked past it every day – so it was well known.

So, I got out the file and had a good look through it I couldn't see anything particularly wrong with it although clearly if they'd missed a payment or two something was going wrong. Anyway, I decided to go and have a look at it so I asked one of my colleagues two accompany me there next morning as it is always good to have another set of eyes and a witness. Then I went home.

Next day we met at the office and decided to walk down to the client's building and try to meet with the business management. I took out the list of our security – fixed charge on the buildings – which of course are fairly difficult to take away – but also cannot realise cash until they are sold. A floating charge on any debtors and stock – which at last valuation was on its own good enough to cover our loan."

"Ah mun what is a floating charge?"

"Och weel it is a useful artifice for bankers and clients. At one time there was only a fixed charge and that meant all sorts of problems for traders as they needed, in theory, the secured creditor's permission to trade – ie to dispose of stock, to process raw materials into finished goods, and or realise debtors – dissatisfactory. A floating charge, by contrast, allows firms to buy and sell goods, use cash to pay off trade creditors, buy new stock and realise their debtors. If I remember my banking training it was described by a judge as 'crystallising into a fixed charge at the point where it is needed.' Of course, this is usually when a business has failed and what value the assets might have at that time is then in the lap of the gods.

I had walked past the office on the way up in the morning and it was clearly there. Although for a client visit you would usually arrange it in advance: where there is – well shall we say a mickle of doubt as to their position – we go unannounced. So, we wandered down and knocked on the door and stood waiting. As we waited the sun got up and it started to get hot, but there was no reply – and no signs of life. This was a bit worrying but, of course, it is a trading business – not a manufacturing business, so their people could be out and about doing things, however I did want to talk to them urgently so I went back to the office and gave them a call. No reply.

I asked my colleague to call several times during the day to see if he could get hold of him: but, at the end of the day, we still had no reply. I, therefore, decided immediate action was necessary. Next morning, I went to the local magistrate and got an enforcement order to enter the premises. We went down and we were, as I had asked, accompanied by the local Inspector so that we had cover from the law. He brought two colleagues with him one of whom brought a ram to breakdown doors, which I thought was a bit unnecessary at the time. When, however, we went down to the office and knocked on the door there was still no reply.

What to do? I didn't really want to breakdown the door – just on case. I said to the Inspector look let's wait a little while – let's come back tomorrow, or in a couple of days?

I went back to the office went through the file and checked all the documentation and account history. As I looked it seemed to me that it wasn't quite such a good account as we had supposed. There had often been hiccoughs – although never for very long. I did notice, however, a definite trend to longer gaps and an increase in hardcore on the overdraft."

"What is hard core – isn't that used in building and so on?"

"Aye – it is an analogy – it means that part of an overdraft which doesn't move. As you know an overdraft is meant to be a temporary thing where the account swings from borrowing – that is deficit - and back into credit. Where this doesn't happen the movement is usually at the margin – say the top 10% or 15% and the rest doesn't move.

I checked out our documentation and looked at the

security we had and I looked at the amount we had outstanding. The security was on land and buildings, fixtures and fittings, as well as the floating charge or debenture, and that seemed to cover the loan plus the missed repayments plus any extra interest and charges two or three times so I was reasonably relaxed about it. The security had been up stamped as was the law locally every time they had increased the borrowings: so I felt quite relaxed about our position with regard to the security. I was still concerned about the decline in payments of course.

During the course of the day, we tried to ring a few times - no reply. I even went down to the office a couple of times and knocked on the door. No reply. I therefore rang the police inspector and when he had answered I said 'I think we need to take immediate action, so once more we went down to the office. As I was walking toward the door the inspector shouted "Kwema! – stop!" he pointed upstairs. "Kuangalia – look!". I stopped and looked to where he was pointing – I could see that two or three the windows were broken

It is curious that nobody at the bank had mentioned this because most of the staff walked past it every day - but I suppose they never looked up as it was a part of the landscape. Of course, if you leave the windows open, or if they are broken: in Africa all sorts of creatures and things can get in so that was a bit concerning. They looked like they had been broken for some time too.

The police inspector signalled to his colleague who was carrying the ram for breaking down the door, to come forward, which was a bit sad, but there we are – needs must and so on. So, he smashed the door down. I took out the list of what we were secured on and we walked into the building."

"What do you think we found there?"

This was greeted with a chorus of 'no idea' and so on and some silly suggestions.

"There was nothing. Absolutely nothing. Nobody, no fixtures, no stock, no office furniture – nothing. We had walked into a bit of scrubby field. The whole thing had been a fraud from the start. The so-called building was just a façade between two others. A salutary lesson."

"What actual lesson did you take from this Mac?"

"Always make a physical check of assets – both at the start, and periodically, across the life of the lending facility. The account had been with the branch for some time and I suspect either there was some sort of collusion originally – or just lackadaisical processes - as everybody walked past it everyday and assumed it was kosher!"

There was much clapping – as much for the tale as for the masterful presentation via puppets by Archie.

Groves filled our drinks again and we all said 'Cheers and Merry Christmas.'

Security

menu

African Fish Stew

Flat Bread

Somalian Goat Curry

West African Lime Cake

African fish stew

Prep time:	20 minutes
Cooking time:	40 minutes
Serves:	12
Method:	medium

Ingredients

- 1.2 kg white fish, hake, pollock or ling
- 4 tbs vegetable oil
- 500 gr tomatoes chopped or 1 large tin chopped tomatoes
- 3 red peppers, sliced
- 1 chili chopped
- 6 garlic cloves chopped
- 1 onion chopped
- 1 tsp paprika
- 1 tsp black pepper
- 1 tsp mild curry powder
- 1 bunch of fresh coriander

Method

- cut the fish into 12 pieces - or get the fishmonger to do it for you
- Using a large saucepan
- add the oil gently heated
- add the onion, red pepper, garlic, paprika, curry powder, black pepper
- cook slowly for 5 minutes

- add the tomatoes
- add the fish
- season to taste
- simmer for 30 minutes
- chop the coriander and add to the dish before serving

Chef's tip: Tilapia is a main fish for this recipe but can be substituted with any other fish.

Flat bread

Prep time:	10 minutes
Cooking time:	4 minutes
Serves:	12
Method:	easy

Ingredients

- 400 gr plain flour
- 1 tbs salt
- 200 ml water
- 4 tbs olive oil
- 1 tsp ground cumin

Method

Using a medium bowl

- add flour, salt, cumin, olive oil and water
- mix well until it forms a dough
- cut into 12 equal pieces

- using a little flour roll the flat bread

In a dry, hot pan

- place the flat bread and cook for 2 minutes each side
- serve hot

Somalian Goats Curry

Prep time:	30 minutes
Cooking time:	3 hours
Serves:	12
Method:	easy

Ingredients

- 100 ml vegetable oil
- 8 tbs curry powder
- 1 tbs all spice
- 3 kg goats stew meat
- 2 large onions chopped
- 2 tbs mace, ground
- 2 chillies chopped
- 100 gr fresh ginger peeled and diced
- 6 garlic cloves chopped
- 4 cans of coconut milk
- 2 coconut tins of water
- 500 gr potatoes peeled and diced into 3 cm chunks

Method

Using a large bowl

- place the meat and season with salt, mix well

- set aside for 30 minutes

Using a large saucepan

- add the oil
- add all of the spices
- add onions, garlic, chili, ginger
- cook for 1 minute at low gas
- add the meat
- mix well
- add coconut milk & water
- cook for 2 hours
- add potatoes
- cook for another hour
- serve with plain rice

Chef's tip: You can use mild curry powder or hot curry powder according to your tastebuds.

You could also use lamb or beef if you prefer - or antelope, ostrich or giraffe.

West African Lime Cake

Prep time:	10 minutes
Cooking time:	30 minutes
Serves:	12
Method:	easy

Ingredients

- 250 gr brown sugar
- 250 gr butter

- 250 gr flour
- 6 eggs
- 6 lime juice and zest
- 1 tsp baking powder

Method

- preheat oven to 180ºC

Using a mixer

- add butter & sugar
- mix well
- add juice of 2 limes: keep the rest for later
- add all the zest
- add eggs & flour
- mix well

Using a medium 8 inch (20cm) square cake tin

- place baking parchment on the bottom and side
- pour in the cake mixture
- bake for 30 minutes
- leave to cool before unmoulding

Christmas Day

The Last Advent Candle

The last of our Advent candles is lit,
And the four now shine together.
There is just one more that is yet unlit,
The candle for Christmas for ever.

The fourth tells us that we are nearly there,
At the special day we remember.
With the birth of a child with wishes and prayer,
In the deep dark depths of December.

The four make a circle around the crown,
The fifth goes into the centre.
We light them all 'til they burn down,
As we wait for the Christchild to enter.

The fourth and the fifth makes the green crown complete,
And they fill the church with their light.
We remember the barn where there was no heat,
and the stars filled the cold wintry night.

The final candle is deep, deep red,
And is the final, sacred part.
It will burn with a light, to drive our dread,
And to make a fire in your heart.

The church bells peal and they chime and they ring,
As we've lit the way from November.
We've seen shepherds and angels: but nary a King,
For we are still in December.

And so now we come to Christmas day,
When the word was made flesh in the stable,
And all five candles shine out in array,
And we praise for all we are able.

Just the fax Ma'am

We had filed into our usual room – it was Christmas Day. All had agreed to go ahead with the meeting even though it was that very special day. We had all spent Christmas Eve and Christmas Morning with our families and friends, and then assembled at the Professor's house, as usual.

Groves was standing in his usual place offering us a choice of beverages. A 'Steam lager' from New England; other US beers which brands I had never heard of; or a Rye whiskey. So that gave us the probable location – somewhere in the USA. Everybody wished each other a Merry Christmas and there was a chorus of 'Cheers' and so on, as we reacquainted ourselves with each other. Many swapped Christmas cards.

We had agreed that the meal would not be turkey, which would have been appropriate as it was a bird whose use had come over from the USA – but most of us would have already eaten it – so, instead, we would revert to the more traditional, in the UK, goose.

So, we sat down and our first course was brought in. It was a soup, although Groves informed us that it was more properly a 'Chowder' – an American soup whose etymology was a little obscure – variously thought to be named after the French 'Chaudiere' – which meant bucket, or 'Chaudron', cauldron; or from a creole word from Brazilian or Portuguese 'caldeirada'. It might also have come from the French word for hot – 'chaud'. I knew that it was usually a fish soup – very rich and often had crackers mixed into it. Clam Chowder was a well-known US East Coast dish, which I had had on occasion when I was there.

Given that the soup was so rich I was not surprised to see that the main course was in fact much lighter. As well as small portions of goose, with traditional stuffing, there was also a selection of traditional US – in fact New York I supposed - dishes. There was pastrami on rye, and hot dogs – with mustard, pickles, relish and sauerkraut. I recalled that once, when my children were small their school had a 'western' themed open day. They were serving hotdogs and I, in my niaivete, slathered the mustard over it – assuming it was American mustard. It was, of course, English and my first bite nearly blew my head off!

I also recalled that when I had visited New York on business – my US colleagues had asked me what I would like to eat. I had said I wanted to try pastrami on rye and a celray – that being my view of New York food at the time. We went to a New York Deli and, when the lady asked me what I wanted, I told her. She said "That's OK dear. It will be up in a minute." And gently laid her hand on my arm.

My two US colleagues, one who was Irish-American and one who was Italian-American, were flabbergasted and Joe Schiro the second generation Italian-American said "I have never heard anybody called 'Dear' in a New York Deli before. It must be your British accent!" Very funny. They were further surprised when I said I had to visit a client and I wanted to go on the subway. They said it was dangerous and nobody took it. I did and it was fine.

Then New York wines were served (State not City) – for those who wished it - both red and white – from Long Island, and they were very drinkable.

Then afterwards there were a couple of cheesecakes and platters of different cookies with coffee.

Then Dryasdust stood up and commenced his tale.

'As you might have guessed this tale is set in New York – a little while ago - and concerns a very good friend of mine – we can call him Andrew. We were at College together – but whereas I went into law – he studied chemical engineering and then went into banking.

Cast your mind back, if you will, to the late '80s – a time of hedonism, big bang and "loads-a-money" being made in finance following the 'Big Bang'. This was also long before we had smart mobile phones and even laptops. In fact, desktop PCs were only just coming in to general use – albeit slowly. It was long before Apple and Microsoft took over the world. There was no integrated 'Office' and the only programmes around were Lotus – a real game changer – and on which XL was based – or reverse engineered; Freelance

– a very low-quality precursor of Powerpoint (but still a radical step forward) and various 'Word' programmes for writing documents and so on. Nobody remembers Lotus 1-2-3 now but it was a major change to the way in which ordinary people could manipulate large amounts of data and engage in number-crunching without needing mainframes or undertaking it manually. There was only one 'sheet', or tab, so developing large calculations was difficult to say the least. Despite the obvious benefits it was amazing how much resistance there was to even this low level of automation.

My friend had been asked to join a Merchant bank – a UK Investment bank we would say now - as Head of Credit and Risk. He had come from one of the big international banks – where, surprisingly and quite radically then, he had been involved in rolling out desk-tops across the international branch network for credit analysis, and seen their utility – quite forward looking of that particular bank. He had, therefore, insisted on having a desk top PC with adequate software and a printer in his new role. There had been some rumblings from the 'old guard' at this – they were opposed to changes of course - but he had insisted: pointing out that if he were to be analysing tens, if not hundreds, of banks for creditworthiness he could not do it manually. The irony is that, once he had had the PC installed (with support from the Head of IT – who was very keen), just about the entire bank came to see it and within a few weeks there were suddenly very many more all over the bank as all could see their usefulness: especially those in corporate finance, derivative trading and other exotic instruments.

Anyway, after a while, it was felt that he should go to the USA and visit some clients and also review the New York branch operations. At this juncture, of course, there were no real mobile phones: and certainly not with the amazing processing power and functionality which we enjoy today such as storing contacts, diaries etc. Instead, everybody used paper-based tools. Mainly the 'Filofax' or similar. For those who do not remember, or have never had one, this was a book-like item within which you could file your items - 'facts/x'. It had a sprung centre with a sort of ring binder with 'teeth': which you opened, put in your pages, and which held the inserts firmly after closing. You would buy whatever contents you wanted – e.g. – a diary (daily, weekly, fortnightly, monthly), blank sheets for writing and making notes, maps of the world, interesting facts, names and addresses, train times, airline details, expense records, tube maps, graph paper, ruled paper and section dividers for clarity and so on. Very useful in fact!

The 'Filofax' became the indispensable tool for Young Upward (or Urban) Professionals – known as 'Yuppies' and, to a certain extent, a way of recognising them. Of course, being a manual record, there was no such thing as automatic back-up to the cloud – as there is today. Back up was a photocopy of various sheets – which of course nobody did as it was a fag.

Given that a Filofax contained so many pieces of information and so much that was important – it came to dominate people's lives – rather in the way that smart phones do now – except that nobody walked along reading their Filofax, or texting – for you couldn't. They always had to have it with them, however, as it had all contact details, diary entries etc. They usually had a plastic ruler in the middle which you could take out and use. If it was forgotten then one either had to manage without it – which could be tricky if you had a busy diary or social life - or go home and get it. Losing it, of course, would cut you off from all your friends' contact details and your business and, more importantly for many Yuppies and Sloane Rangers of course, your social life. It also had pockets for keeping other things in – such as business cards and, if you wanted to, credit cards etc.

Andrew was no exception to this norm, and always had it with him and kept records of everything in it. It was often said that the Filofax would be the death of him – to which he responded with a wry smile. They were about the same size as – oh I don't - know a bible, about A5, and similar in looks generally: a leather bound outside and about 1 inch or 1 ½ inches thick, depending on what information you kept in it. It was fairly heavy – but a Barbour was useful for carrying it around as it had good sized pockets – also part of the Yuppie identity. Of course, then, long before Covid and work-from-home dress down, everybody wore suits – and I mean everybody – even female yuppies – often with big shoulder pads!

So, Andrew flew to New York, Business Class, which was a new experience for him and then took the train from the airport to central New York and went to his hotel. It was late December – so the Christmas lights and decorations were out, and, as anyone knows who has been to New York in December – it is freezing, so warm coats, scarves and gloves are a must. Having checked in and dumped his case and briefcase in his room he went for a short walk to get the feel of the 'Big Apple'. On the way he had one of those apocryphal encounters with a couple of down and outs - male and female – who asked him for a light. He responded "Sorry I don't smoke." To which the women said, leaning close to him with her bad breath, which was disgustingly alcoholic "We asked you for a light – not your life story!"

So, a little wary now, but not too concerned as he was a karate black belt, he carried on walking for a bit, then returned to his hotel and took his evening meal. Next day he went to see a couple of clients – counterparty banks - taking the traditional yellow cab and putting up with the endless and meaningless chit-chat from the driver, but in reality, switching off. Fortunately, he had a Walkman (an early portable music player) bought on the way over Duty free, "Remember those?" so he put on his headphones, inserted a cassette "Remember those too??", - no portable CD players, no streaming and no music on mobiles then! -and was able to listen to music.

That day's meetings concluded, he stood inside the lobby of the bank building – too cold to stand outside - and checked his Filofax for the next day's itinerary, saw it was with three more banks, one of which was giving him dinner, grabbed a cab, and went back to the hotel. In his room, which was rather too warm for a Brit used to somewhat lower heating: as in America they whack the heat up high, he carefully wrote up his notes from the meetings. He had taught himself shorthand, so was able to take them down almost verbatim, and now converted it into long-hand reports. His secretary would type it up back in the UK. He had a graduate PA, which he shared with the MD – oh those were the days! Then he wrote up all his expenses – carefully accounting for every dollar and cent with requisite receipts. For large items he had a bank Amex – but for smaller items such as cab fares, and the inevitable tips for everyone you encountered, it was cash. He had planned to be there for about ten days and would be able to see quite a few banks as well as some non-banking US clients. He also needed to visit the New York branch on Wall Street – a swanky office he had been told. A couple of colleagues from the UK office were also due to join him and they would be arriving the next day, staying in the same hotel.

He then put everything in his Filofax and retired.

Next day his colleagues arrived and checked into the hotel. He was waiting for them in the lobby, making notes and checking details in his Filofax. The saw him and strode up, shook his hands and one said "I see you are holding your Filofax?"

"Yes, it has everything in it that I need. My diary, my notes, my expenses, my contacts, maps of New York etc. I cannot manage without it!"

"That Filofax will be the death of you!"

"Ha-ha. Go up to your rooms and drop your things off, shower etc. I shall wait here and then we can go for lunch." And he carried on making notes in the Filofax. After a while he put down the Filofax on the table and wandered over to the concierge's desk and picked up a paper. the Wall Street Times – essential for anyone in finance. As he came back to his seat a young lady was walking past and she smiled at him saying, in an American accent.

"Hi. I see you have a Filofax. Me too. I can't manage without it."

"No, me neither. It has changed my life so much."

"Well. I am staying in the hotel too – perhaps we can meet for a drink one evening. I am here all week." And she smiled again and went to the lifts.

When his colleagues came down, he was still smiling at the thought of the lady as they went out for lunch: in the inevitable yellow cab.

After their lunch and, as he had no other meetings that day, he decided to hit the gym - one of the corollaries of hotel life is that you tend to eat and drink too much – so keeping fit and in shape is essential. He didn't take his Filofax – left it in his room – but to his surprise that young lady was there on a treadmill. So, he took the one next to her, put his headphones on and started to run/jog.

She stopped running after a while and hovered round him. He slowed down to a walk and then she placed her hand on his arm saying "How about that drink tonight?"

"Yes of course. I have a couple of colleagues here too – but we are not living in each other's pockets."

"Sure – shall we say 19.00?"

And she smiled again and went out of the gym.

Wow he thought! And carried on running.

At around 18.30 he went down to the hotel bar, and ordered a glass of wine. A nice dry New York wine - state that is not city. In fact, the wine that is being served tonight – a different year obviously! He sat down and started flicking through the Wall St Journal - the US equivalent of the FT. He took a sip, it was nice and chilled, and was just wondering when the gym lady would show up when a hand touched his shoulder and said

"Hi."

He turned round and saw her looking radiant in a little black dress (as per Coco Chanel he thought.) and he smiled back saying

"Would you like a drink?" and then mentally kicked himself – of course she would – he should have said what would you like to drink – this was a bar after all.

She smiled again

"Why, yes thank you. Might I have a gin and tonic?"

This surprised him as he had always thought of that as a quintessentially English drink, not even British, and especially not an American preference.

"Of course. Any special type of gin? Or tonic?"

He has noticed an impressive array of both gin and whisky (Scotch, US, Irish and curiously Japanese) behind the bar.

"Gordons please. And ice and a slice."

Again, he thought, that was very British.

The barman complied.

"If I might say," he said looking at her, "that is a very British drink and a very British expression?"

She smiled again

"Yes. I work in London. In investment banking and

I have picked up some of your British habits. It is a nice drink. I do love a gin – don't you?"

"Yes indeed. I will join you."

"Sure," she said "just so you know, this is a Doubles Bar."

But I am single he thought – then twigged.

"Ahh just like our army messes and indeed the Albert Hall! Extra tonic then please barman."

"Cheers!"

"Mud in your eye!"

Well, he thought that was a US expression.

"So tell me," he said "what are you doing in London?"

"No – first things first, my name is Stacey – what is yours?"

He was so flustered that he had forgotten to introduce himself.

"Andrew. I live and work in London, but I am originally from Hampshire, if you know it."

"Yes I have been to the Noo Forest – real lovely."

Well, that was American for sure.

"Where are you from?"

"I am a Maryland girl - from Bal'more."

Which he correctly interpreted as Baltimore.

"Ah, I haven't been there. What is it like?"

"Well, it was originally a port city and was very important for both trade and for immigration, with about

2 million people on the greater area. It is not so much of a port now, of course, and much of the old part or dock area has been redeveloped and is now a very nice shopping centre with restaurants and so on."

"Ok I have been to Washington DC, which is the same state isn't it?"

She nodded and he signalled the barman to replenish their drinks.

The drinks came and they clinked glasses.

"I think I need to eat now, after 2 double G'n'Ts."

"Sure thing!"

She carried on telling him about Baltimore

"It has a long history for example it had the first post office in the USA, it was the first to really cultivate sugar and tobacco and the success lead to sugar being grown in the Caribbean. It is also famous for brewing and its beers, due to its central European immigrants – National Bohemian being a major brand – knowns as 'Natty Boh'."

Dryasdust indicated his beer and said 'This is that very beer - Natty Boh. Cheers' and he carried on with the tale.

'They went into the restaurant and set the evening getting to know each other. It turned out that, fortunately she didn't work for a client bank, which could have been awkward, but for another US bank.

They then parted with the promise to meet the next night for dinner again.

"Wow!" he thought as he cleaned his teeth "Who would have thought it?

Next day he met his colleagues over coffee and juice – but just before they left he said

"I have forgotten my Filofax. It is in my room I must go and get it."

and he went and fetched it before rejoining his colleagues and spending the day with various banking clients, but anticipating the dinner very much.

As usual during the meetings he took copious notes, in shorthand, and in between, wrote them up in longhand in his Filofax. His colleagues who were using A4 noteblocks teased him about his Filofax, trotting out the same cliche – "It will be the death of you."

He ignored them.

That evening he met Stacey for dinner and again they got on very well. So well in fact that he suggested that on the following day they go out to a restaurant for dinner.

They went into the restaurant were ushered to a table and the waiter come over bringing the menus and they ordered a couple of glasses of wine. They looked at the menu and Andrew realised it was an Italian restaurant– the name of the restaurant hadn't been Italian as it was just a number. He presumed it was the address. Some of the dishes were unfamiliar to him and he supposed they were Italian-American derived – he remembered that chop suey, thought by the British to be Chinese, was in fact American.

As they looked at the menus was looking around the restaurant out of interest and he noticed two very strange people talking to the owner. Unbelievably they looked like Italian gangsters out of a film. They had the thin moustaches, what you might call sharp suits, and porkpie hats.

He just presumed it was just some sort of fashion trend in and turned away. He carried on talking to Stacey and jus then the first course came. They chatted at length throughout the meal and then they left – in a yellow cab. They were getting on really well and he suggested that given that the food was so nice and that it as better and more ambient than the hotel, that they come back the next night. Stacey agreed wholeheartedly, and giving him a big hug and a kiss, she went up to her room.

Next day he went with his colleagues to see some non-banking clients but couldn't get his mind off Stacey: which meant that occasionally he lapsed into a sort of dream state musing on her.

He hadn't forgotten his Filofax today, but his colleagues still teased him about: it trotting out the same old line "That will be the death of you!" but wrapped in the warmth of Stacey's smile, he ignored it.

That night, full of expectation of another fantastic evening over dinner, he went down to the hotel bar to wait for Stacey. He had been to the gym, but she hadn't been there. He had his Filofax with him: as he had a lot to write up and he didn't want to lose time, so he made his notes, did his expenses and added in the new client contacts whilst he waited. He saw her coming across the bar and waved to her, which was a little unnecessary as she was coming straight at him. They had a G'n'T, grabbed a cab and made their way to the same restaurant.

The waiter welcomed them back with great pleasure ad gave them a very nice table, in a quiet corner. He was wearing his Barbour with the Filofax in a pocket which he had left in the cloakroom. They ordered different meals as he was keen to try different dishes and their evening progressed as well as the day before. As he was signalling to the waiter for coffee, he noticed that the same two strange characters from the previous evening were again standing with the owner. One of them was clearly making emphatic gestures. Suddenly there was a big altercation and he looked round and could see those two people having a huge argument with him. Odd he thought and then he had another thought – was this some protection racket of some kind? He said as much to Stacey who suddenly looked alarmed and said. "I think we should go." Urgently, but smiling. So, he paid the bill and they left. The argument was still raging.

"Should we do anything? It looked like a protection

racket – what do you call it – extortion?" he asked "Like call the police?"

"Yes, let's do that!" and she pulled out a phone from her bag, which he wasn't expecting, for he had no mobile of course and flipped up the lid. She made a rapid call and then closed the phone and said

"It is out of our hands now."

They stood talking and recovering from the minor, but unsettling, incident and then he shivered and realised that he had left his coat and thus his Filofax inside.

"I have left my coat inside. I must get it."

"No no. Don't go it might be dangerous."

"Why? I am sure I will be alright – and anyway the police are on their way."

He kissed her and ran up the stairs.

A few moments later there was a shot and then seconds later the two oddly dressed chaps came flying out of the restaurant door – luckily just as the police arrived and straight into their arms.

"Drop the weapon and place your arms above your head."

They didn't and the police opened fire, shot them and they both dropped

Stacey was beside herself and screamed.

"They shot Andrew, they shot Andrew!!"

The policeman nearest her said "Please stay here

ma'am." And both police went up the stairs. But she of course followed them.

As she entered the place was in uproar and lying on the floor was Andrew. She screamed again and ran across to him thinking that Filofax was the death of him and tears welled up.

She bent over him but, as she did, he moaned and slowly sat up.

She hugged him very tightly so that he couldn't get his breath. The policeman came over and gently asked her to let go of him.

"Ok Sir. What happened?"

He gulped a few times and then to her amazement sat up.

He held up his Barbour. I grabbed my coat and, as I came out of the cloakroom, they hit the owner with a gun and then turning round, fired once at me, and then fled."

"You should be dead!" said one of the policemen "The guy who shot you is a professional hitman. A crack shot – especially at that sort of rage. He never misses!"

He didn't answer but held up his Barbour and from the pocket extracted his Filofax. A bullet was embedded in it.

"It saved my life!"

"You idiot!" shouted Stacey and smothered him in kisses. As soon as there was a break he grabbed her hand and said "Will you marry me?"

"YES, yes, yes you stupid boy. I thought you would

never ask, and then when I heard the shot that you would never get the chance!" and she covered him in kisses again.

He made a statement to the police, as did she and then they went back to the hotel.

On the way back a punk stopped them and said "You got a light mac?"

"No." he said "but I have a dark brown overcoat!"

And Dryasdust sat down to applause and a chorus of Merry Christmas and much chinking of glasses.

Just the Fax Ma'am

menu

New England Festive Chowder

Texan Pecan Rice

Maple Pumpkin Dinner Rolls

Cheesecake

New England festive chowder

Prep time:	15 minutes
Cooking time:	60 minutes
Serves:	12
Method:	easy

Ingredients

- 4 kg clams
- 500 ml white wine
- 2 bay leaves
- 4 garlic cloves crushed
- 1 kg potatoes diced
- 600 gr parsnips
- 250 gr smoked bacon
- 2 onions chopped
- 300 gr sour cream
- 4 tbs chopped parsley

Method

Using a large saucepan

- place the white wine, salt, garlic, bay leaves,
- bring to the boil
- add the clams
- cook for 3 minutes
- retrieve the clams and set aside
- pour the liquid through a sieve
- remove the clams from the shells

- keep a few clams on the shell for effects

Set aside

- place the potatoes and parsnips in the pan
- cook for 30 minutes
- using a food processor
- blitz the soup
- add the clams, cream & parsley
- season to taste

Texas Pecan rice

Prep time:	30 minutes
Cooking time:	60 minutes
Serves:	12
Method:	easy

Ingredients

- 200 gr butter
- 300 gr mushrooms sliced
- 2 medium onions sliced
- 600 gr brown rice
- 4 garlic cloves crushed
- 300 gr pecan toasted
- salt & pepper
- 1 tsp cumin
- 1 tsp thyme
- 1 .5 litre chicken stock
- 6 rashers of streaky bacon cooked

Method

Using a large saucepan

- add the butter
- add mushrooms, onions, garlic
- cook for 5 minutes
- add the rice
- stir well
- add cumin, salt & pepper,
- add chicken stock
- stir well
- add the pecan nuts
- cook for 20 minutes
- stir occasionally
- check the rice is cooked
- season to taste
- add the bacon
- serve hot

Maple pumpkin dinner rolls

Prep time:	30 minutes
Bake time:	15 minutes
Serves:	12
Method:	easy

Ingredients

- 1 pack of dry yeast
- 200 gr polenta
- 200 gr brown sugar
- 1 tbs pumpkin pie spices 'see chef's tip 2'
- 600 gr plain flour

- 150 ml milk
- 100 ml maple syrup
- 100 gr butter
- 200 gr cooked pumpkin 'tinned in the US' see chef's tip 3

Method

Preheat oven to 200*C (Gas mark 6)

Using a large mixing bowl

- place the polenta, sugar, dry yeast, pie spices & flour
- mix well
- warm the milk
- add maple syrup
- pour the warm mixture to the dry mix
- mix well until it forms a soft dough
- leave to rest for 20 minutes
- turn the dough into a floured surface
- knead for a few minutes
- divide the dough into 24 small balls or 12 larger ones
- place in a greased 10 inch (25 cm) cake tin
- leave to prove for an hour
- bake for about 15 minutes
- leave to cool
- brush the hot rolls with butter for a shiny effect
- serve with the pecan rice

Chef's tips:

1. Do not warm to milk too hot you will kill the yeast - lukewarm at best

2. If you can't find pumpkin pie spice: make it yourself...

Ingredients

- Cinnamon, Nutmeg, Cloves, Ginger

3. Non-tinned pumpkin

Method

- place 200 gr pumpkin in water cook for 20 minutes
- drain well and let it dry out
- mash with a fork

Cheesecake

Prep time:	30 minutes
Cooking time:	60 minutes
Serves:	12
Method:	easy

Ingredients

- 250 gr digestive biscuits
- 100 gr butter
- 1 kg cream cheese 'full fat'
- 250 gr sugar
- 3 tbs plain flour
- 4 eggs
- 3 tbs vanilla extract

Method

Preheat the oven to 160*C

- place the biscuits in a plastic bag and crush with the

bottom of a pan or rolling pin
- melt the butter in a saucepan
- add the crushed biscuit
- mix well
- place the mixture in a 9 inch cake tin
- spread equally and firmly

In a large bowl

- beat together cream cheese, sugar, eggs & flour
- pour the mixture in the cake tin
- bake for 45 minutes

Chef's tip: Once the cheesecake is cooked. Turn the oven off and open the door. Leave the cheesecake in the oven for around 20 minutes. This will allow the cheesecake to settle.

Boxing Day

Tree

The day is cold so too the nights
We brighten them with Christmas lights
We hang them round about the tree
With tinsel, baubles, Wise Men three

We look ahead to Christmas time
With carols, songs and bells that chime.
But central to our time: the tree
With presents there for you and me.

It brings a breath of pine inside
Of living greenery.
To cheer us at the Christmastide
Bedecked for all to see.

Fine garlands trace out every bough
The baubles hanging low.
The lament tumbling sparkles now
Like icicles in snow.

Never a cross word

So, it was the 26th December - Boxing Day - when next we gathered together for our tale telling and meal. The day that historically and traditionally, in the UK anyway, presents were given to staff to say thank you for their efforts over the year. It isn't celebrated in all countries as it is quite unique to the UK and countries which share the tradition – usually Commonwealth countries. It is of course also the Day of St Stephen – traditionally the first Christian martyr and is celebrated as St Stephen's Day many other Christian countries. Indeed, the carol 'Good King Wenceslas' is set on that day.

Occasionally our days for our meals fell on 'special' days. When this was the case, we discussed the date and whether people would like to meet on that day. Usually, but not always, the answer was yes – as it was usually only one day in some calendar years that fell on these special days. On this occasion when it had become evident that one of our potential meetings would fall on Boxing Day, there was unanimous agreement that we should go ahead. Thus, a story was offered to the Professor, well in advance, with the setting to reflect this particular day from the Christmas period.

As we had filed into the dining room we had, as usual, been offered a selection of drinks by Groves. He was wearing a cap of sorts, which he explained was Omani, as well as having a curved dagger at his belt – which looked a little incongruous, but reinforced the feeling of where the tale was set. He explained that it was called a Khanjar, and that The Professor had asked for permission from the Omani Embassy for Groves wear it. They had been delighted to agree. The Christmas tree was filling one end of the room, by the roaring fire – twinkling - this year in blue and gold colours.

On offer was Arak – the aniseed flavoured traditional Arab spirit and Laban, a salty yogurt drink, which I confess was not to my taste. Beer is also brewed in Oman and is a major export product, so that was on offer too – more to my liking I must say. I had been to Oman and had enjoyed my time there very much. It has a lot of history with the UK, it was a protectorate – known as the Trucial States of Muscat and Oman, and we have many armed forces there, and train theirs too.

Once we all had a drink of some sort the Professor raised his glass and wished us all a Merry Christmas for - given we only met monthly - this was the first time we had got together in the Christmas period this year.

Before we ate Groves washed our hands by pouring a stream of water over them into a bowl. It was flavoured with Frankincense – which is the traditional spice from Oman and made our fingers smell very nice – very Christmassy.

And we recalled that Frankincense was one of the gifts from the wise men. It is known as the tears of the gods and is said to have originated in Oman, in the Darfur region. It comes from the sap of a tree known as Boswelli sacra – according to The Professor – the latter part of its name presumably reflecting its use in religious rites.

There were also one or two candles burning which also gave off that frankincense odour – but it was not overpowering.

The cleansing was because this evening we were to eat with our hands in the traditional Arab manner.

Omani cuisine is rich and varied reflecting the fact that it has always sat astride a whole series of trade routes criss-crossing its lands, especially the spice trade, and bringing many flavours and interesting dishes which are based on chicken, fish, and lamb served with bread and or rice. Many Omani dishes have a rich blend of spices and herbs reflecting its situation on the spice routes. Groves explained that the difference between herbs and spices is that, by and large, herbs are the leaves of a plant, whereas spices are from the other parts, seeds, bark, stalks etc. Many of us had not known that exactly.

There was a selection of dishes to choose from. First there was an appetiser - small cups of soup – called Sakhana - and made from wheat, dates, molasses, meat and milk.

This was followed by a thick meat stew which was very

tasty. Only afterwards did we learn that it was stewed camel and took 48 hours to cook! This was accompanied by rice and flat bread – so ubiquitous across the middle east. I wondered where they had obtained the camel meat from.

Then, to our amazement Groves brought round a piece of paper to each of us. As we looked at it, we saw that it was a crossword skeleton with a set of clues, and on the other side a set of numbers – intriguing.

The Professor said 'Please attempt the crossword. It is germane to the story.'

So we did, helping each other. It was fairly hard and required some concentration, however, it is much easier to complete a cross word when there is more than one person as we all think in different ways, have different vocabularies and different ways of looking at things.

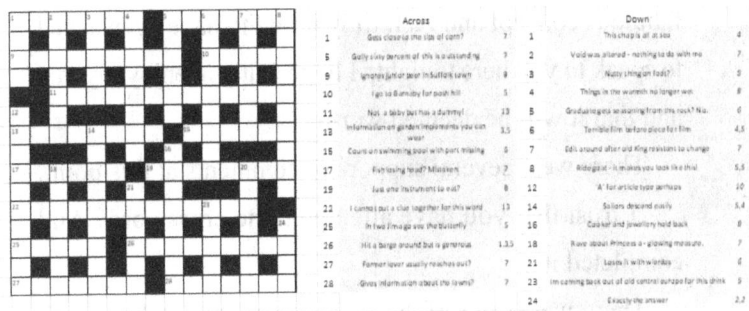

After this we were offered - Kahwa - an Omani coffee mixed with cardamom powder, served with dates and Omani halwa, as well as more usual coffee for those who were less adventurous. Arak was also offered again - as a digestif.

Well, I thought, that this meal, alongside the Kazakh food we had had some time ago, was one of the more interesting meals we had enjoyed!

Then the Professor stood up and introduced our speaker.

He was a guest of The Professor and to me looked like a very hard, competent ex-military man.

'Hello – I am very pleased to have been invited to speak at this august body of people.'

At this there was an undercurrent of 'No we are just a group of normal people who get together for amusement and entertainment.'

He raised his hand placatingly

'Quite, quite. Forgive me, I was being polite. My name is not important – you can call me David. I believe that you meet occasionally and are regaled with interesting tales? A fabulous concept and I am truly proud to have been asked to speak to you here tonight. I hope that you enjoy my tale and that it will be deemed worthy.'

There were several supportive comments at this point.

'I trust that you have attempted the crossword? And completed it?'

There were cries of "yes!" and even "no!" although it wasn't clear whether that was referring to an attempt or completion.

'Well, this relates to an enigma or a mystery which I was tasked with solving. I am ex-special forces and I was attached to the Omani Government, Energy Ministry as a security adviser. As you are probably aware Oman is in a fairly unstable part of the Gulf (which part isn't I hear you say!) with the former colony of Aden (Yemen) being a hotbed of terrorism and a de facto civil war going on. Oman is at the bottom of the Arab Peninsula, where inter-state boundaries are pretty loose as it is mainly desert away from the coast. It is bordered in the north by the UAE, in the west largely by Saudi Arabia and in the south west by Yemen. This border is very dangerous and many firms are no longer trading down there because of the danger, I was also advising a pipe manufacturer whose business in that region had dried up as the population moved away, or ceased investing in pipes to bring water for crops as it was just no longer feasible given the incursions.

Not far away across the straits is Iran – a terrorist state which delights in fomenting war, strife and general unrest and insurrections amongst Shia populations and especially aimed at Sunni governments. For those who do not know – Islam is separated into two main sects. Shia and Sunni. The latter is the overwhelming majority accounting for 90% of all Muslims – but the Shias are often concentrated in an arc around Iran and the two sects are bitterly divided. The Shias have a long history of, as they see it, "glorious martyrdom" leading in our modern age to use of explosives, suicide bombings with which we are all too sadly aware.

I understand that one of your previous tales was set in East Africa and near Zanzibar – well Zanzibar used to be the capital of Oman before two brothers split it off into a separate kingdom, later incorporated with Tanganyika as Tanzania, and it was the centre of the eastern slave trade – stopped by the British using the Royal Navy as muscle and subsidies as bribes - successfully.

Returning to the story: it concerns some other work I was doing on behalf of the Omani government. The civil war in Yemen has caused all sorts of issues and spilled over into Oman as you might imagine. It is suffering from threats from Al Quaeda and from the Houthis who attacked the Yemeni capital. They then installed a revolutionary government and dissolved parliament. They caused much trouble in the past and this eventually led to an outright civil war, which has been raging for several years, and also led to a food crisis with an estimated 20 million people (out of 30 million!!) needing famine relief. In addition, some 6 million been uprooted from their homes. Sadly, the UN cannot send in peacekeepers as it in an 'Active Warzone' and thus intervention is proscribed by its rules – which seems perverse and ridiculous.

Nine countries led by Saudi Arabia are opposing the Houthis to try to restore the legitimate government. Iran is supporting the Houthis (of course it is I hear you say – it is causing trouble wherever and whenever it can). So it is also a proxy Sunni : Shia war, as well as being part of the continuing struggle for mastery of the Gulf. Yemen is 65% Sunni and 35% Shia (largely the Houthi). The Houthis are largely in the north of Yemen which is odd as it borders Saudi Arabia which is Sunni. There is also no oil in Yemen and, therefore, it is not very high on the global geopolitical radar. It used to be called Arabia Felix - Lucky Arabia - how inapt is that nowadays!

It is situated at the base of the Red Sea and Aden as it was then called – or the southern part anyway - was an important base for Britain until it withdrew in 1967. It was also significant in ancient times for the spice trade and is also, purportedly, where the Queen of Sheba dwelt in all her glory before she visited Solomon.

Well, the Omani government alongside some agencies were sending food to the starving and I was advising on security. Several previous convoys had been intercepted by Houthi rebels and the Omanis clearly didn't want that to continue. The information they appeared to have received was so precise that I suspected foul play, but in fact that we had absolutely no idea as to who might be involved. I looked at who was involved in planning the convoys and, unfortunately, there were many, many – including government officials, the armed forces, the agencies and so on. Too many in fact and it would have been a Herculean task to investigate everyone. The logistics and detailed preparation involved many tens if not hundreds of people, however, not all would know, nor need to know the precise details. Security had been lax to say the least initially and whilst there had been a little tightening up of information after the first attack, it was still not good enough in my view. Of course, politics, personalities and what we might call 'sensitivities' were involved: as so many thought that they were important and should be involved, and some just wanted to help.

I, therefore, proposed a plan where those involved would only be given details on a need-to-know and just-in-time basis – a pyramid of knowledge if you like. Only a few at the Apex would know the critical details i.e. when convoys would leave, the route, etcetera: and only at the absolute last minute. This narrowed it down to a possible handful of people in the short time prior to the convoy leaving.

It was clear to me that someone (or maybe more than one – never discount that possibility: look at Burgess, Philby and Maclean) must have been tipping off the Houthis but who? We didn't even know if it was one of the few left within the new apex, or someone else, now excluded. A puzzle.

We obviously couldn't take the risk of sending another convoy, until we had solved the puzzle, because the last convoy had been slaughtered to the very last man: all the drivers, the loaders, the guards, everyone. I, therefore, decided to work down from the Apex, cross-correlating all the key information – what little we did have that is - with all personnel. So, I started by excluding those that would not, probably, know.

We could exclude ordinary solders etcetera as rankers would just go when and where they were told and were unlikely to wish to be killed. But not the officers involved as they would need to know details in order to arrange things.

I asked for transcripts of all messages sent out just before the convoys left. Fortunately, the date was a relatively well-kept secret until just before it left so that reduced the number of messages I had to go through. Many were in Arabic which fortunately I can speak and read and a surprisingly number in English. One or two in Farsi, the language of Iran, and I was immediately suspicious of these and got them translated straight away. Luckily one of my colleagues had been in Iran and translated them for me – but they were just innocent meaningless, in this context, messages.

So far three convoys had been attacked and the second one had repulsed the attack, for after the first one, they had sent soldiers as an escort; but by the time we sent the third one they were thoroughly prepared to deal with the escort and that was the one where all were slaughtered. A very tragic fate for those who were only delivering aid. We just could not let that happen again and indeed I was determined that it would not happen again on my watch. – apart from anything else people were now becoming afraid to be a part of the convoys.

It was clear that we needed to find out a little more about how the bandits or terrorists or insurgents whatever you wish to call them, would react. Accordingly, I decided to lay a false trail to try to precipitate them into showing their hand, and let it be known that another convoy will be sent soon and I, accidentally on purpose, let slip the date and route. In the meantime, I had secretly spoken to one of my British army colleagues and arranged for drone surveillance over the route. We had identified the only two possible places for an ambush.

Sure enough when the Intel came back there was a definite build up and movement of armour and forces at one of the locations. No tanks but they clearly had RPGs and SAM missiles. Of course, we did not send any convoy and in due course the drone surveillance showed them dispersing. Round two to us I thought – a small victory – but nevertheless a victory of sorts.

During this time, we had monitored all messages by phone and email (there were no faxes) in and out. There was the usual groundswell of pointless messages that are so prevalent nowadays – but some looked very interesting and stood out. Of especial interest were the ones that went out and then subsequently had a flurry of return messages. I took those which were unusual in their content. Short messages would not have been able to give enough details so they could be excluded.

Of course, we were not sending a convoy but the Intel, however, confirmed that there was a leak. Sadly, there are no messages saying 'the convoy will leave at X' - that would've been too easy!

What struck me particularly was one in French that purported to be a set of lottery numbers, and which received a flurry of short inward messages to the mobile number which were meaningless for analysis.

I inquired and found out that the phone belonged to one of the Omani army officers who was of North African origin : Tunisian or Moroccan I think. His family had been in Oman for some time and, therefore, he would have grown up speaking in French. This in itself is not suspicious, probably – mais non - but unusual when the general language in the Gulf and The Maghreb is Arabic and French was seen as a colonial vestige and frowned upon by nationalists. Indeed, Algeria has recently instructed schools to stop teaching French and switch to English - which is fascinating.'

I went back to my hotel room, had a beer, and logged onto the main aid organisation's website. There is a section of puzzles to encourage you to log on and surf the site and read about what it does - so fun at the site if you like. I started to do some of the puzzles out of that boredom. One was a that very cross which was distributed here today. I wondered who had developed it so I rang the web guru who gave me a name. I sat up for it was the army officer from North Africa. I had spoken to him already and whilst it was clear that his English was ok - it was, in my opinion, not good enough to have construct this, really quite complex, crossword. I was suspicious straight away, but a suspicion is not proof and anyway compiling a crossword is not an offence. I have also done it myself in the past and it takes some effort, requires a very good understanding on English and its vagaries, and it takes time.

So, if somebody else was compiling it had a potential conspiracy, possibly, although we didn't have any proof. It might just, in any case have been copied from somewhere else - for example The Times or the Telegraph (it was definitely British English). I pulled his messages from the file again and re-read them. In each of the messages shortly before the convoys to the same person whom he addressed in endearing terms, there was a series of numbers purporting to be lottery numbers.

Thus, there was a definite pattern.

They could have been many other things such as map references, bank details possibly, but almost definitely a code.

It was unlikely to be map reference for, whilst that might give a location for attack, there were simply too many - and how would that convey time and dates? And too many for bank details – and who would have so many accounts? I checked the numbers differed in each message.

So, what were they? Were they linked to the crossword for example

I reproduce the message numbers here.'

At this point he gave out a series of numbers.

0308021107050102
0315130210070510
0509050507070301
0913080505151413
1112111011131315
1307110305031303
1501070315071409

'These are the numbers from a message – clearly not really lottery numbers and not telephone numbers either – as far as I can tell – but there we are…

I checked with the Webmaster and apparently there was a new crossword only every three months, therefore, this must mean that, if the numbers and the crossword were connected, then there should be some correlation – but I couldn't see it. I went back over the messages but still could not see any connection or Pattern in them. The lottery numbers seemed random.

My brain was by now hurting so I went to the bar and had another beer or two then turned in. It seems that I would have to keep looking through the messages and maybe revisit some of his others. Perhaps he was, after all, innocent. Next day I reviewed all the relevant messages which had been sent just after I had laid my false trail. No others seemed at all likely but I went through the longer ones again - just in case. Nothing. I was stumped.

There was some pressure on me to achieve something quickly, so aid shipments could re-commence; but, as I explained to the CEO, it would take time as whoever was involved would be taking care not to be caught.

A word on compiling crosswords. If you've never done one, on the face of it, it looks very simple but really it isn't. What you have to do is look at the longest answers and complete those first, and then fill in the shorter ones: as you go you don't want to put the short ones in first and then be trying to find a 17-letter word with two 'X's three 'K's and a 'Q' in it. As you go along you often have to jiggle some of the words around, or change them to fit in. You never do the clues first for that reason. If there is a bit of a theme like Christmas or something, paradoxically it makes it harder. But whatever it takes time and then you have to write the clues to go with the crossword and the clues have to be all of the same level of consistency and difficulty. It is no good having 10 easy clues and 20 really hard ones of it is meant for general consumption, as they will not be able to do them, so you need to know the audience and aim your clues at it.

I decided that to free my brain I would do something different - so I decided to compile a crossword myself. It seemed appropriate. I used XL as a template and here is the template I created.'

He then handed out a sheet of paper to each of us with. It had the blank spreadsheet crossword frame on it. He said 'I created this as a beginning and then I took a call on my mobile about the next convoy and had I found the issue and when might it be safe to send it. Obviously, I was unable to give them the all clear, which disappointed them.

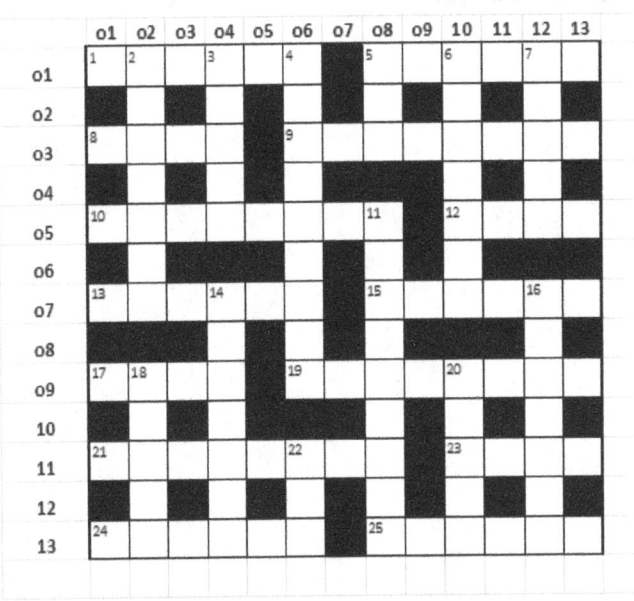

As I took the call put the blank frame, which I had printed out, on the table next to the one from the website. When the call was over I decided to go and have dinner and I went down to the restaurant where I had a meal, and a couple of beers and then went back upstairs to my room.

When I came into my room I saw the template lying next to the crossword puzzle, and the numbers and I had a eureka moment. I had cracked it. I checked the numbers in the message and: yes the mystery was solved – the code was cracked. We arrested the Officer and agreed for the next convoy to be sent.'

Professor thanked our guest and then said

'Now whilst we have our pudding – Mannasama - can you crack the code?'

Never a Crossword

menu

Sakhana

48 hours Camel Stew

Mannasama

Sakhana

Prep time:	20 minutes
Cooking time:	60 minutes
Serves:	12
Method:	easy

Ingredients

- 600 gr lean mince beef
- 2 large onions diced
- 4 large carrots
- 6 garlic cloves chopped
- 500 gr kidney beans cooked 'tinned'
- 2 large tins of chopped tomatoes
- 3 litres beef stock - see 'chef's tip'
- 200 ml white wine
- 3 bay leaves
- 2 tbs fresh basil chopped
- salt & pepper
- 200 gr peas
- 200 gr vermicelli

Method

- pre heat oven to 180*c (gas mark 4)
- place the meat in a roasting tray
- add salt & pepper, garlic
- mix well
- bake for 30 minutes
- place the beef in a large saucepan

- break the beef into mince again
- add carrots, tomatoes, beef stock, white wine, bay leaf
- add beans
- season to taste
- cook for 20 minutes
- add vermicelli & peas
- cook for another 10 minutes
- season to taste

Chef's tip: To make a beef consommé add 6 beef stock cubes per litre of water. You can add 1 tbs of chili paste to the soup for heat.

48 hours camel stew

Cooking time:	48 hours - see chef's tip
Prep time:	20 minutes
Serves:	12
Method:	easy

Chef's tip: You could use lamb or goat for this recipe

Lamb cooking time:	3 hours
Goat cooking time:	4 hours

Ingredients

- 1.4 kg camel meat 'see chef's tip'
- 3 litre of chicken stock
- 150 ml oil

- 2 tbs cardamom
- 2 sticks of cinnamon
- 2 tbs cloves
- 4 bay leaves
- 2 tbs crushed garlic
- 2 tbs chopped ginger
- 1 tbs turmeric
- 1 tbs garam masala
- 2 green chillies chopped
- 2 tbs fresh mint chopped
- 2 large onions chopped

Method

Using a large sauce pan

- add oil
- add all the spices
- cook gently for 1 minute
- add the onions
- cook for another minute
- add the meat
- add the chicken stock
- mix well and put the lid on the pan
- simmer gently for 48 hours
- check for liquid
- add water if the meat is not covered
- remove the lid for the final 4 hours
- serve with plain rice and flat bread "see recipes index"

Mannasama

Prep time:	15 mins
Cooking time:	N/A
Serves:	12
Method:	easy

Ingredients

- 100 gr caster sugar
- 300 gr brown sugar
- 100 ml boiling water
- 1 tsp vanilla extract
- 1 tsp salt
- 3 egg whites
- 1 tsp ground cardamom
- 100 gr butter
- 2 tbs rose water extract
- 200 gr mixed pistachio, walnuts, almond chopped
- 300 gr icing sugar

Method

- dissolve the sugars in boiling water
- add vanilla and butter
- bring to the boil and cook until syrupy
- leave to cool
- whip the eggs until firm
- pour the syrup slowly into the eggs
- fold the cardamom, nuts & rose water into the mixture
- place greaseproof onto a shallow tray

- pour the mixture into the tray
- leave in the fridge overnight
- cut into squares
- place the squares into icing sugar cover well
- 350 gr brown sugar
- 2 tablespoons water

Little New Year's Eve

Winter 2021-2022
So, winter starts its icy grip
with frost on tree and haw and hip.
It crackles on the path and lawn
when we go out in early morn.
All creatures lie snug in their lair
awaiting spring's earth warming air.
And we inside, the fires bank up
and share a warming winter cup.
We sniff the air - a freezing blow
but will it bring us rain or snow?

We get our greatcoats, boots and hat
and walk around, see this and that.
See Robins on a tree branch sat
with feathers plumped up round and fat.
But winters now are warm and wet
white Christmases we do not get.
Except for some years in the north
When Boreas his wind sends forth.
Although it's sometimes freezing cold
it's not the same as years of old.

And Covid made us lock the door
self isolating - what a bore.
For two years running, worried, sweating,
Deep concern, we all were fretting.
Double vaxxed and boosted too
But still the virus could get through.

So now we hope the peak has passed
and we can socialise at last.
And go out in the wintry sun
and say hello to everyone.

Blue Eyes

S o, it was the 30th of December, known on the continent as little New Year's Eve - but not a big event in the UK – in fact not an event at all, except as one of the 12 days of Christmas. We assembled in the usual room where the Christmas tree was, of course, still filling the corner of the room with its welcoming, warming, twinkling lights. It doesn't come down till 12th night of course and it glowed delightfully: highlighting the beautiful decorations which were, tonight only in two colours – blue and silver/white.

The meal we had on this day was very interesting as it was British food with an Australian twist. We had all had several 'traditional' Christmas meals over the Christmas – i.e. turkey - and we didn't really want another one. Mrs Groves had excelled herself on this occasion reaching back into the traditional Victorian Christmas, as articulated so well by Dickens, and served up honey roast goose, still however, stuffed with thyme and parsley. As a starter we had a very thick and tasty soup called 'Proper West End Broth' - a curious name I thought – and accompanied with a chilled Australian white dry wine. It was delicious and we were offered either Mango and Coconut tart or 'Caramel Tim Tam balls' – which Groves assured us were traditional Australian puddings, served with custard, ice-cream or cream. The goose was served with a fine red wine from Australia, with an Australian 'sticky' wine with pudding. Then coffee.

After we had eaten Angel rose to tell the story. As a nurse, of course, she had been often been involved in many sad or interesting cases and I wondered if this would be one of them – I suspected so – but I was wrong.

She stood up looked around at everyone, smiled, and said

'Imagine, if you will, a young man in his late 20s. He is a bit of a drifter, a bit dissolute and is living really on a small income left to him by his father, who had died of cancer when he was a teenager. His father had realised that he was probably a waster, and had left the bulk of his fortune to his second wife, this young man's step-mother for her life, then to go to his son. We'll call him James. His father had married his second wife, later in life, some years after his first wife had been killed in a tragic car accident. His step-mother was a very good person, who also knew that this boy was a waster but, for the sake of his late father, she wanted to try and 'turn him around', so she insisted on him coming to visit her once a quarter or so for dinner and to stay the night in the house. She would then discuss what he was doing, and try to persuade him to 'make something of his life' – by, for example, getting a job.'

She paused and took a sip of water, then continued.

'I am telling you this story which was recounted to me by a doctor friend of mine who was involved towards the end. James had dropped out of a good school (expelled in fact – but his step-mother hadn't been aware of it at the time although his father did know) went to a college, passed some sort of exams, got into a minor university and then dropped out after the first year and then just drifted. Then his father had been diagnosed with the cancer which killed him in short order, but he had had time to make a new will. At the reading of the will James had raged at the terms – but it was incontrovertible.

James, of course, hated this arrangement as he felt so beholden to his step-mother, living in, as he saw it, his house, and also living on, as he saw it, his inheritance. He kept asking her for money, as an advance on his inheritance, but she would always refuse his request, saying

"No, you won't inherit until after I die, as your father insisted in his will."

He became increasingly desperate because the money he had was just not enough to live on - in the way he wants to live – i.e. by loafing. He wondered about doing away with her – but realised that he was bound to be found out and then would lose both his inheritance and his freedom. Then he had an idea: not a pleasant idea, but an idea. One of his friends was schizophrenic and sometimes became a completely different person and, although you might have known the face, you wouldn't have recognised him from his behaviour. James thought: well, if I can create a new personality, that is, a new person wholly separate from me, and totally different in all aspects, I could dispose of my step-mother without being discovered and, therefore, I would inherit. He was looking into a mirror in his bathroom as he thought this and his cold blue eyes looked back at him. Clearly, he had by then passed over the threshold into madness.

He, therefore, went to a number of different shops and bought various different accoutrements such as a wig, a beard, some clothes and a pair of glasses with just plain glass in the frames from an optician. The optician asked why he wanted them and he told him that he was appearing in a play where he had to play an old man wearing glasses. The glasses he was looking for, of course were not going to have plain frames, as he decided to get something very outlandish: again very different from how people would normally see him. When the optician asked him what colour he wanted he replied

"I don't really know as I'm colour blind."

"OK…" the optician said "…right, well in that case, I recommend a dark frame: as it will stand out better on the stage under the lights."

So, he took a pair of quite garish, but black framed, glasses.

He had very fair hair so he had chosen a wig and beard of a very different colour – dark brown - and when he had put them on and looked in the mirror with the glasses perched on his nose, he could see that looked completely different – albeit still with his blue eyes staring back at him, unblinking, like a lizard. Naturally he had paid cash for all items to ensure that there was no evidence trail.

He then rented a flat in a very different part of town from where he would normally live, in his new disguise, giving out that he was only looking for temporary accommodation and started inventing and building the new character. He called himself Bruce Barrowclough: choosing it as being a memorable name and, as his stepmother had originally hailed from Australia, he put on an Australian accent. To support his plan he wove a tale of having been for some time a farmer in the Outback with his uncle, then a spell in insurance in Sydney and that he had now been transferred to the UK office in London. He visited several local wine bars, cafes, and so on, in his new persona, and went out of his way to make himself known. To do this he initially made conversation with people but then, when people tried to talk to him subsequently, when he returned to the same places, he was quite rude to them saying things such as

"Go away - leave me alone yer bludger!"

Then next time he would apologise saying "I acted like a bogan!", when, being polite people, they would say it didn't matter and he would say "No worries mate. Would you like a drink?" and then, when they assented, he would say "Bonzer." And so on, keeping in his Australian persona. He had invested in the bible of Australian slang "Let's talk strine!" which had useful phrases he could use.

But then again he would be rude when next they spoke to him.

With his new persona, his dark-framed glasses and his strange clothes which he had adopted he was sure that they would remember him. He had bought some hideous ties for example but he drew the line at flip-flops.

After a couple of weeks, he decided he was ready to start his campaign. He, therefore, sent a letter to his step-mother claiming that he had known her in Australia and threatening to expose her past. Of course, she had no past to be ashamed of and he was making it all up - but this is part of his plot. The so-called shady past was not the objective – it is to fix in everyone's mind that it was the character of Mr Bruce Barrowclough who was in correspondence with her. He did not use the address of the flat where he was staying as part of his new persona, initially, as he didn't want anyone to follow it up just yet in quite that detail as he didn't know how long this would take.

He had read several detective novels about fraud and blackmail and other crimes, and so he wrote the letter with his left hand, copying the words from an original he had already written out in block capitals, turned upside down, to disguise his handwriting: because his step-mother would obviously recognise his.

James spent a couple of days each week at the flat giving out that he had to travel a lot with his job. He had bought, a small overnight bag for verisimilitude, which of course he used to carry his change of persona before he arrived at his flat. The bag was of a very different type from the ones he would normally use – being much cheaper and more garish. Each time he would travel from his home in his real persona and then, at a pub which he knew had several exits, he would enter, have a drink as James, and then go to the loo, change into his new persona, and then leave by another exit.

Thus, he would turn up at his new flat in the new clothes, with his wig and beard, and wearing his glasses, stay a night, then go to the wine bars and the local shops, then come back.

Next day he would travel to another pub in his new persona, again one with several exits, with the garish bag and change into his normal clothes. He would put the 'new' clothes and accoutrements inside the new bag, and then place that bag inside another one, bigger, which he had carried inside the newer bag, folded up, before returning home. Obviously, he did not want anyone to see him as

Mr Barraclough coming out of the pub and going back to his flat - just in case.

He continued to visit his step-mother periodically as usual, obviously, and to allay any possible suspicions on her part kept asking for further advances on his inheritance which she naturally kept refusing. During the next couple of visits, after he had sent the letter, she didn't mention to him that she had received the letter, and naturally he couldn't ask after it. He began to wonder if she had in fact received it, but then, the third time he came, she mentioned, en passant, that she had had a letter from someone calling himself a Mr Barraclough and claiming that he knew her in Australia and threatening to expose some undisclosed thing from her past and, naturally demanding money for his silence. Of course, she knew that she had no 'past', she was a very respectable lady and, moreover, she didn't know any Mr Barrowclough. This of course was just what James wanted to hear.

"What did you do with it?" he asked feigning only a token interest.

"May I see it?"

"No, no!" she said "I burnt it. It was just some larrikin nutter sending menacing letters." Using an idiomatic Australian term – which in fact showed that she was actually a little bit rattled by it.

"Oh, ah, okay, what did this, ah larrikin, say precisely?"

"Well, as I said, he claimed to have known me in Australia and he was threatening to expose me. Haha. Me!"

"Did you know him?"

"Not a chance!

"Are you sure?"

"Of course I am sure: and also there's nothing in my past to concern me nor anybody else."

"Well - of course not - but don't you think you should tell the police?"

"Why what would they do? – Nothing! Pointless."

"Well. I think you should."

"No, no, no. It is probably a prank. It'll be apples."

He wasn't quite sure what this meant, as she had never used such terms before – but he made his excuses and left and went to make sure of his next step. When he got home he decided what to do next and his blue eyes looking out at him from the mirror seemed to be shining in anticipation.

A few days later he composed another letter, in the same way, making quite salacious allegations and threatening to kill her if she didn't pay him because of some imagined slight or wrong. This was to encourage her to tell the police because obviously he wanted the deception to be strong and he wanted the police to know about it so that they would investigate the strange Mr Barrowclough and throw them off his scent.

He then visited his step-mother a few weeks after the

second letter, but obviously could not ask about the next letter, but casually said

"What have you done about the letter from the – what was it you said he was – a larrikin? Have you called the police?"

His step-mother became quiet and then said

"Actually, I have received another letter from that, that drongo: but much worse this time.

And quite reluctantly she showed him the second letter, which this time she had kept.

He read it – feigning ignorance of the contents, although clearly he was very well aware of what it said.

"I really think that you should call the police now – this is not a prank or joke – it looks very serious. Are you sure you do not know him?"

"Of course not – didn't I say so already? Very well. I will call them tomorrow."

He stayed the night, as was his usual custom and, as he was cleaning his teeth, his eyes seemed to look back at him with a self-satisfied glow. Next day she called the local police; and in due course a female Inspector came around. The Inspector listened to her story, read the letter and said

"I will take this away to test for fingerprints."

"Okay…" she said "…but it will have both my and my step-son's prints on it, as we have handled it quite extensively."

"Right, thank you, we'll bear that in mind." said the Inspector "Do you have the envelope as well?"

"Yes, yes. It is in the Bureau over there. It is on the second shelf behind the large piece of cardboard. I would have said the green piece, but James is colour blind." She added to the Inspector.

"I will get it step-mother." said James a little too hurriedly, although luckily nobody noticed, and he went across to the bureau and took out the envelope, making sure that he picked it up with both hands and put his fingerprints all over it: as he had thought that he might have forgotten to put gloves on when sealing the envelope.

Luckily for him this had given him the opportunity to cover that mistake. He could have kicked himself. He had also used the most common paper and envelopes from bought from a major High Street store as they would be untraceable, he had thought. He had also used self-adhesive stamps.

The Inspector, who was wearing gloves, as is normal in these types of incidents, took the envelope from James, placing it in a clear plastic wallet which she had taken from her bag, adding

"We can't even test the stamp for saliva or DNA because they are mainly self-adhesive now, as are many of the envelopes."

The step-mother said

"But presumably, in any case, criminals would know not to lick them and use plain water instead?"

"Yes, probably," said the inspector "but this is almost certainly a crank and cranks do not always act rationally and would not necessarily think of that."

James certainly hadn't thought of that but, luckily it had been a self-adhesive envelope. He let out a bit of a sigh of relief and tried to keep the emotion out of his voice as he said

"What do we do next?"

"We'll get back to you, as soon as we have finished our investigations. He must be a nutter as he (assuming it is a he) has put his address on the letter. This means we can investigate in some depth. We shall start with the address, and talk to neighbours and so on. I will put some lads onto it immediately. In the meantime – please be very careful when opening the door and always put the chain on."

James saw the Inspector out and then said good-bye to his step-mother and went home. He made a mental note to get rid of the remaining stationery envelopes and stamps as soon as possible by burning them.

A couple of weeks later and, as it was coming up to Christmas, he visited her again to see what, if anything had happened, and ostensibly to help her to decorate the Christmas tree and house.

His step-mother said that the police had contacted her

but only to say that they were making inquiries and would let her know if anything came up.

He started taking baubles out and hanging them on the tree. After a while she stopped him, taking the bauble box away from him, and saying

"Your colour blindness means you cannot see the different colours and you are making a bit of a mess of things. You just put the lights on the tree and I will decorate it."

"I see you have a real tree."

"Yes, of course, as usual. It is a little expensive, but it is my Christmas treat to myself."

"As long as you are not wasting my inheritance."

"Ha! Your inheritance. Don't be silly."

He left. He had intended to kill her then but had decided to wait till after Christmas - not from kindness you can be sure - but because he had had an invitation from an old friend whom he hadn't seen for some time and so he decided to come back later – in fact just before New Year. Also, by then, the police would probably have carried out some investigation into the mysterious Mr Barrowclough and discovered some things about him and so it would be safer for him he reasoned. He had, of course, in the meantime, disposed of anything and everything to do with the other persona. He had gone on a couple of quite long trips and deposited the various bits in bins quite far apart from each other. The clothes had had given to a couple of charities, as well as the bag. The glasses he left in a sad part of London assuming they would be stolen and/or smashed by local yobs.

He went home and changed to go out to see his friend. As he washed his face in the bathroom his blue eyes stared back at him with, he felt, a hint of anticipation that he would soon be very rich.

A few days later he went back to his step-mother's. It was little New Year's evening, which meant little of course, except that it was dark, as he had planned. He had dressed in very dark clothes, with a dark scarf swathed around his neck and face, so he would be very difficult to see, given the absence of street lights there. He was nervous as, although he had planned, everything, he had never actually done anything as insane such as murder before, not even any major crime. He had, however, crossed the line into madness: so he steeled himself and pretended to be pleasant. Casually he drifted around the room, moved behind the chair in which she was seated and then, suddenly, he took off his scarf, wrapped it tightly around her throat and tugged it very tight, as she struggled, until she ceased drumming her feet on the floor and clawing at his hands. He pulled it even tighter to make sure and then, when he was certain she was dead, released the scarf. He was wearing gloves so that there were no marks on his hands from her nails. He intended to dispose of the gloves in due course. He took a glove off and felt for a pulse. Good. There was none.

He quietly left, leaving the front door open, and vanished into the night. Next day he disposed of the clothes he had been wearing, the gloves and the scarf, and then made his way to his step-mother's house later that morning. It was New Year's Eve of course. He arrived to find two police cars outside and police tape across the gateway. He had expected this of course, but he feigned surprise. A policeman stopped him

"Excuse me Sir. Where do you think you are going?"

"This is my step-mother's house – what is going on?" he asked in wholly feigned innocence.

Just then the same female inspector came out of the house and beckoned him inside. The policeman let him through and under the 'Do not Cross' tape. She let James precede her into the house and then surreptitiously signalled to the policeman to come in as well. He did so and stood just behind James whilst the Inspector spoke with him.

"Well, what has happened. Why is there tape across the gateway?"

"There has been a murder: that is your step-mother has been killed. Strangled we think but the doctor will confirm that."

"Oh my God." he ejaculated "Is, is it that nutter Barrowclough? The one she got that letter from?"

"We believe so."

"H-have you found him yet? You were following up on the address I recall."

"Yes. Please sit down."

He did so, and the policeman who had been on the pavement, and another (rather large and quite young) who was also in the room moved, discretely, a little closer to him.

"We went to the address – but the bird had flown as they say. There was no-one and nothing there at all. The landlord said it had been only a temporary rent as the chap was looking for somewhere more permanent."

"Did you ask around at the local shops etc?"

"Yes. We did and we got an absolutely accurate description of him. We went to local shops and to local cafes and wine bars. Many there knew him. They said he was a very strange chap who was often quite unpleasant. Australian they thought."

"Really? She was Australian you know."

"Yes, we know that."

"So, you are certain that you will be able to find him?"

"Oh yes – we are sure." And she picked a piece of imaginary lint off his collar.

"Not only that but we had an extraordinary piece of luck. As we were asking around and describing the unusual clothes and appearance to the neighbouring businesses, we had a call from another police station. Apparently, someone had found a pair of odd-looking spectacles in the street and, being a public-spirited citizen, had handed them in. As we had put out an APB to all stations including the description of the glasses, they had recognised the glasses and called it in."

At that James shifted a little uncomfortably in his chair. She carried on.

"Luckily the glasses had the name of the optician upon the arms so we roused him out and had a long chat. A long and very productive chat. He was able to give us a very clear description of the person who had bought them. The sale had, unsurprisingly stuck in his mind. Along with the others he was also able to give us a very good description in detail of the eyes. As an optician this was an area he would have focussed on, obviously."

James felt a little uncomfortable at this as he wondered if his blue eyes were really that outstandingly different – but then he thought – no – at least 25% of the population has blue eyes. It will not matter.

He sat back in the chair a little more.

"How did he describe them?" he asked with more nonchalance than he felt.

"Oh, quite well – and it matched what everybody else had said too."

"W-what exactly?"

"Well, he said that they were some of the most distinctive

eyes he had ever seen – in colour terms. The left was red and the right was green."

"What?" James cried in relief.

"Yes, and, moreover, he said that the red eye had a blue-black fleck in it. He had been in the Royal Navy and described it as being the same as the lights on a ship. Port on the left, that is red; and starboard on the right, that is green."

"Well then in that case you should be able to get someone with eyes like that very easily I would have thought." He said allowing a little bit of smugness to creep into his tone.

"Yes. I think we shall have him very soon. Very soon indeed."

The Inspector nodded her head slightly and the two policemen each grabbed one of his arms.

"I arrest you for the murder of your step-mother. You are not obliged to say anything, nut anything you do say will be taken down and may be used in evidence against you."

"B-but…" he expostulated "…you cannot mean me, that I did this – my eyes are blue! Not at all as you described them."

"Ah. Well. You suffer from colour blindness I believe? Your step-mother said so when we were chatting."

Yes – but what has that got to do with it?"

"Well, the optician, as I said, had examined your eyes, as he placed the different spectacles on your face. He had noticed that you were unable to differentiate red-green and he said that in his opinion you were suffering from Deuteranopia."

"W-what is that?"

"It is an inability even to see red and green at all, and in fact those colours look blue to your eyes. As you said your eyes are blue. But they are manifestly not. To everyone one else your eyes are as the optician described - one red and one green. A little like David Bowie's eyes were, too I am told. Everyone we interviewed said the same thing."

His face became horror-struck.

"We have you bang to rights."

The police cuffed his unresisting hands.

"Take him away."

Well. that is it. the doctor confirmed she had been strangled, the day before and James later on confessed. A sorry and sad tale.

"What about his inheritance?" asked Fruity – as a criminal he could not inherit

'Ahh yes. I forgot. His step-mother was wise. Although the monies had been left to her for her lifetime to go to James on her death, there was a codicil, which although James knew about had forgotten, or ignored in his madness. It said that, if she felt that he was never going to "mend his ways", then his step-mother could change the will to leave the inheritance to charity. She had come to that conclusion not long before, and had left it to a couple of cancer charities in memory of her late husband. So, it was all for nothing in any case.'

'Crime does not pay! Your health!'

Blue Eyes

menu

Proper West End Broth

Honey Roast Goose

Caramel Tim Tam Cheesecake Balls

Or

Vegan Mango & Coconut Tart

Proper West End Broth

Serves:	12
Method:	easy
Prep time:	15 minutes
Cooking time:	60 minutes

Ingredients

- 1 whole chicken (1.5 kg)
- 4 carrots peeled and sliced
- 2 celery sticks cubed
- 1 leek cubed
- 1 parsnip peeled and cubed
- 1 large swede peeled and cubed
- fresh thyme
- 4 chicken stock cubes
- 4 litres of chicken stock "see method"

Method

Using a large saucepan

- pour in 4 litres of water
- add chicken cube, salt
- bring to the boil
- add the whole chicken
- simmer for 1 hour
- remove the chicken
- leave to cool then peel all the meat from the chicken
- cut into rough pieces
- add the chicken to the broth

- add all the vegetables in the pot
- simmer for 1 hour
- season to taste

Honey Roast Goose

Serves:	12
Method:	easy
Prep time:	30 minutes
Cooking time:	1 hour

Ingredients

- 2 whole geese
- 200 gr butter melted
- 2 cinnamon sticks
- 200 gr fresh ginger peeled and diced
- 2 star anise
- fresh thyme
- fresh rosemary
- 2 oranges cut into halves

Method

For each goose wash thoroughly inside and out and dry well.

- place all the ingredients inside the goose then place the stuffing - well packed
- preheat oven to 200*c (gas mark 6)
- rub salt all over the goose
- brush the butter all over the goose
- place the goose on a roasting tin - 'see chef's tip'
- roast the goose for 30 minutes breast side down

- turn the goose around carefully
- turn the oven down to 170*c (gas mark 3)
- then cook the goose 30 minutes per kilo
- if the skin colours too fast cover the birds with tin foil
- rest your bird for at least 30 minutes before serving

Chef's tip: Start roasting the goose breast side down. Keep the fat for roast potatoes by placing your goose on a small upside down tray, so the fat drops to the bottom of the roasting tin. Retrieve every 30 minutes to avoid the fat burning. Ideally get your butcher to completely bone out your geese this makes it a lot easier to slice on the day.

Stuffing

Ingredients

- 1.5 kg sausage meat
- bunch of flat parsley chopped
- bunch of fresh thyme chopped
- 150 gr breadcrumb
- 150 gr dried cranberries

Method
Using a large bowl

- add the sausage meat
- add parsley, thyme, breadcrumb, cranberries
- mix well

Caramel Tim Tam cheesecake balls

Prep time: 30 minutes
Cooking time: N/A
Serves: 12
Method: easy

Ingredients

- 400 gr chocolate/caramel digestive
- 300 gr cream cheese
- 300 gr milk chocolate melted

Method

Using a blender

- put the biscuit in and blitz until crumbed
- add the cream cheese
- roll into tablespoon balls
- leave in the fridge for at least an hour
- melt the chocolate

Using a toothpick

- dip the balls in the chocolate coating well
- place on a greaseproof paper
- leave to cool

Chef's tip: You can use dark chocolate if you prefer rather than milk chocolate. You may struggle to find 'Tim Tam' caramel biscuits in your country, so use any caramel/ chocolate base biscuit for this recipe.

Mango & coconut tart "Vegan"

Prep time:	15 minutes
Cook time:	N/A
Serves:	12
Method:	easy

Ingredients

- 2 cans coconut milk
- 250 gr fresh mango
- 1 lemon juice
- pinch of salt
- ½ tsp ground cardamom
- ½ tsp ground Sichuan pepper
- 1 fresh mango for topping

For the crust

- 400 gr dates
- 80 gr grated coconut
- 150 gr oats

Method

Using two 9 inch (23 cm) tart moulds

- grease the mould with vegetable oil
- place the dates in a bowl, cover with hot water
- leave to soak for 5 minutes
- drain well
- put the dates into the food blender
- add coconut, oats, salt
- blitz until it forms a dough

- spread the dough evenly across the tart mould making sure to raise the sides
- set aside in the fridge

Using a food blender

- add coconut cream, mango, lemon juice, cardamom & Sichuan pepper
- blitz until thick & creamy
- transfer into the tart mould
- place in the freezer ideally overnight
- take the tart out of the freezer a few minutes before slicing and serving

New Year's Eve/Sylvestre Abend

The year grows old
The year grows old, the nights are dark
The wind is cold in town and park.
The wintry season now draws nigh
And stars bedeck the dusky sky.

Long skeins of geese fly by on high
And creatures struggle to keep dry.
The barns are filled with hay and straw
To feed the cows and warm the floor.

The crops have all been gathered in
We wear thick shirts against our skin.
The clocks go backward – lengthening night
November flames are burning bright.
The summer coats respond to night

And change from brown to wintry white.
Warm nests are built and dams repaired
The beaver's lodge is warm and aired.

Loud fireworks are everywhere
they split the night and rend the air.
It's dragon's breath as we exhale -
we warm ourselves with good mulled ale.

Some children go for tricks or treats
and gorge on sickly chocolate sweets.
We alter settings on the heating
Autumn's haze is swift and fleeting.

The darkling sky brings winter rain
That lashes door and window pane.
And we begin to set our sights
on Christmas trees and Christmas lights.

Substance and Shade

It was New Year's Eve. Also called Sylvester Abend in Germany and Austria and a big celebration there. It is St Sylvester's Day, hence the name, but largely unknown in the UK and in fact most countries. He apparently was a Pope and was, allegedly by some accounts, responsible for the conversion of Constantine: the Roman Emperor who made Christianity the formal religion of the Roman Empire. The 31st December celebrates the date of his death. We were in our usual room. Being winter: indeed, a particularly cold and foggy day; the heavy curtains were closed and a very merry fire burned in the grate. We had been served a glass of schnapps by Grove as we filed in. This was very welcome to drive out the damp from our bones. This was our first clue as to the location of our main story tonight.

Once we were seated Grove came in with an extremely large tureen from which he proceeded to serve a very thick soup (Pumpkin). This spicy German soup further served to warm us up and further hinted as to where we might expect the tale from; along with the broad-brimmed green Alpine hat which he was wearing which was a bit of a giveaway I felt. Groves explained that the soup was, unusually flavoured with coriander to reflect the Christmas tide feeling. This herb, he further added, although often thought of as Asian or even Meso-American, has long been used in European cooking and a reference to it was found in the Linear B tablets: where it weas called ko-ri-ja-da-na in its odd syllabic language. That was very close to our pronouncement and I wondered where he got that information from: as it was more than a little arcane! It was accompanied with coriander dumplings.

For those of us that had been skiing in Germany, Switzerland and Austria fond memories of the Alps were brought back; maidens in dirndl serving dunkelbeer and aging ski instructors that could ski better at 70 then I ever could at 25. Indeed on offer for beverages were that very beer; as well as a light lager and a fine Austrian wine. Soon the conversation was flowing and the cold was left outside to fester in its misery. Reminiscences about times in southern Germany, that is Bavaria, as well as Austria and Switzerland were soon being swapped. It seemed as though everyone had been to the region and there was a lot of coincidental visits where members had been there when other members were also there but had missed each other.

The heart-warming soup was followed by a main course of roast leg of duck with spiced red cabbage and duck fat potatoes that are so symbolic of Swiss/Austrian and Bavarian cuisine. Plenty of beer was poured into those alpine tankards with the lids and talk flowed. Groves then cleared the plates away and a fine peach and apple strudel was served with cream. Glasses of sweet German pudding wines: a trockenbeerenauslase; and an eiswein; were also available.

Then we were offered gingerbread and coffee.

Shamus then arose and, clearing his throat, set the scene. He spoke crisply and tersely: not wasting his words. Shamus was one of the older members of our little group and had made a name for himself, when in the force, by solving some extremely difficult and high-profile cases. He was rumoured to be in the running for a Knighthood; but with due modesty pooh-poohed any such suggestion.

'Imagine if you will a couple. Married for many years; he a Diplomat, she a language teacher. They had had three children and, due to his work, the family had lived in many countries and, therefore, had a cosmopolitan outlook on life. The children had, accordingly, boarded in the UK for much of this time. This story concerns his final posting to Germany. They had been in the country for many years and, because in this case he was covering trade, they were based in the south of Germany; Bavaria in fact. By this time his children had completed their education and were now living and working in the UK. The eldest was married with twin boys and a younger daughter; and the second with two young girls. They were immensely proud and fond of their grandchildren, visiting them or hosting family get-togethers in Germany whenever they could. His posting had only another year to go before he and his wife could look forward to well-earned retirement back in good ol' Blighty and to years of enjoying their children and grandchildren.

It was just after New Year's Eve, the Sylvesterabend as it is known there, which, as in Scotland, is a major festival in those parts. All the family had been together and their children had flown or driven back home to the UK: having spent the Christmas and New year's break there. They decided to take a walk in the woods as it was a beautiful crisp day and they felt the need to walk off the festive food. The walk they chose was a good long walk as they were fit and they both enjoyed walking. It took them into a range of foothills and then back to their house. About half way round, however, the weather suddenly took an unexpected turn for the worse. Due to the surrounding hills there is a unique micro-climate in the valley: but, once out of the protection of the slopes, it could change, sometimes dramatically.

As they walked out of the shelter of the hills there was a terrible storm. They were still a couple of miles from home and, although well wrapped up against the cold, for it was, after all January: they hadn't been expecting such a downpour. Soon they were soaked and, although the area was well wooded: with no leaf cover due to the time of year, it offered little protection against the driving torrents. There was nothing to do but press on and try to get home as fast as possible. This they did and, hastily changing into dry clothes and sitting before a fire, they tried to recover and get warm. They were a bit shaken by this so they went to bed early, having turned up the heating to keep out the cold; for the weather had changed back to a dry evening with no cloud cover and as the temperature had dropped rapidly there was a severe frost.

During the night his wife slept fitfully, waking him up and, when he checked her brow, it was burning.

Worried, he rang for a doctor and then sat holding her hand.

''Don't worry.'' he told her ''It is just a fever from the storm. I have called a doctor and he will be here soon. You will be fine, I am sure''

His wife clutched his hand tightly, coughed and replied

''Hold me close, dearest, I feel very cold and the world seems very dark and overbearing. I fear it is the end. If I die, please bury me here. We have had such lovely times here that I should like to stay.''

This uncharacteristic gloom alarmed him very much and, stroking her face gently and kissing her brow, he said reassuringly

''Don't be like that, you will be fine. It is just a bit of fever.''

The doctor arrived and examined her, and although he was cheerful enough when talking to his patient, his face, when he turned back to her husband was grave. They moved a little way out of her hearing and he said quietly. ''It is a fever. Either it will break or it will not. I can do no more.'' and shaking his hand, and embracing him, the doctor left.

He sat down next to his wife and spoke comfortingly to her holding her close. She fell asleep for a little while; then sat up suddenly saying quietly again

"I feel so cold and it is so dark. Hold me close; for I fear it is the end."

He held her tightly murmuring reassurance in her ears. She cried a little and then died in his arms.

Naturally he was terribly upset and for a long time just sat there holding her hand; unaware of the coldness creeping over it. Eventually he pulled himself together and put things in hand. In due course the funeral was arranged locally: for she had asked to be buried in the village graveyard there. After the funeral he went back to UK to live near his children; but his grief hung heavily on him. His wife's name had been Rose and, before leaving, in her memory he planted a rambling plant of that family. Over time his grief, while not lessening, became something that whilst it was with him all the time: he could live with it; but he would, of course, visit the grave from time to time and pay his respects and remember. Over that time the local river had changed course and moved nearer the graveyard; and, as it wasn't contained within pre-defined banks, there were several years of heavy rains and each year the flood waters carved out variations on the river's course. As there were no dwellings in the immediate vicinity and, as it was a small and fairly isolated village, the authorities did not do anything about this.

On a time, just before his visit, there had been a major series of floods due to increasing melted snow water from the Alpine glaciers, driven by El Nino and its attendant consequences for global climate change; and so much water had swollen the river that it had burst its banks in parts; and much of the ground was a marshy swamp. Rose's grave, however, was raised above the general level of the land, on a slight hillock and was safe. There was also a raised path to that area of the graveyard that avoided the low-lying areas which were now marshy. On the day of his visit there was again a massive storm. It hit him as he was almost at the grave. Visibility soon fell to virtually zero and he was, of course, soaked - even through the heavy Loden coat he was wearing. It was very reminiscent of that fateful day: and the memory sent a cold chill down his spine as he recalled the unhappy consequences of that walk in the rain. He struggled on in the pouring rain, reached the grave and, placing the flowers that he had brought upon it, stood with his head bowed for some time; heedless of the water pouring off his hat.

Then he lifted up his head and, saying a soft ''Farewell

my lovely Rose." he turned to walk out of the graveyard and back to where he thought the path was. In the meantime, however, the rain had made the ground into a heavy morass, despite it being raised; and he was soon floundering knee deep in mud and became progressively tired and hopelessly lost. He started to panic, for he couldn't see through the teeming rain and his breath caught in his lungs, as he floundered in a morass which must have been similar to the First World War Flanders trenches at their worst.

He paused to catch his breath and to try to see where he was; but it was all in vain as visibility was just about zero, and he started to become very worried. He leant wearily with one hand against a tombstone and cried softly to himself: feeling the hopelessness of his situation, as he realised that the storm didn't look anything like close to abating. his shoes were now so wet that they were oozing water out when he walked through the mud. Then he noticed that the river was rising yet further; and encroaching rapidly on the raised path, where he was standing. Suddenly a figure appeared before his eyes, shimmering into hazy view out of the spray and rain. He could see it, but it was tantalisingly out of reach. He called but his voice was carried away on the wind by the rain-rich gusts. He squeezed his eyes and peered at the figure and was just able to discern that it was a woman wearing black. She beckoned to him without speaking. He was reluctant at first but as her gestures were increasingly insistent, and as the waters were swirling around his feet he felt that he had no other course but to move toward her. The rain seemed to worsen so that he could hardly see at all and she faded in and out of his vision.

As he moved towards her, however, slowly at first, then with increasing confidence, he could feel the ground progressively hardening underfoot with less water and mud and he was able to plant his feet more firmly with every step and soon ceased floundering and began to be able to stride boldly forward, although still slowly as he was very weary indeed from his efforts in the mud. There was a slight lessening of the rain and, as he looked ahead, she again beckoned and he followed her; now certain that he was on the path. The rain now lashed down harder than ever and she was obscured, but he could feel hard ground underfoot. The path, however, suddenly started to twist and turn amongst the graves and trees, and the visibility was now so low that he wandered off the path again slightly.

Then she reappeared up ahead again and beckoned him on. He struggled out of through the mud to where she was pointing and, as he followed her, he found that she had directed him once more onto the firmer ground of the path. He could feel the cinders of the surface beneath his feet and wondered how she could see in the storm when he couldn't; but assumed it was a local who was very familiar with the way. He continued to follow her calling to her to wait a moment until he could catch up: but she continued on; only pausing when he paused and then starting again when she was sure he was following.

Occasionally he stumbled and fell; for even the path itself was under attack by the angry floodwaters; but when he did so: each time she stopped and waited for him. He could see her up ahead each time he picked himself up; shimmering slightly in the rainy starlight. He thought that she was wearing one of those heavy German shiny waterproof coats – just like his: a Loden.

He carried on, cursing at the cobwebs that continually pushed into his face where they had grown across the path which was narrow at this point. After a while it broadened out and he could, once more, see her gliding along; almost seeming to float along the path. Then the path narrowed again and he was forced to claw at his face to remove the cobwebs spun between the bushes. He cursed again, then stopped in amazement as the potential implications hit him. "I wonder why she hadn't broken them – spiders can't spin that fast?" and he began to be concerned, just a little.

He held up a hand to her, as if to say 'Wait just a little whilst I rest.' then paused and rested on a tree trunk to catch his breath; and he looked at her intently as the rain began to lessen. She seemed to waver and appeared slightly less substantial; but he just put that down to his fatigue and dizziness and so he shook his head and hurried to catch up with her where she seemed to have stopped. She was waiting where the path joined the main road. He reached her and called out

''Fraulein: please who are you? What is your name? How can I thank you properly for saving my life? Please wait a moment.''

He had nearly reached her and put out a hand to stay her; but just then the sun came out: it was dawn and the light made him stumble; catching his hand on a thorn from the bush nearest the road. He picked himself up, sucking at the scratch; but she was gone. He walked forward in amazement; but tripped and, as he fell, masses of petals tumbled down onto his head and body, sticking in the wet. They were petals from the bush. it was a rose bush and he realised where he was with a start. It was the one he planted in her memory. But there were no flowers on the bush. It was the wrong season for roses. he followed the path back to where he was staying, had a hot bath and a stiff whisky and lay in the bath pondering on the events of the day. He got out, dried himself, put on a thick warm dressing gown and then sat in front of the fire staring into the flames. After a while he got ready for bed, and shaking his head he went to bed, disquieted.'

Shamus took a drink and sat down heavily. He reached behind him and brought up an object. He opened his briefcase, for that is what it was, and took out a folder. He stood up once more and opened it, showing it round to us. In it, pressed between two preserving sheets, were several rose petals.

'It was her. My mother. I know it. She saved my father's life. He pointed at the petals.

'My father gave these to me just before he died. They were on his clothes when he got back to where he was staying and he preserved them. We took his body back to the graveyard and buried him alongside her. The river has now swallowed both of them up and they are united once more.'

Shamus was a hard ex-policeman and had a no-nonsense approach to life but, as he sat down, grief-driven tears filled his eyes.

We all walked out very quietly that night.

Substance and shade

menu

Pumpkin soup

Coriander dumplings

Roast Duck leg, spiced red cabbage, duck fat potatoes

Peach and apple strudel

Ginger bread

Pumpkin soup

Prep time: 15 minutes
Cooking time: 30 minutes
Serves: 12
Method: easy

Ingredients

- 100 ml olive oil
- 100 gr butter
- 2 large onions chopped
- 3 kilos pumpkin peeled and diced into cubes
- 6 garlic cloves crushed & chopped
- 3 litres chicken stock
- black pepper
- salt

Method

Using a large saucepan

- add oil & butter
- add the onion & garlic
- cook until golden
- add the pumpkin
- add the stock
- bring to the boil
- simmer for 30 minutes
- blend the soup until smooth
- season to taste

- place the warm dumplings on top of the soup

Chef tips: You can add a tablespoon of garam masala to the oil and butter to make this soup lightly spicy

You can add chopped red chilli on top of the soup before serving.

Coriander Dumplings

Prep time:	10 minutes
Cooking time:	12 minutes
Serves:	12
Method:	easy

Ingredients

- 300 gr self-raising flour
- 150 gr suet
- 1 tbs coriander seed
- 1 tbs turmeric
- 1 tbs chopped fresh coriander
- 150 ml cold water
- 1 tsp salt
- 1 tsp chilli powder 'optional'

Method

Using a large mixing bowl

- pre heat oven to 180*c (gas mark 4)
- add the flour, salt, turmeric, coriander seed and fresh coriander

- mix well
- add water and mixed into a dough
- if sticky add flour - if too dry add water
- cut into 12 balls
- bake for 12 minutes or until golden

Roast Duck Leg, Spiced Red Cabbage, Duck Fat Potatoes

Prep time:	20 minutes
Cooking time:	45 minutes
Serves:	12
Method:	easy

Ingredients

- 12 medium potatoes peeled and cut in half
- 12 medium duck legs
- 150 ml olive oil
- fresh thyme
- garlic cloves crushed
- 1 large red cabbage finely shredded
- 100 gr brown sugar
- 400 gr redcurrant jelly
- 1 (large) orange
- 4 cloves
- 1 tsp mixed spices
- 150 ml vinegar
- 1 litre orange juice

Method

Duck & potatoes

- preheat the oven to 200°c (gas mark 6)
- place the potatoes in a large saucepan of cold salted water.
- bring to the boil and cook for 2 minutes.
- drain, rinse under cold water and dry well with paper towel.
- toss in 1 tablespoon of the oil.
- lay thyme and garlic in a roasting pan,
- place duck on top and scatter potatoes around
- season and roast for 45 minutes, turning potatoes occasionally, until duck is cooked and potatoes are golden.

Spiced red cabbage

Using a large saucepan

- place the vinegar, orange juice, sugar into it
- ad in the mixed spice, red currant jelly
- cut the orange in half and insert the cloves into the skin
- add to the mix
- mix well and bring to the boil
- add the cabbage and simmer for 2 hours - 1 hour covered and 1 hour without the lid
- add water if the cabbage runs out of liquid

Chef tips: The cabbage is best made a few days earlier and can be served hot or cold.

Peach & Apple Strudel

Prep time: 20 minutes
Cooking time: 30 minutes
Serves: 12
Method: easy

Ingredients

- 6 eating apples - peeled and cubed
- 2 cooking apples - peeled and cubed
- 6 peaches cubed or 1 large tin of peaches drained and cubed - keep the syrup
- 150 gr brown sugar
- 1 juice of an orange
- 1 tsp ground cinnamon
- 100 gr sultanas
- 12 sheets of filo pastry
- 200 gr butter melted

Method

Preheat oven to 180*c (gas mark 4)

Using a large saucepan

- place all the apples and peach in it
- add sugar, cinnamon, sultanas
- add the orange juice
- cook for 10 minutes
- leave to cool

Using a large baking tray

- place one filo sheet on the tray and brush melted butter
- repeat 6 times and keep buttering the sheets
- add the apple mixture
- roll gently around the apples
- the buttered sheet will seal the strudel
- bake for 30 minutes or until brown

Chef's tip: Cooking the apple prior to rolling into the filo melts all the flavours together - however you can skip this and place the mixture directly onto the filo. You can use the syrup from the tinned peaches as a sweetener for whipped cream.

Ginger Bread

Prep time:	30 minutes
Cooking time:	10 minutes
Serves:	Makes 24 gingerbreads
Method:	easy

Ingredients

- 400 gr plain flour
- 1 tsp bicarbonate sodium
- 1 tsp cinnamon
- 3 tbs ground ginger
- 150 gr butter
- 180 gr soft brown sugar
- 2 eggs
- 4 tbs golden syrup

Method

Using a food processor

- add flour, bicarbonate, ginger, cinnamon,
- add butter, sugar, eggs & syrup
- blitz together until mixture binds
- remove and knead gently

Using a floured surface

- roll out the dough about ¼ inch (0.5cm) thick

Using a cutter

- cut as many as you can – depending in the shape(s)
- place the biscuits on a baking tray
- bake for 10/12 minutes or until golden brown

Chef's tip: You can freeze the dough Preparation time. Once you have made the gingerbread it can be made into all sorts of shapes – and with several flat pieces you can construct houses etc using icing sugar for 'glue', sweets for decoration/window etc.

New Year's Day

Close the Door
Close the door upon this year
Christmas gone, the new one's here.
Do we remember or forget?
The best so far – the worst one yet?

Upon the year we close the door,
The New Year's peeking in to view,
The last year lying on the floor,
Its day is done – its time is due.

So that is that: what's done is done,
The old year slips into the night.
New Year's Eve – a time for fun,
The song rings out so clear, so bright.

We'll take a cup of kindness yet,
Or so the old song says.
And here's a hand and don't forget,
Friends lost along the ways.

What message will the New Year bring?
What's gone before is past and old.
How will we view each coming spring?
Will it shine forth so bright, so bold?

We tend to live inside our past,
But treat each new year with respect.
Each year drags on – but flies so fast,
More rapidly than we expect.

The New Year brings a ray of hope,
To lift us from our gloom.
The New Year dawns - how will we cope,
As it brings in our doom?

Some Damned Foolish Thing in the Balkans...

It was a rainy night as the members assembled at the Professor's house. Many were in raincoats, some in wellington boots – others with umbrellas and so on. Where relevant, things were deposited in the entrance hall in stands or on pegs and then all progressively filed into the dining room. Everyone had been double vaccinated against covid – and also received their booster. The Professor had checked before we assembled. A wet New Year's Day! The start of a new year – we all hoped it would be better than the last one! Many had lost loved ones, or watched them suffer from covid and its effects.

Tonight, the dining room was festooned in an amazing array of army uniforms around the walls and in niches: which looked like they were of early 20th Century vintage. On one side there was the ridiculous blue coat and red pantaloons of the hairy poilu – French infantryman from pre- and early WWI whose officers had also worn white gloves! Then there was the khaki British uniform of the ubiquitous and long-suffering tommy; a white uniform topped by a helmet with an eagle – so obviously a German cavalry version of the pickelhaube; and what could only be described as a Turkish outfit complete with waistcoat, fez, balloon shaped trousers and upturned shoes. On the other side was the white uniform, lance and hat of a Russian cavalryman and next to it the strange Austrian uniform – kepi and blue jackets; then the khaki uniform and soft hat of an American 'doughboy', as well as an Indian army sepoy uniform with its smart turban helmet.

Well - we all thought – that sets the tone – clearly WWI context – but the uniforms covered pretty much the full panoply of warring sides - but where exactly will tonight's story be set?

Groves then served the food explaining what it was as he did so.

The first course was a soup, called 'Begova Corba' Groves explained, and containing chicken and vegetables – more like a stew really, served with a sour cream in a clay bowl. This was followed by Cevapi - small, oblong-shaped kebabs made from lamb which were served with or rather in Bosnian pita bread – Somun - with raw onions – fortunately not too strong! This gave us an initial clue as to the likely setting – how intriguing! Alternatively, there were vegetable Dolmas with aubergines (eggplant), peppers and courgettes (zucchini) stuffed with rice and spicy seasonings accompanied by a lemon-based sauce.

For pudding there was either an apple boiled in sugar and stuffed with walnuts served with syrup and whipped cream in a large glass – called, so Groves told us, Tufahija; or Baklava – endemic across the Middle east and Mediterranean and in this case looking like a small cake with layers of nuts, syrup and honey.

This was served with thick black Turkish coffee to complement the sweetness of these types of puddings. There was also more 'normal' coffee for those not much liking Turkish coffee – myself included. Finally, there was a couple of small strange cheeses – called 'Pule' – a white, smoky, crumbly cheese – which was very nice and made, so Groves took great delight in telling us after we had tried it, from donkey milk. He also told us that it was the single most expensive cheese in the world – hence the small portions.

To drink there was a selection of wines - Radgonska Ranina from Slovenia, just east of Maribor - its second city or town, and where I, at least, had been: a fresh white wine, pale lemon in colour with, I thought, a hint of ginger – but I could have been imagining things. There was also a red – a Peljesac Kvalitetno we were told – although it meant nothing to any of us – but it was a good 'big' strong red from the Croatian area. I remembered that Tito – Philip Broz – the Communist dictator of Yugoslavia had been half Croatian and half Slovenian and I wondered if that was a pointer as well. After his death the area had erupted into some of the cruellest fighting seen in Europe since WWII. He had apparently been the glue holding it all together. I also recalled that, despite not being the most effective partisan leader, he had been given eventual backing by the Allies as opposed to all others as there was a British Communist spy in the British Regional HQ in Cairo who was falsifying reports about the Yugoslavia/Balkan situation and the lack of success of the Royalists and attributing their success to Tito.

There was also beer. A dark beer and a light lager – from Serbia we were told – pivo in the local language.

So – clearly there was a Yugoslavian (I use the term to embrace all of those unhappy countries) – or at least Balkan theme – and clearly linked to WWI or the early 20th century we all thought.

Then, as we sipped our drinks, Angel arose and started her tale.

This story is far-reaching both in terms of time and distance. It concerns both my grandfather and my father.

First, I need to set some context. I quote from Sir Edward Grey – the Home Secretary in 1914.

"The lights are going out all across Europe.

We may not see them lit again in our lifetime."

As you are probably all familiar with this was his alleged comment as what was to become 'The Great War', or 'The War to End All Wars', and what we now call WWI, started. As we now know it lasted four and a half years and cost the lives of millions, in turn laying the unhappy roots of, and leading into, the Second World War – which was far more global in its impacts and resulted in far more deaths across the world.

But what was the cause? We know what the ostensible trigger was – the deaths of the heir to the Austro-Hungarian throne (an unloved individual by all accounts) and his morganatic wife. This led to the Austrian ultimatum to Serbia; the 'blank cheque' from the German Kaiser – giving unconditional support to Austria; mobilisation by Russia in support of Serbia; and then mobilisation by France to whom Russia was bound by a treaty. Then the stated neutrality by Italy – bound by treaty, in theory, to the Central Powers (Germany and Austria-Hungary) – but which got cold feet – and subsequently changed sides; but not mobilisation by Britain which had no treaties of alliance. This was then followed by the invasion of France by Germany – incidentally violating Luxembourg and Belgium and thus, finally and very reluctantly, but not unexpectedly, bringing the British Empire into play. Britain had, paradoxically or ironically, along with Germany, guaranteed Belgium's sanctity and also, from a more strategic point of view, could not let Germany take possession of French ports which would have been a direct threat the Royal Navy. The USA and Japan joined a little later. Thus, all major powers became involved in a major European conflagration which, as Bismarck had predicted, was caused by "some foolish thing in the Balkans" and which subsequently became global.

A question often asked is: why did the murder of such an unliked person, on a visit to Bosnia-Herzegovina, recently annexed by the Austrians and a seething hot bed of different religious and ethnic tensions involving, inter alia, Orthodox Serbs, Catholic Croats, Muslims etc, but where he had been generally well received, cause the biggest conflagration then seen?

There are many millions of words and hundreds of books devoted to this question – and few agree on the real drivers. Contributing factors include German militarism and the quest for both an empire and recognition of it as a world power by the 'older powers' (Britain and France – but especially Britain). Then there was the naval rivalry between Britain and Germany, driven by the Kaiser's megalomania and his paranoid wish to be 'liked by the British': where the King was his cousin, as was the then Tsar. In his memoirs he claimed to be Victoria's favourite grandson – but he wasn't invited to her Diamond Jubilee, nor her 80th birthday celebrations, and thought of him as tiresome and capricious. He also treated the Tsar as a retard and hectored him with condescending letters and telegrams which the latter resented. (I also recalled that the influence of Julius Caesar was so great that the word Kaiser, Tsar and Shah all came from his name – although as at today there are none bearing that variant title.) The French desire to recover the provinces of Alsace-Lorraine – lost to Prussia (the antecedent state to the German Empire) in 1871 after the Franco-Prussian war which was a humiliation for France and France's global standing.

Also, German generals wanted to attack Russia before it modernised to the extent where it became an existential threat (as they then saw it) to Germany. Poland did not exist at that time having been absorbed - mainly into Germany and Russia – so there was a long border between them. Finally, mention could also be made of Austria's fear of a growing Serbia, with its desire to unite all Balkan Slavs under its leadership – and in turn breaking up the Austro-Hungarian Empire – known also as 'The Sick Man of Europe': and, thus, it wanted a pre-emptive strike to finish it off. Even the Hungarian members of the Austro-Hungarian Empire – so often at odds with Austria, supported this - as they dominated many non-Hungarians (mainly Slavs) in their 'part' of the Empire. At the same time Serbia was trying to foment unrest in the Slav portions of Austria-Hungary for its own ends.

In the years running up to 1914 there had been much unrest in the world: attempted revolutions; communism was rearing its ugly head; and there had been several high-profile assassinations; regicides; and civil wars. In the 20 years up to WW! There had been assassinations of 6 Presidents (including both France and the USA), 7 Prime Ministers (including Spain and Persia), and 7 Royal rulers (including The Empress of Austria-Hungary, the King and Queen of Serbia who had been killed, hacked to pieces with sabres and then thrown out of their palace windows by the Serbian Army, as well as the Shah of Persia, and both the King of Italy and of Greece). On average one head of government or state had been assassinated or murdered each year. it was not an unusual thing – especially in the Balkans.

Into this hot bed of dissent, anarchy and general unease some Serbs had got together to force the pace of Serb unity. There were many secret societies which talked of political murders and assassinations and wanted to 'do something'. They were largely drifting, naive youngsters – but there were dark sinister shadowy figures at the top – and it is still not clear how heavily the Serbian government was involved: despite a total denial – suspicion was strong. A small group of Bosnian Serbs had got together and were agitating the Serbian heads of the secret societies "to be given something to do".

They were introduced to a secretive Major Tankovic who headed up the Black Hand – ostensibly a cultural society – but secretly dedicated to Serbian hegemony on the Balkans.

The story goes that a group of Bosnian Serbs – separated into two groups of three - were given rudimentary training, a few pistols, some bombs and poison for suicide and sent into Bosnia-Herzegovina to (try to) assassinate the Archduke.

Reportedly there were two failed bombing attempts, most lost their nerve, and then one of the Serbs was idly standing at the side of the road, eating a sandwich when the Ducal procession, having taken a wrong turn drove by. If we can believe it: he then fired two shots without looking (his words) and managed to kill both the Archduke and his wife with one shot each.

This has always seemed to be an unlikely coincidence, although not impossible, but it beggars belief to a very great extent to think that a 19-year-old consumptive, with virtually no arms training, and no military service could manage to kill two people with just two shots especially given how unreliable hand guns were then.

Certainly, my grandfather had his doubts and, unlike many, he decided to undertake some investigation to satisfy his curiosity. He was in the army and involved in ballistics, so in a quiet time in the late 30's – but before Anschluss, he decided to visit the Austrian Military Museum where the artefacts relating to the assassination were kept. His German was good and so he was able to read the notes, and engage in conversation with the curator. He saw the blood-stained uniform; three of the alleged four pistols – which were Belgian Brownings; an apparent bomb; a few pictures of the event (with a snap of what purported to be Gavrilo Princep – the assassin being arrested – but which in fact was later found to be someone else); the car in which the Duke was riding; and…

… the bullets.

This was what caught his eye. Two bullets only were apparently recorded as having been fired by Princip. One was taken out of the Archduchess – but the second had been lodged in the Archduke's spine and couldn't be taken out and was left in when he was embalmed and then buried. But there they were – two bullets openly on display. He started asking questions about them – but at that point the curator became difficult and he was asked to leave. Fortunately, he had sketched them by then, before he was escorted out.

He then left Austria, World War II started later on, in which he was involved, and so he was unable to return to Austria, even after the war, and the he died.

He passed onto his son, my father, however, his discoveries and his disquiet. In those days, of course, there were no such things as mobile phones with cameras and he had not been allowed to photograph anything – but, being a ballistics expert, he could see that the bullets were wrong. They were not from a pistol – but from a rifle he believed. He was sure that they were from a rifle – and a German at that – a Mauser in fact' - and she looked down at a note she was holding in front of her and read out: "The 7.92×57mm Mauser S Patrone cartridge which was loaded with a new 8.20 mm (.323 in) 9.9 g (154 gr) spitzer bullet." She looked up again and carried on.

'It was this bullet, or rather these two bullets, he earnestly believed, which were on display. The Browning pistols, which were Belgian or American it wasn't clear, and well documented as being used by the assassins, in fact fired a different bullet – a '45. The Mauser had a range of around 110 yards with high accuracy.

My father Inherited these notes about the bullet discrepancy on my grandfather's death along with some other investigation which he had undertaken. My grandfather had wondered if there had been another person, or persons involved in the assassination – and now he wondered if they had been armed with perhaps longer-range rifles, from a longer distance, which would have given them the chance to get away easily in the confusion caused by Gavrilo Princip's shots. He had found no conclusive proof of this but had later had researched into many German documents – at least those which had survived the destruction of Berlin by the Allied bombing and then the Soviet attacks in WWII.

What he found was quite amazing and I share this with you today almost in disbelief. He researched documents in Germany, in Austria, in Hungary, in Russia, and in Serbia. It took him many years as, not only did WWII and the subsequent Soviet occupation of Eastern Europe, interrupt his work, but also, they were in a plethora of languages and he had to get them translated, carefully, bit by bit, without giving anything away.

I have only fairly recently been given access to my father's and his father's, my grandfather's notebooks – they were held under a moratorium for many years. I wondered why – now I know!

It is clear from his notes and his conclusions that there seems little doubt from these documents that there was in fact an international conspiracy of sorts to start a war. Not a major war – and certainly not the war that occurred – who would have foreseen that? There was no precedent for such a conflagration. Although given the industrialisation of 'killing' it was all too apparent that this might be the case – as demonstrated by the slaughter in the US Civil War, which lessons were, however ignored. Only Kitchener seemed to think, and then only once it had started, that it would be a long war and urged the British Government to prepare for a war of many years' duration.

No - what these conspirators wanted was a quick 'localised' war: as had been the Austro-Prussian war in 1866 or the Franco-Prussian War in 1871. A quick defeat of Serbia: "Stop in Belgrade", no territorial annexation, punishment of that country and reduction in its local power; then a neutralisation of Russia without a war. Certainly, no war against France (Germany's fear, or nightmare, of a two-front war) and certainly not a major (World) war involving all the Great Powers. The precedents for local wars were strong as there had been several short wars in the Balkans prior to 1914, as the Balkans had freed themselves from the Ottomans and then argued over the spoils. No 'Big Powers' had been involved. The Serbians wanted a war in which they would beat Austria-Hungary and "free the Slavs" (although they wanted them [Bosniaks, Croats, Slovenes etc] to be the subjects of a Greater Serbia "Yugoslavia"). Austria Hungary wanted a local war - they wanted to beat Serbia.

Germany wanted a war to destroy Russian power; even the Russians wanted a war. The Austrian notes are the most interesting. The heir to the Austrian throne, the Archduke Franz Ferdinand was not at all a well-liked man. The then Emperor, Franz Joseph (also called Kaiser-King under the political pretence – in reality a shambles - of the Dual Monarchy) disliked his heir and, as an insufferable snob, loathed and hated the Archduke's wife whom he thought was beneath the throne's dignity. His own son, the original heir, had killed himself in a very risqué scandal with a dancer or prostitute of some description. He had even forced Franz Ferdinand to have a morganatic marriage so his children couldn't inherit. His fear was that after his death the Archduke would disavow his morganatic marriage and change the inheritance etc.

The Austrian army had no particular love for Franz Ferdinand seeing him as an obstacle to war with Serbia –

so were probably were quite indifferent to him - but really wanted a war with Serbia. The leader of the General Staff had urged a "Preventative war" with Serbia many, many times. They did not want to World War, let's be clear, as they knew they could not beat Russia, the 'protector' of Serbia, on their own – hence their treaty with Germany.

The Hungarians absolutely and utterly hated Franz Ferdinand because they knew from his own statements that he wanted to change the Austro-Hungarian Empire from a dual monarchy into some sort of tri-partite state "trialism" giving Slavs equal power with Austrians and Hungarians, with Slavs having much greater autonomy. This was not at all to the Hungarians liking because they exercised hegemony over a large number of Slavs and other non-Hungarians (Czechs, Poles, Ukrainians, Ruthenes etc) and this would have reduced their authority. They had a key phrase "No more Slavs in the Monarchy" and were afraid that the annexation of Bosnia-Herzegovina – mainly Slavs - would dilute their power. They would have only been too keen to see him go.

In turn Franz Ferdinand loathed the Hungarians and was a major recidivist and a very old-fashioned and pious catholic. He wanted to turn the clock back: undo the independence of (secular) Italy; recover the Austrian territories there; and reinstate the Pope as ruler of the former Papal territories, and destroy the Italian state. He wanted to get back the German territories lost to Prussia. He had made it known that he wanted to give the Slavs more power and equality, and reduce the influence of the Hungarians. He had no friends.

The 'Court' in Vienna also loathed him and made his and his wife's life an absolute misery – she was not allowed to sit with the Archduke at functions but was made to sit in inferior places – below many others. The German Kaiser, however, was a friend of Franz Ferdinand and invited him up to Germany and stayed with him and treated him and his wife with the respect that the heir thought his wife deserved. He regarded him as a friend, if Kaiser Wilhelm actually had any friends, however, the German generals had no time for Franz Ferdinand and particularly wanted a "Teuton" war against Russia: but which they felt that the Kaiser and the Archduke would veto. They were all lobbying for something to happen.

Serbia clearly wanted a war and was only too happy to do anything it possibly could to cause it. It is clear, from the documents that my grandfather read, that the Germans, Austrians and Hungarians had got hold of news about the potential plot to assassinate Franz Ferdinand – presumably the Austrians had passed this on to Germany. Normally you would think they would do something about this because it would be appalling if any heir to any throne was assassinated, however, it suited their means and they were clearly men without honour. It is likely that the German Kaiser was not informed: as he would almost certainly not have allowed an assassination of any Royal personage, least of all someone who he regarded as an ally and a friend.

Not only did the Austrians and/or Hungarians not do anything to stop it, but in fact when Franz Ferdinand and his wife toured Bosnia there were virtually no precautions taken – such as the street aligned with troops and police – as is usual practice when any monarch visits any country; and particularly one that only been annexed recently. Nothing at all was prepared properly - it looked very, very lax.

One of the reasons why the Archduke was so keen to go to Sarajevo, where he was to watch army manoeuvres and to inspect troops, was that, as it was not an 'official' part of the Austro-Hungarian Empire, he and his wife would be treated as befitted their station: as Heir Apparent and Consort.

So, all things were in place for a tragedy.

In one of the documents my grandfather found, and detailed in his notes, without giving the name of the document (which he may not have known); there was a reference (but not direct proof) to the fact that the Russians were also part of this plot because they too wanted a war. They had to support Serbia, and they wanted to beat Austro-Hungary, its rival in the Balkans. They knew they had to fight Germany at some stage and the generals were keen to precipitate it before Germany, as they saw it, got stronger. Russian generals had an optimistic view of the qualities of the Russian military men. The French had invested a lot of capital in Russian railways: especially to facilitate mobilisation quickly against Austria-Hungary and Germany.

Curiously enough Germany had the same sort of paranoid fear - that Russia was going to get stronger. It saw the railways being built and thrusting like a dagger into the heart of the German Empire and too it was fearful of Russia's seemingly inexhaustible manpower and its, reported, but in fact untrue, weapons build up. In the event many Russians went to war with no weapons or ammunition, being told to take them the off dead soldiers. It is certain that Britain, USA and Belgium did not want a major conflagration: and certainly not one involving them.

France wanted to win back its lost provinces – Alsace and Lorraine - which was described as a "festering sore" between Germany and France, but was banking on a quick charge into those provinces – based on the French army's fateful and disastrous philosophy of "elan": to win them back and achieve the status quo antebellum the Franco-Prussian war of 1871 – after which it had lost them. Unfortunately for France, in a clash between "elan" and machine guns, there are no prizes for guessing which will always win. Britain did not want to go to war at all – as this was especially bad for trade and as the world's leading trading nation it had much to lose. Although it had the most powerful navy in the world – even after Germany's disastrous ship building race - it had virtually no army only what was called the "British Expeditionary Force" designed to quell unrest in the Empire: but not to fight major wars.

Thus – from my grandfather's and father's notes - it was clear that the other Central Powers definitely were involved but they could find no reference to the Ottoman Empire's involvement. It is possible they were involved as they were the historical power in the Balkans, and no doubt still had many spies there. One might think perhaps they could have been involved in order to take back parts of the Balkans but we don't know.

So, I have drawn up a list of suspects – and judged them accordingly. It is doubtful that, whatever his feelings about Franz Ferdinand and his wife - the Emperor of Austro-Hungary would have overtly consented to an assassination of his heir – that would set a bad precedent – but (guilty of a] knowing – or b] involvement) – too difficult to be definite now that over 100 years and two hot wars and a cold war have passed by:

Country	Guilt
Austrian Government	guilty
Austrian Army	guilty
Austrian Court	guilty

Hungarian ruling class	guilty
Serbian secret society 'black hand'	guilty
Serbian government	probably
German Government	probably
German Army	guilty
German Kaiser	unlikely
Russian Army	probably/not proven
Russian Tsar	probably not guilty
Bosnian government	not proven – unlikely
Ottoman Empire	no information
France	unknown/not proven – unlikely
Britain	not guilty

Furthermore, some of the documents my grandfather found seemed to indicate that, the Hungarian government, having heard about the plot, decided that they very much wanted it to succeed and in fact dispatched an unknown number, of what are we presume are snipers, to Bosnia and Sarajevo to ensure that the assassination actually happened.

This is clearly appalling and if true is evidence of a massive conspiracy to commit an assassination; and yet the documents show this. Now, although I am talking about "the documents in the case", I do not have these documents, nor even copies. My grandfather had seen some documents and taken notes, or rather wrote them up later, when no-one was watching. My father then went back to try and find these documents, but unfortunately, they had all been destroyed in the Second World War or possibly even taken back to Moscow by the Soviets.

My father was unable to find any of the original documents to which my grandfather referred, except for one. A copy of an (anonymous) letter that was sent to the Serbian Prime Minister, Pasic, which stated that there was an Austro-Hungarian plot (army and politicians) to assassinate the hated Archduke (but not necessarily his wife) and blame Serbia, and thus give them the trigger and excuse to start a war. The Serbian government did nothing with this letter, as far as we can ascertain, which indicates an involvement of some sort – overtly, covertly or tacitly.

So, on the balance of probability, we can say that, based on the investigations by my father and grandfather before him, there was a plot to assassinate the Archduke. We know that Bosnian Serbs were definitely involved and too a Serbian secret society; and that at least Austria-Hungary (or some people there) and possibly some German Army generals were also involved; and moreover, that it is likely that several snipers were sent to Sarajevo to "shadow" the Bosnian Serbs, or to take individual action as they saw fit, ensure that the job was executed (no pun intended) properly. And they did.

The result was, as we all know, four of the five empires

involved disappeared in the immediate aftermath of WWI: Russian, Austro-Hungarian, German and Ottoman. It also unleashed communism on the world and resulted in something like 40 million deaths during and in the epidemic aftermath. The greatest tragedy is that the genesis of the "local war", as originally envisaged especially by Germany, was to ensure the survival of the Austro-Hungarian as a great power. It achieved the opposite effect.

For the Austro-Hungarian Empire it was clear that it was on completely the wrong side of history. The world had, by and large, moved to the position where most entities were now nation states (Italy, Germany, France etc). Austria-Hungary, by contrast, was a ramshackle collection of many nationalities, many religions, many languages and many oppressed (and often sizeable) minorities with inequitable and inadequate representation in politics and power. Furthermore, many could look to nation states outside the empire and see states to whom these minorities should belong and wanted to belong – e.g. Serbia, Bulgaria, Romania etc. In addition, there were many that had been states and wanted to recreate them – e.g. Poland, Ukraine and these many-layered, strong tensions were bound to tear Austria-Hungary apart sooner or later. The war merely exacerbated the position and led to the creation of many small states which had scores to settle and whose boundaries were disputed and lead, partly, to WWII.

A tragedy!

To the Archduke – an unloved man and an innocent pawn! Prosit! And ekerkeshedra!'

She sat down.

Well, that was an eye opener – but no definitive proof of course – but the facts could easily be fitted into that theory.

Some Damned Foolish Thing in the Balkans...

menu

Begova Corba

Cepavi (Bosnian Kebab)

Stuffed Aubergine

Baklava

Begova Corba

Prep time:	20 minutes
Cooking time:	60 minutes
Serves:	12
Method:	easy

Ingredients

- 600 gr boneless chicken thighs
- 400 gr carrots diced
- 1 large onion chopped
- 1 beetroot diced
- 2 celery sticks diced
- 100 gr okra sliced
- 200 gr sour cream
- 1 tbs salt
- 1 tbs black pepper
- 1 tsp ground nutmeg
- 1 cinnamon stick

Method

Using a large saucepan

- place the chicken thighs
- cover with water
- season to taste
- simmer for 30 minutes
- remove the chicken
- leave to cool
- add all the vegetables

- add the black pepper, carrots, beetroot, onions
- add celery, okra
- add nutmeg, cinnamon,
- bring to boil
- simmer for 10 minutes
- shred the chicken then add to the soup
- simmer for a further 10 minutes
- serve with a spoon of sour cream

Cepavi - Bosnian Kebab

Prep time:	15 minutes
Cooking time:	10 minutes
Serves:	12
Method:	easy

Ingredients

- 600 gr lean minced beef
- 600 gr lean minced lamb
- 6 garlic cloves chopped
- salt & black pepper
- 1 tsp chili powder
- 1 tsp thyme

Method

Preheat oven to 180*C or hot BBQ

In a large bowl

- combine the beef and the lamb
- add all the spices
- add salt & pepper to taste

- mix well
- shape the mixture into thin sausages
- brush the kebab with olive oil
- grill of bake the kebab for 15 minutes
- serve with flat breads 'see recipe index'

Stuffed Aubergine

See chef's tip'

Prep time:	15 minutes
Cooking time:	60 minutes
Serves:	12
Method:	easy

Ingredients

- 6 large aubergines
- 1 tbs harissa paste
- 2 onions chopped
- olive oil
- 600 gr lean lamb mince
- 2 tsp cinnamon
- 1 tsp oregano
- 1 tsp chilli powder 'optional'
- 250 ml red wine
- 1 tbs tomato paste
- one 500 gr tin of chopped tomatoes
- 250 gr feta

Method

Preheat oven to 180*C (Gas mark 4)

- halve the aubergines lengthways
- scoop out the flesh and set aside
- rub the aubergine with olive oil
- place in a baking tray upside down
- cook for 15 minutes

Using a large saucepan

- add oil, garlic, onions, and aubergine flesh
- stir well add all the spices
- stir well and add the mince lamb
- cook for 20 minutes and stir until the mince is crumbed
- add the tomato paste, harissa
- stir well
- add the tin of chopped tomatoes
- cook for 20 minutes
- place the mixture carefully in the aubergines
- sprinkle the feta over the top
- bake for a further 20 minutes

Chef's tip: You can use courgettes instead of aubergines - follow the same process

Baklava

Prep time:	30 minutes
Cooking time:	60 minutes
Serves:	12
Method:	easy

Ingredients

- 250 gr butter
- 250 gr pistachios
- 100 gr walnuts
- 100 gr pecan
- 50 gr hazelnuts
- 2 packs of filo pastry

For the syrup

- 2 tbs spoon orange water
- 1 tbs rose water
- 3 cardamon
- 100 gr honey
- 200 gr sugar

Method

Preheat oven to 180*C (Gas Mark 4)

Using a food processor

- place all the nuts and blitz until crumbed
- place in a mixing bowl
- add honey and stir well
- set aside
- melt the butter

Using a large baking tray

- place a sheet of greaseproof paper
- place a filo sheet the brush well with melted butter
- repeat 6 times - one over the top of the other - well

buttered
- spread the mixture evenly on the filo
- repeat the filo process 6 times
- press well so it is reasonably packed
- sprinkle sugar over the top of the last one
- turn to oven down to 150*c
- bake in the oven for 30 minutes
- leave to cool
- cut into squares

Syrup

- place all the ingredients in a pan
- bring to the boil
- simmer for 10 minutes or until honey like consistency
- leave to cool

Drizzle over the Baklava

Perihelion

Winter

The tall tense trunks of trees
against the greyish wintry sky
Stand starkly bare in frosty air
and softly draw one's eye.

No leaves protect the branches now,
No flowers festoon its bough
The east wind bites, its fingers chill,
Its wintry touch a bitter thrill.

The crow sits proud atop its nest,
to feel the sun: it faces West.
Whilst on the ground a heavy frost,
lies over autumn's leaves ere lost

A robin chirps its merry air,
whilst hopping, seeking wintry fare.
The clouds go scudding past the sun,
Their snow soon spent, the snow storm done

Tho' little stays up on the ground,
but here and there an object crowned
With melting snow,
so soon to go.

The lowering sun gives wintry light,
Ere giving way to bitter night
Whilst creatures shiver in their lair,
escaping freezing frosty air.

The starlings fly to summer climes,
while children practice Christmas rhymes
Though we enjoy the festive cheer,
we all look forward to next year.

When the Finger Points!

As we entered our usual room, we could see the Christmas tree twinkling in the coroner: a lovely blend of red, green and gold. Crowning it was a very large star, golden and shining out. There was obviously a bulb from the general Christmas tree lights inside it. The effect was rather good I thought. This was clearly intended to reflect the star which guided the Wise Men on their journey from the east, and which led them to Bethlehem – where, as the carols have it, it hung over the stable. On the roof was a projection of part of our solar system – the earth the sun and the moon. That was unusual. In fact, a first, and more than a little intriguing. Groves was, as usual, on hand to offer us a selection of drinks. There was Italian beer, Italian wine: a deep red, a fine Sicilian; and also a white a very nice chilled Pinot Grigio. There was also a cocktail which Groves explained was a Harvey Wallbanger. We had all heard of it, of course, but only a few had tried it.

The Professor motioned us to be seated and then said a few words by way of introduction.

'Welcome my friends. It is the 4th January – the perihelion – and Shamus will go into a little more detail about that in due course.'

So, we knew who was telling the tale tonight and where it was set.

'As you have almost certainly perceived, there is a strong Italian flavour – both literally and figuratively - tonight. The cocktail on offer features Star Anise, which also features in our food – as a reflection of the star which led the Magi in keeping with our Christmas festivity theme. Star Anise is a wonderful spice, shaped like a star and there are two types – Chinese and Japanese. Both bear similar fruits, but the Japanese, which is called Shikimi, is poisonous. Naturally we are using the Chinese version.' and he smiled at us.

'The tree is 'Illicum verum' and the fruits are picked just before they ripen and dry. It is used in many ways in the Far East: tradition has it that by placing a star anise fruit in each corner of each room in your home it will bring you luck. A similar claim is that placing a star anise beneath your pillow will induce prophetic dreams and also help you sleep. It has a sharp aniseed flavour and this along with its shape gives us its western name. It is also used to flavour the Italian liqueur Galliano – which is a key ingredient in the cocktail you were offered – the Harvey Wallbanger. You can also, apparently, make a sachet of star anise and bay to put into your bath water to purify and cleanse you. Buona salute - cheers!'

At that Groves served the meal explaining that the food was from the Calabrian area as well as Tuscany.

We had a good but light garlic soup to start – lightly flavoured with star anise – so the flavour was a delicate hint rather than overpowering. For the main course we had baked courgettes a tasty dish with mince and a hint of chili. For pudding there were star shaped biscuits, or cookies, which Groves informed us were called Canestry, accompanied by an Italian lemon curd dip, as well as home-made ice cream with the option of a delicately star anise flavoured warm sauce; and a selection of cheese with a chutney which also featured star anise – but again delicately so that we did not feel that we had been eating nothing else. A strong Italian red wine was on offer to go with the cheese, and for those who wished it a glass of Galliano. I took the red wine with my cheese alongside some parmesan flavoured biscuits.

Then Shamus arose and started to speak.

'Forgive me if I start with a little bit of an information dump – it is background to this story and interesting in an arcane way. At least I hope you think so!' he added.

'Earth reaches its closest point to the Sun approximately two weeks after the December solstice – which is the shortest day and thus the longest night. Tonight, is that night.

Conversely the summer solstice is the longest day and shortest night. In between are the equinoxes - where days and nights are of equal length. These were key events in the year ancient times and were known in Britain as Alban Elfed or cyhydnos yr hydref and cyhydnos y gwanwyn.

There were also other key events:

- May day – known as Beltane in Welsh and Celtic – which is halfway between the spring equinox and summer solstice. There were lots of traditions associated with this date;
- Lammas — and which comes from Anglo-Saxon for 'loaf mass': which celebrates harvest and falls half way between summer solstice and the autumn equinox - in Cornish/ancient British and Welsh is called Gŵyl Awst and celebrations took place in all societies.

This point in Earth's orbit around the Sun is called "perihelion". Interestingly the earth is closest to the sun in northern hemisphere winter (when it is usually very cold – at least historically that was the case, but this has not been so in more recent years) and farthest away in northern hemisphere summer (when it is hot). The opposite holds true for the southern hemisphere of course. The term comes from Greek: peri (near), not to be confused with the Victorian word for a fairy; and Helios (God of the sun).

The opposite is aphelion – meaning furthest away. It is a paradox that in winter for the northern hemisphere the earth is nearer and in summer – when it is hotter – furthest away! It is similarly paradoxical that the winters are shorter in the northern hemisphere (about 89 days) than in the south - whereas summer is longest at 93 days in the northern hemisphere – although it really doesn't feel like that!

As the earth does not revolve around the sun in a perfect circle these dates are moving and have moved. Thus in 13,000 years' time (when you and I almost certainly won't be here to see it) they will have changed places in the calendar year and perihelion will be in July and aphelion in January. How this will affect the seasons is not yet clear – and, moreover, whether humans will still be around at all for this is also a moot point!

In the mid-13th century – the winter solstice and perihelion were on the same day/date but this changes by about a day every 60 years or so, due to the "erratic" wobble in the Earth's orbit, and the perihelion moves forward from the solstice. Thus, we have the approximate two week gap nowadays.

In addition to this – there is also the perigee – probably only a word you heard in an incantation in the Disney film Bedknobs and Broomsticks – but it means when the moon is closest to the earth. This does not in fact cause much of a difference at all – but there is an old Italian and Roman Catholic legend that when the Perigee and Perihelion concur – the dead can rise and talk to the living. Not all the dead: only those who died when it was either perigee or perihelion. Curious what superstitions are even now still rife.

On this date the Roman Catholic peasants, a superstitious

lot by all accounts, go out and, where they know that a non-Catholic was killed, or died on those days, and buried, they hammer a stake into ground to 'hold the spirit in its grave'. If fact for good measure they often just stake all non-Catholic bodies. During the Peninsula War the peasants did this to the graves of British, Dutch and German troops so killed: on the assumption that they were Protestants. This was not always true, of course, as some Germans were Catholics, as were many of the Irish troops. Small thanks for saving them from French domination! Just why I am telling you this will, I hope, become apparent as the story unfolds.

Now the real meat and drink – our story.

This is a sad story. I have pieced it together from a diary and from an interview with a member of the family, whom I knew slightly from one or two ventures in Italy. I have Anglicised certain aspects for better intelligibility for this group.

An Italian couple were to be wed, and there was high excitement, tinged with a little apprehension on the part of her family. She was from a very wealthy family from Calabria; whereas, he was from an old and aristocratic – but now impoverished - Tuscan family. After the marriage, a full Catholic mass lasting some three hours I am told, they moved into his slightly run-down villa in Tuscany. A part of the marriage was that she would get to become a

Contessa, and her family money would be used to restore the villa gardens and grounds. The marriage seemed to be made in heaven. They were blessed with two children in due course, and the villa was restored, if not to its full Renaissance magnificence, at least to a very comfortable condition. With time however, and is often the case, things started to go wrong. The husband became even poorer when a couple of his business ventures went belly up, and one or two of his family properties, providing at least some rental income, were destroyed in an earthquake, but it turned out that he had not insured them. What can one say – living in an earthquake zone – e stupido!' And he shrugged his shoulders.

'The two children went to school, boarding, and as soon as they could left home to run their own lives. They were on good terms with their mother, but not their father; who increasingly came to resent his family's lack of money and his reliance on his wife's monies. His drinking increased and he dissembled, however, and pretended all was fine to her and anyone on the family who visited, although these visits were discouraged and became progressively fewer. He had persuaded his wife earlier on in the marriage, when he seemed to be making some money, to make a will putting all their monies in joint names.

Twice a year they would go on holiday: in winter skiing in the alps, where her family had a chalet; and in summer

- cruising around the med – he was a culture vulture of some sorts.

They were also, gradually, restoring the gardens, buying interesting plants that thrived in the warm summers and other shady trees that lined the path and provided a cool walkway when it was too hot.

All in the local town knew them as they often shopped there, and ordered goods to be delivered to their villa.

After a while, the villagers noticed that they had not seen his wife, Signora La Contessa, for some time. On occasion, when asked, he replied that she had left him and gone back to her family in deepest south of Italy – Calabria. The villagers expressed surprise, as they had no idea that anything was amiss, and sorrow, as she was generally well liked.

Time passed.

Then one day her brother turned up, concerned that he had heard nothing from her for some time and wondering why and demanding to see her. Her husband told him the same story as he had told the locals and other neighbours – that she left him and returned to her family. Her brother is mystified and stated that this was not true and that no-one in the family had heard from her nor seen her for some time now.

The husband replied, not too kindly "I am only telling you what she told me. Good riddance, adulterous bitch!"

and he turned away from her brother and shrugged his shoulders. "Ptchaa!"

He then motioned to her brother saying "Come. See." And he took him into her dressing room, stating that it has been untouched since she went, apart from cleaning: her clothes gone and overnight bag missing.

"She never sent for any other clothes – but why should I chase her? A large sum of money was taken out of the joint account, on her written instructions, and transferred abroad not too long before.

He points to a scrappy piece of paper on the dressing table – weighted down with a brush

It said "Non posso andare avanti" – "I can't go on".

Her husband said "I was pretty sure that there was another man involved: as I found some correspondence which could be interpreted either way, from someone I didn't know. It could have been friendship, or something more…"

He sighed then carried on

"Even though she has left me for someone else - I have planted a tree in the grounds in her memory. Come and see."

He led her brother down the stairs and out into the courtyard, and from there they walked into the woods forming part of the estate until they came to a clearing, where he showed him a tree, set in a circle of earth with a diameter of about six feet, that is just under two metres.

"What tree is it?" her brother asked

"It is a Maidenhair Ginko. To remind me of her golden hair." He replied

Here Fruity paused the narrative and added

'It has golden/yellow foliage in autumn, has a capacity for prodigious growth and, curiously, has unpleasantly scented yellow fruits. It is the last living species of the order 'ginkogoales' which appeared over 300 million years ago (I looked it up).' he added to explain this piece of trivia.

'It starts off thin but can grow huge and wide – it can live for hundreds and thousands of years.'

He took a sip of the Calabrian wine, cleared his throat, and resumed his tale.

'The Contessa's brother was dissatisfied with the explanations and went into the village to ask around. There was sadness that she was no longer around but he found nor heard nothing untoward reported by anyone. Nobody had heard of any arguments, nor any issues – just that she went away some time ago, leaving the Signor Conte. They had never heard nor seen anything from the children either – not for a long time.

"E Triste!" was the most common phrase. The local grocer added "la famiglia del conte è qui da molti anni." – his family have been here for many years – as though that settled the matter for him.

Her brother remained dissatisfied with the situation, but was unable to take it any further. He took his leave, not in a friendly way, and said that he will get in touch with the children, his nephew and niece, and that he will return. "Be assured that I will drop in from time to time."

"Bene. Feel free. If you hear anything of her then please let me know, as I cannot divorce her 'non posso divorziare da lei' - without knowing where she is, nor have her declared dead if that is the case: until we know."

Her brother left and, in due course, called each of the children in turn – but they could only confirm that their mother had indeed stopped contacting them a while ago and that their letters and calls had gone unanswered. They were as mystified as he was as to where she might have gone.

The call from their uncle unsettled the children, not surprisingly: and for the first time in a long age, they called their father to find out what had happened, individually. He told them that he was pleased to hear from them, after such a time, but told them each the same story: that their mother just walked out on him one day and he has heard nothing from her. He explained that, as their monies were joint, he can still run the house, and that, of course, in due course they will come into their inheritance from the money, after he has died. This did not satisfy them and they both decided, after talking to each other, to visit together and see for themselves what the position was.

A few days later a car pulled up in the drive of the house and his children got out. Whilst he was pleased to see them – they were not friendly and immediately demanded to know what was going on. He patiently told them what he had said on the telephone, and took them into her dressing room, showing them the scrappy piece of paper, in her handwriting, and then the tree planted in her memory in the woods. The daughter burst into tears on seeing the tree and they both left feeling dissatisfied with everything.

Time passed.

Then he started receiving odd things in the post.

The first thing he received was a copy of a Rolling Stones record. This was odd as he wasn't a fan, and didn't know that his ex-wife had been ether. There was no name on it – nor any way to trace it.

In the following week he received a sheet of lyrics by the English group 'The Christians' of whom he had never heard.

Then a week later he received a package of chocolate biscuits - every day for a week. Curious as he didn't particularly like chocolate biscuits and he wasn't sure why he was getting them. It was very strange. Again, no name, no indication who sent it, nothing to identify who the perpetrator was.

In the following week he received the same set of lyrics.

A little while later he received 13 cards in the post, every day for a week. A random set of cards. Very bizarre and again he had no idea what this meant, again for 7 days.

Then a week later he received a packet of frozen seafood every day for another week. Quite bizarre. He put them in the freezer - he didn't quite know what else to do with them. He was by now more than a little concerned as to whom might be sending them to him, and more importantly – why?

Then there was a week where nothing happened and he began to relax; but then a week afterwards he got the lyrics again, along with five cards in an envelope 3 aces and 2 kings. Bizarre. The cards were received every day for a week following exactly the same procedure, but not the lyrics.

He was now beginning to worry so he told the police. The police said "Sapristi - Well what can we do?" and shook their shoulders. The Capitano said "There's nothing illegal in this. It isn't threatening – that is you haven't had any threatening letters - have you?"

He shook his head.

"Bene. You can eat the food; you can use the cards: you have got two packs by now – so play bridge or something."

And they left with wry smiles on their faces.

Then the following week – again the lyrics, and then a week's gap and it started again. He received 5 small green vegetables in the post, the same thing every day. Okra - vegetables he didn't really like, but in truth had no real feelings about them one or another. He was by now hitting the sauce quite heavily. He was convinced that someone was sending him a message – and about his ex-wife. He was sure of it.

Then the lyrics arrived again accompanied by a bunch of 5 bananas – the same bunch every day for a week. Now he was getting paranoid and he started moving on from white wine to heavy red wine – at least a couple of bottles a day.

As they say "Just because you are a little paranoid – doesn't mean that they are not out to get you!"

Then the lyrics once again.

Then the next week he received several small sweets in the post – long thin and covered in chocolate. Once more every day for 7 days.

Then he received an LP by a Northern Irish group – of whom he had never heard – a different CD every day over the week but no more lyrics.

It was all becoming too much and he moved onto strong spirits – grappa - and a tipple he loved: Scotch Whisky. Now this was serious drinking and he put on weight, was sleeping badly, and his face took on that red flushed hue of the lush.

The things kept arriving. The following week more chocolate biscuits – long thin and flat - sometimes in twos others in fours; the week after, on each day, a multi shaped large piece of ginger.

Then his brother-in-law called to see him. It was the

4th January – the perihelion – when, as has been mentioned, Catholics believe that the dead can rise.

"You look terrible. What has happened?"

And he told the brother-in-law, who was not sympathetic.

"Come show me the tree you planted. I want to remember my sister." He shuffled out, leaning on the brother-in-law's arm and they went to the tree.

On the way he noticed – or thought he saw some of the things he had been receiving. One of the chocolate biscuits lying on the ground. He pointed it out to his brother-in-law, who said " è solo un ramoscello o un piccolo ramo" a small twig.

Then he saw a piece of ginger root – his brother-in-law gave the same response adding "You are a little paranoid aren't you?"

Then turning a corner – they saw a banana. He gasped and pointed at it and his brother-in-law said

"Si - Sì, posso vederlo, ma è solo una banana!" - 'Yes I see it – but it is just a banana.'

Then they came to the tree. Nailed to the tree was a set of five cards. The Count started jabbering and moaning.

Then his brother-in-law grabbed his arm saying

"Look!" said the brother-in-law, pointing to the soil beneath the tree. "Down there. I know you buried her there now – her fingers are sticking up through the ground."

And sure enough there were what seemed to be several small fingers pushing up through the soil, beneath the tree!

The Count gave a terrible scream, ran back indoors and flung the door shut and refused to open it until much later: when he had drunk yet more, partly sobered up and the brother-in-law had long gone. He paced around the house muttering to himself.

Next day the cleaner came in and then rushed out screaming and called the polizia.

The local Magistrate who was also the coroner was called in and examined the cadaver. The husband was dead. Suicide: a serious sin in Catholic Italy – which means he cannot be buried in a church yard.

The husband left a diary. Most of what I told you comes from this. The final entry in very shaky handwriting said "Ma l'ho seppellita a faccia in giù." But I buried her face down…

So, said Shamus – that was all clear then. He had murdered his wife and buried her under the tree, as her brother suspected.'

He sat down.

'No, no, no, this won't do.' said Archie. 'What were the items in the post all about?'

Of course, Shamus had left this bit out deliberately, then he said

'Well, if I tell you that the fingers were, in fact, a fungus growing out of tree roots does that give you any clue?'

There was a pause, then:

'Dead Man's Fingers!' shouted Mary who was a bit of a botanist. 'Ha. Ha. Excellent. – or maybe Dead Moll's Fingers?' Shamus just inclined his head.

'Yes…' said Janus 'but what about the others…ohh the fruit was bananas - in a hand.'

'The chocolate biscuits were chocolate fingers.' Added Dryasdust.

'The 13 cards were also "a hand" yes, I see.' Added Marley

Then the realisations came thick and fast

'Dead Man's Hand – what Jesse James was reputed to be holding when he was shot playing poker – a Full House I think it is called.' Said Angel

'Kit-kats!' said Eddy

'Ginger roots!' added Marley

'Okra, are also called Ladies' Fingers!' said Eddy enthusiastically

'The Rolling Stones' Sticky Fingers LP!' said Marley

'Fish Fingers! And Fingers of Fudge, I imagine.' shouted The Boffin

Then our Northern Irish member, Podge called out in triumph "Stuff Luttle Fungers!!!"

And Shamus sat there feeling quite pleased with himself.

'But the lyrics, I do not know the songs of the Christians.

Is it a religious group?' asked Mary

Shamus smiled and said 'They are a pair of brothers with the surname Christian, and the third member, curiously, is called Priestman – but they are not a religious focussed group – they sing very nice songs – sort of pop/rock – very sweet tunes and good lyrics.'

'Yes, yes: but what were the lyrics?'

'Oh they were from the song "When the Fingers Point". It goes on "Too much to take, too much to take."

'Very apt and very poignant.' said Marley

'The brother-in-law clearly knew in his heart what had happened so he ran that campaign of intimidation to get a confession out of the husband, culminating in the Dead Man's Fingers fungus appearing under the tree. We presumed that he had forged the bank transfer purporting to be by his wife, and subsequent investigations proved that the new account was his. We also presumed that the note had been written by her as part of a letter she never finished – perhaps to her brother, or children. Possibly discovered by the husband as he stormed in to kill her and shall we say adapted for his use. So cold blooded.'

But Fruity, also a bit of an amateur botanist and gardener, said 'But that fungus doesn't grow under a tree such as maidenhair gingko – it grows under northern deciduous trees!'

'I know!'

When the Finger Points!

menu

Roasted Garlic Soup

Baked Courgettes

Canestry - with

Italian Lemon Curd Dip

Italian Parmesan Biscuits

Italian Chutney

Roasted Garlic Soup

Cooking time:	40 minutes
Prep time:	20 minutes
Serves:	12
Method:	easy

Ingredients

- 500 gr peeled garlic
- 150 ml olive oil
- 100gr butter
- 2 tbs fresh thyme chopped
- 2 litres of chicken or vegetable stock
- 4 medium onions sliced
- 400 ml double cream
- salt
- black pepper
- 4 star anise
- 2 large potatoes cubed
- 12 slices of baguettes

Method

Preheat oven to 180°C (gas mark 4)

- place the sliced baguette onto a baking tray and drizzle with olive oil
- cook for 15 minutes or until golden

Using a large saucepan

- add olive oil and butter

Baked Courgettes

Prep time: 30 minutes
Cooking time: 40 minutes
Serves: 12
Method: easy

Ingredients

- 12 large courgettes cut in half
- 2 large onions chopped
- 6 garlic cloves crushed
- 100 ml olive oil
- 1 kilo lean mince lamb
- salt & black pepper
- 1 tsp chilli flakes
- 1 large tin of chopped tomatoes
- 1 tbs tomato puree
- 4 fresh mozzarella balls

Method

Preheat the oven to 180*C (Gas mark 4)

- cut the courgettes in half
- scoop out the inside
- chop the flesh and add to the minced lamb

Using a large frying pan

- add olive oil
- garlic, onion, chilli flakes
- cook for 5 minutes
- add the mince lamb and chopped courgette flesh

- cook for a further 10 minutes breaking down the meat into mince
- add the tomato puree & chopped tomato
- cook for 30 minutes uncovered
- slice the mozzarella into 24 pieces
- place the mince into the courgettes
- add the mozzarella
- bake for 20 minutes

Lemon Canestry lemon curd dip - Classic Italian Shortbread

Prep time:	25 minutes
Cooking time:	15 minutes
Serves:	12
Method:	easy

Ingredients

Biscuits

- 8 egg yolks, hard boiled
- 400 gr plain flour
- 200 gr cornflour
- 400 gr unsalted butter cut into cube
- 200 gr icing sugar
- zest of 2 lemons
- 1 tbs vanilla essence

Method

Preheat the oven 180*C (Gas mark 4)

Using a large bowl

- add flour, cornflour, sugar, lemon zest
- add cold butter
- grate the egg yolk
- mix until it forms a dough
- roll the dough to about 1 cm thick

Using a pastry cutter

- cut as many shortbread as you can rolling the pastry again with the left overs
- place in a baking tray
- cook for 15 minutes
- leave to cool

Chef's tip: Canestry should remain quite pale so avoid browning.

Italian Lemon Curd

Prep time:	30 minutes
Cooking time:	30 minutes
Serves:	12
Method:	easy

Ingredients

- 8 Italian lemons and zest
- 300 gr caster sugar
- 200 gr unsalted butter
- 6 large eggs beaten
- 1 tsp cornflour

Method

Using a medium bowl

- add the beaten egg
- add sugar & cornflour

In a large sauce pan

- add the lemon juice & zest
- bring to the boil
- reduce to low heat
- add the egg mixture
- mix well to avoid lumps
- cook slowly until it thickened
- remove from heat
- pour into a cold bowl
- keep mixing occasionally for 10 minutes to avoid over heating
- can be served hot or cold with the Canestry

Parmesan Cheese Biscuits

Prep time:	10 minutes
Cooking time:	15 minutes
Serves:	12
Method:	easy

Ingredients

- 500 gr plain flour
- 250 gr butter
- 150 gr grated parmesan cheese

- 1 tsp chilli flakes
- 1 tsp smoked paprika
- salt

Method

Preheat oven to 180*c (gas mark 4)

Using a large bowl

- add the flour, salt, chilli flakes
- mix well
- add the butter
- mix until it forms a dough
- roll out and cut into 1 cm thick
- bake for 10 minutes
- leave to cool

Italian Chutney

Prep time:	20 minutes
Cooking time:	1 hour
Serves:	12
Method:	easy

Ingredients

- 1 kilo cooking apples peeled & diced
- 1 kilo pears peeled and diced
- 150 gr dried cranberries
- 150 gr sultanas
- 100 gr dried cherries

- 200 gr sugar
- 100 ml apple cider
- 100 ml white wine
- 100 ml water
- 1 tsp mustard powder

Method

Using a large sauce pan

- place all the liquids in the pan
- bring to the boil
- add the dry fruits
- add the apples & pears
- mix well
- simmer for about an hour
- stir occasionally
- leave to cool

Chef's tip: Chutney will keep well and for a long time in a sealed container – once opened keep in the fridge.

Epiphany

No Kings

There were no kings at the virgin birth,
when angels sang across the earth.
What king would leave their crowns and lands,
to follow stars across the sands?
The shepherds came so brave, so bold,
and left their flocks there in the fold.
They may have brought their dogs along,
but this is not told in the song.

The travellers came from the east,
To Bethlehem but not to feast.
Not from the north, nor south nor west,
They set out on their fateful quest,
To see the birth of all that's best.
But did they go with zeal and zest,
Or were they frightened, scared, distressed?

They brought great gifts to offer there,
To that young child in stable bare.
With ass and oxen standing by,
And Angels singing from on high,
They dropped in homage on the ground,
and so the glory shone around.
But still we wonder who were they?
A mystery still unto this day.

Were three Kings kneeling on the hay,
As we recall on Christmas Day,

Or were they Savants, Wisemen all,
Who journeyed long to that small stall,
To see a babe, led by a star,
Travelling, travelling out so far?
The gifts they brought, if gifts they were,
Of gold and frankincense and myrrh.
Strange things to bring a babe new born,
On that especial Beth'lem morn.

So will we ever get to know,
From whence they came so long ago?
The tale is told each Christmas time,
And sung in songs, proclaimed in rhyme.
That on that ancient starry night,
A babe was born that brought the light.
With shepherds, ox and ass inside,
A lonely byre at Christmas tide.

With Advent calendars, each door,
Will tell the story less or more.
Becloaked and dust-grimed, starlight led,
They journeyed long to that poor shed.
They bent their knee, the babe to see,
And then before the light of day -
They turned around and rode away.

A Cold Dish

It fell to me, Angel, to act as MC that evening, as we occasionally took it in turns to introduce the evening, and then the speaker: although the Professor, naturally, remained the host. I had spoken to our speaker for this evening to understand what might be involved, so that I was prepared for anything – but it had all seemed very straight forward, although I was not aware, obviously of the detailed content of the tale. The Professor read out the poem composed especially for this meal – called 'No Kings'.Several of the Club had been to Canada and they were reminiscing about their times there. Not a few had been skiing in the west around Banff, Whistler and Lake Louise.

It was the 6th of January – Epiphany - when the three Wisemen, or Kings if you prefer, are believed to have arrived at the stable, in Bethlehem, to worship the Baby Jesus. They were, traditionally, guided by the star which led them west – from the east - unto Bethlehem and then it hovered over the stable. I like to think of them on Bactrian camels, rather than Dromedaries as that makes it more exotic.

A fabulous tale of course, and one of the cornerstones of Christian belief and of the Christmas celebrations. It is also the day when people of Spanish extraction receive their

Christmas presents – unlike everywhere else of course in the Protestant and the Roman Catholic churches – where they get them on Christmas Day. This of course makes a lot of sense, in one way, as it was the Wisemen who brought presents and thus started the whole idea of gift giving. In the other countries the gifts are given on Christmas Day (25th December) to celebrate the birth, rather than the arrival of the Wisemen. Both are, of course, reasonable, perspectives. It is tough on the Hispanic Christians if they are with those that get presents on the earlier day, of course.

Traditionally we see three Wisemen – but curiously their numbers are never mentioned. It is a presumption from the gifts that they are said to have brought gold, Frankincense and Myrrh symbolising in some accounts, virtue, prayer, and suffering respectively. It is only the Gospel of Matthew that even mentions them. As there are three gifts mentioned the number of Wisemen has been extrapolated out. But, of course, it could have been two or indeed many more, we have no record. Neither are their names recorded, nor what they look like – even though hymns and writings talk of Caspar, Melchior and Balthazar.

The Wisemen are also called Magi – which refers to the priests of Zoroaster – another monotheistic religion that was extant at the time of the birth of Jesus, and comes from the Persian word for priest. We get our words magic and magician from it. The Magi spent a lot of time looking at and analysing the stars and trying to foretell things from them. This is Astrology which at the time was almost considered as a science. The religion still exists in Iran and India, where they are known as Parsees – a corruption of Persian, and also close to Farsi – the Persian language. Freddie Mercury, from the rock group Queen, was born into a Parsee family (as Farrokh Bulsara) in Stone Town, Zanzibar, now part of Tanzania after the 'bloodless revolution' where it was forcibly acquired by Tanganyika. I have visited Zanzibar and it was very pretty and very historic.

This Christian complexity is further compounded by those adherents to the Orthodox churches (mainly Slavic peoples such as Russians, Serbs and Ukrainians – but also the Greek churches) who still use the older, Julian, calendar which does not celebrate Christmas until many days later as they did not accept the Gregorian reforms (attributed to the then pope – Gregory) to re-align the calendar with actuality and adjust for the misalignment. This was also adopted by Protestant churches as well who had been seeking this reform for some time based on rational scientific analysis. The Orthodox Christmas Day usually takes place 13 days after the 'Western' Christmas Day: on January the 7th, a day after the 12 days of Christmas are over!

Indeed, my next-door neighbours are Orthodox Ukrainians, and we often hear them singing their beautiful

Christmas songs on that date – the day after we have taken down our decorations and, with sorrow, removed the Christmas tree. Of course, they now have far more sorrow than the taking down of a Christmas tree after Putin's illegal invasion of their country.

Interestingly in some Eastern (Syriac Church) accounts there are 12 Wisemen, and there is also an old Armenian legend that states that the three were none other than the sons of Noah - Japeth, Ham and Shem - come to pay homage for all humanity: as in the bible they are the precursors of all races after the flood. So many legends and tales!

"Now enough history – let us eat."

Unusually that evening, we had had a buffet style meal, rather than a formal seated dinner, consisting of what we might call 'Tex-Mex' food. Beer - Cerveza, and, if you wished Tequila and Mescal – made from Agave, which is a cactus plant apparently. We had a Tex-Mex meatball soup to start - a traditional Mexican dish with rice, tacos, avocado guacamole, sweetcorn fritters, soured cream, and black beans, so the conversation had been quite animated as we circled around sampling the various dishes. Some of us had been to Mexico and others to Texas so the conversation about food, and poor hotels was interesting. There were items such as Churros and Jerricala – and of course various flavours of ice-cream, which although not a Mexican invention, was very popular in the hot Central

American countries, unsurprisingly, for pudding. One had had an authentic chilli kick, I had noticed, and helped myself to a glass of water and a mouthful of beer, whilst wiping my eyes. The main pudding was Corn cake which was new to me.

All had then seated themselves in their customary places, with a drink, and waited. Although there was no allocation of seats there had been a tendency for some to prefer a location over others, interestingly enough: we are all creatures of habit I suppose.

I introduced the tale.

'Now that we are all fed and watered, we can commence with the real serving tonight. Our tale. This is the story of something that is a recurring theme across mankind and down the ages: virtually since mankind walked the earth. We have called this tale "A cold dish" - but of course this is no reflection on the tasty, spicy food which was hot - both figuratively and literally – which we have just had. It also tells how the Professor came to meet one of our esteemed company. As you have probably guessed from the food, there is a Spanish/Central/Southern American connection. And that most hot of emotions – revenge!

So let us move on - step forward, please, Podge: or rather stand up.'

At this Podge rose smiling and started to speak.

'As you all know – I teach Spanish and Portuguese,

under the rather broader banner of Iberian and Hispanic studies. Therefore, most of my students are usually not fluent Spanish or Portuguese speakers, nor usually nationals of those many countries using these languages. But not all. There are some who enrol for the course as they think that being native speakers they will fare better. This is probably so for the language part – but most of the Hispanic studies are, in fact, conducted in English obviously: as most are not natural 'Hispanic' speakers and we are generally studying it from the academic, non-native speaker, literary, point of view, so that balances it up a bit. And their literature understanding is often risible. An interesting aside – more people speak Portuguese globally than French – which the French are in denial about. Bouf!'

And he placed his thumb behind his front teeth, and moved it forward in a very Hispanic gesture which I have never understood – just for show of course – being totally British in antecedents!

'In this particular year I had a very eclectic mix of students, the majority, of course, were British and non-Hispanic European, but with some from Spain and Portugal; a couple from Brazil; an Angolan; and several from Mexico. Two of those from Spain were in fact Basque – which is an extremely interesting language – non-Indo European and full of fantastic consonants - Xs, Zs Ks and Qs etc - and sounds – and whom hated to speak Spanish - as imposed by Franco and the Fascists. Another spoke Catalan as her first language, rather than Castilian which we study. One of the Portuguese was Galician with that as his first language. So, this gave an interesting political and national mix to the group and also meant that few, if any, had a major linguistic edge over the rest. A very eclectic bunch indeed.

Now let me see. We were about half way through the second term, and we had just finished a lecture on Cervantes (not Don Quixote though) when there was a bit of a disturbance out in the street which, it being a hot day and as the windows had been opened, and as we were only slightly above ground level, we could hear very clearly.

I sauntered over to the window and looked out and, as we were slightly raised, I had a good view and, thus, I could clearly see a man lying on the ground with a small crowd standing around it. Just then a police car and an ambulance pulled up and two police and two para-medics got out.

They were too late, it seemed, as he was dead: or so I assumed from the fact they covered his face, and the police then collated everyone to take statements. They had looked up and, seeing me gazing out of the window, asked me, by signalling to me, to come out and give a statement. I acknowledged the request and, having asked the class to read on in the work, I went downstairs and talked to the police. Of course, I had seen nothing of any interest, and said so once I was with them in answer to their question.

I was preparing to leave, when one of the policemen said to the other ''Two of the witnesses appear to be Spanish or Hispanic perhaps and do not, or at least claim not to, speak English."

At this my ears pricked up and I explained that I taught Hispanic studies and I offered to translate for them. They, unsurprisingly, immediately took me up on this offer. The policeman, or detective I suppose, who by then had arrived and taken charge of what was now a death rather than an accident, asked me to explain to the pair that he would like to ask some preliminary questions, and that he would question the witnesses separately.

I started off with a few pleasantries and answers:

"Hola?"

"Que Tal?"

"Como estas?"

"Muy bien gracias"

"Si bien gracias"

"De donde es?"

"Soy Mexicano : somos Mexicanos de hecho."

"Que estas haciendo in inglaterra?"

I then told the police that they were Mexican – although they probably guessed from the reply.

Then I explained what the police wanted to do and, at the detective's request, asked one of them to step over a little way from the other, out of earshot, to commence the questioning. He asked me to translate several questions, which I presumed were of the standard witness diagnostic type: Where are you from? What are you doing here? What did you see? Etc, etc. I had already asked some of these, so I answered for them and then asked the other questions of both of the witnesses, one after another, and the police recorded their answers, along with the odd further clarification question.

It appeared, from their answers, that they knew nothing of the dead man and were just 'passers by' as it were. The police then took down their details – passport number, where they lived at home in Mexico and where they were staying in the UK etc, and let them go.

There were several other people nearby – one of which, I noticed was a man in a wheel chair with what seemed to be a wooden leg stretched out in front of him – funny - he looked Hispanic too. Poor chap I thought. The police had questioned all of the witnesses, but it appeared that nobody had seen anything material. The man in the wheel chair also turned out to be Mexican – but as he spoke reasonable English, they hadn't needed me to translate. The policeman had mentioned that he had had a curious scar on his arm – it is the sort of distinguishing mark that they are trained to notice and record. It looked like a knife wound, but when asked about the man had said "De nada. It is nothing."

The detective then thanked me for my help and asked

me for another favour.

"We have searched this poor chap's clothing and found some documents. They are in Spanish. Can you tell me what they mean, please?"

"Certainly officer."

And I took them from him and read them.

They turned out to be surprisingly interesting as I read them, although in a sad way.

I explained to the police that the documents showed he too was Mexican and, rather coincidentally, from his name it appeared that he was the father of a female student on my course. This was a little strange, but not improbable, and I informed the police of this: and suggested that we go back into the college, get one of the Safeguarding female members of staff, confirm that this was indeed her father, and then tell her what had happened. This would not be a pleasant thing to do, so I was glad the police didn't need me, as I had told them her English was excellent.

I asked the police was there any indication of cause of death.

"No sir. Not a mark on the body – except for what looks like a sting on his hand, which had swollen up and must have happened just before death. Nothing else – although from his face it looks like he was in some pain or even agony."

"Perhaps it was a heart attack. Or even a reaction to

the sting? I have heard of that."

"Well, we won't speculate. The autopsy will no doubt show us what happened."

"Yes of course. Well, if I can be of any further assistance please do get in touch."

And I gave him a card with my details on it. They had already taken them down but I thought it would help.

As it happened our esteemed host, Professor Belvoir, was on the spot, just passing by and offered to conducted the inquest for the coroner. He had been interviewed as well but, as just a person in the crowd, had seen nothing, although he had heard a gasp of pain from, or appearing to come from, the dead man. That was how we met and we discussed the case and I told him all of the details of which I was aware, including the two Mexican quasi-witnesses and the wheelchair bound man. I thought it would assist him when he had conducted the autopsy and was looking for clues, answers and so on'

And he bowed a little to the Professor, who acknowledged it with a smile and a little wave of the hand.

'Having chatted about the case we then parted, I having agreed to join this little club, which the Professor was just in the process of establishing.

So - a few months later I met up with our host to discuss the club further.

We chatted in general terms about how it might function

and then, being a good host, he offered me a glass of wine and sat down with his in hand, staring into its depths – it was a rich ruby red – clearly deep in thought and then he lifted his head saying

"Did the police ever come back to you about that case? You remember - that chap who died? You know the Mexican?"

I replied that indeed I did remember – it is not very often that a Mexican drops dead outside one's school and that sort of incident tends to stick in one's mind.

"Yes Well. They never came back to me – even though the autopsy had shown an unknown substance in his bloodstream, which I was, sadly, unable to identify and which I could not say for certain had been a definite cause of death – although probable. But, however, by an extraordinary coincidence I was the pathologist on duty when, some months later, a body was brought in for an autopsy. It was the 3rd of January – getting on for the end pf the 12 days. As I started to undertake the autopsy, I immediately recognised it, from your description of the curious scar on his left arm, as the chap who had been in the wheelchair when the Mexican chap unfortunately died. He was still 'wearing' the wooden leg as well. It was clear that he had died of cancer and must have known about it as he had some sort of medication – the text was in Spanish, but I think that they were just pain-killers of some sort, as the description of the pill contents was in Latin and was the same as others I have seen."

"Ahh ok." I said. "One of those strange coincidences I suppose?"

"Well - yes and no." he replied somewhat enigmatically.

I leant forward my interest piqued and he carried on.

"I was intrigued about the leg for, on removing it, it felt wrong. That is: the balance was all wrong for a wooden leg. As a pathologist you come across all sorts of false appendages, naturally." And he made a wry face at his attempt at a joke.

"The weight was dispersed in the wrong places. I was fiddling with it, trying to get a feel for what the difference was, when suddenly I noticed that it was hinged in the middle so it would 'break open'. I called in a colleague, for it is always good to have another pair of eyes when dealing with anything out of the ordinary, and we explored it further.

What we found was more than interesting and so I called the police. Luckily, I had kept the details of the Inspector who was leading the investigation. He came over next day and I showed him what we had discovered. He immediately asked me to accompany him to the dead man's house, as he wished to explore it for evidence. We went there but there was no-one in. He then turned to me, disappointed, but not, I suspect, surprised, saying.

"I will apply for a search warrant; would you mind

coming back with me when I have obtained it?"

"Certainly officer. Please call me when you are ready."

The detective rang next day and we agreed to meet and explore the house. It was the 6th of January – twelfth night of course – but there was to be no gift giving on this particular day.

On entering we were astounded at what we found. The whole of the walls of one room were covered in plain paper but in turn covered in writing – sometimes just slogans, other times in patterns, and all different size letters – sometimes capitals, others mixed, but however it was written it contained the same three phrases in Spanish: 'Venganza!'; 'La Venganza es Mia!' and 'Tendre Mi Venganza!' and all in red ink.

I need not explain that these are all variations of 'vengeance!' and 'vengeance shall be mine!' in English.

Clearly obsessed and not a little insane I thought. In the same room we found a glass aquarium type tank with little frogs inside. I recognised them as the South American poison tree frog – which confirmed my suspicions as to how the chap died outside your classroom – poisoned – clearly that 'sting' on his hand was something more. In a drawer we found a set of darts, such as you see for use in air guns.

We also found correspondence from his son or at least we found out that this was who it was, after we had them translated. Now I can reveal what it was that caught my eye. When I examined the false leg I had, as I mentioned, noticed the hinge in the middle. On examining it further we found, by removing the rubber cap at the tip that there was a metal barrel inside the leg and, when we opened the leg by undoing the screws along its length, we found a complete air gun mechanism inside it. The hinge on the leg was to cock it. The barrel showed traces of the same substance I had found in the dead body. When I analysed it further it proved to be the poison from the tree frogs. The darts could be inserted and then it would fire a short distance only, as it had been adapted to fit inside the false leg, and the power of the spring had diminished accordingly. By being in the type of wheel chair he had it meant that the leg would stick put in front of him, slightly at an upward angle, and be steady. There would be hardly any sound and nobody would notice anything. Quite ingenious in a malevolent, evil way.

The police contacted the son and I was asked to interpret for them. It turned out that his father had had an old grudge against the dead man. They had been in the army together and he felt that he had been betrayed by him into an ambush – where other man ran away. This sense of betrayal had festered until it quite consumed him. He had tracked his foe across the world and over the years, and as soon as he had found out that he was in the UK to be with his daughter, he had moved here and rented his place. Then he had lurked outside the school until the right opportunity presented itself. He killed him with a poison dart fired from his false leg. Then the cancer had got him.'

Podge shook his head: as too did the Professor.

Not quite the tale we might have expected for Epiphany.

A Cold Dish

menu

Tex-Mex Meatball Soup

Sweet Corn Fritters

Avocado Guacamole

Black Beans and Rice

Corn Cake

Tex-Mex Meatball Soup

Prep time:	30 minutes
Cooking time:	60 minutes
Serves:	12
Method:	easy

Ingredients

Meat balls

- 800 gr lean mince beef
- 300 gr grated cheese
- bunch of coriander chopped
- 4 garlic cloves crushed
- 2 jalapenos chopped
- 2 eggs
- 1 tsp cumin seed
- salt & pepper

Soup base

- 2 tbs olive oil
- 2 onions chopped
- 1 red pepper chopped
- 6 garlic cloves crushed
- 1 tbs chilli powder
- 1 tin of sweetcorn
- 4 tomatoes into quarters
- 1 bay leaf
- juice of 1 lime
- 2 litres chicken stock

Method

Meat balls

In a medium bowl

- combine the meat, cheese, jalapenos, garlic, eggs, cumin,
- mix well season to taste
- form into 24 meat balls
- preheat oven to 180*c
- place in a baking tray
- cook for 15 minutes
- leave to rest

The soup

- add olive oil
- add onions, garlic, peppers
- cook for 5 minutes
- add garlic, chilli powder, cumin,
- cook for 5 minutes
- add sweetcorn, tomatoes, bay leaf
- bring to the boil
- add meat balls
- cook for 45 minutes
- season to taste
- add coriander

Sweetcorn Fritters

Prep time:	20 minutes
Cooking time:	10 minutes
Serves:	12

Method: easy

Ingredients

- 1 kg sweetcorn tinned or frozen
- 6 eggs
- 300 gr plain flour
- 1 tbs baking powder
- bunch of spring onions chopped
- 2 red chillies
- bunch coriander chopped
- vegetable oil

Method

In a medium bowl

- keeping a cup of sweetcorn aside
- combine sweetcorn, eggs, flour, baking powder, spring onion, coriander, chillies
- blitz the mixture in a food processor
- add the sweetcorn
- season to taste
- preheat a large frying pan with 4 tbs oil
- add a tablespoon of mixture to the pan
- repeat several times until pan is full
- cook for 2 minutes each side

Avocado Guacamole

Prep time: 5 minutes
Cooking time: N/A
Serves: 12

Method: easy

Ingredients

- 4 large avocados diced
- juice of 1 lime
- 1 tbs olive oil
- salt, pepper
- 1 tsp smoked paprika

Method

In a medium bowl

- add avocado, lime juice, chilli, smoked paprika olive oil
- mix well
- season to taste

Black Beans & Rice

Prep time: 10 minutes
Cooking time: 20 minutes
Serves: 12
Method: easy

Ingredients

- 100 ml coconut oil
- 1tbs chili powder
- 1tbs garlic powder
- 1 tbs ground cumin
- 1 tbs ground coriander
- 2 celery sticks chopped

- 3 tomatoes chopped
- 200 gr sweetcorn "tinned or frozen'
- 2 tbs fresh oregano
- 2 tbs fresh coriander
- 500 gr cooked black beans 'tinned'
- 800 gr white rice
- salt& pepper

Method

In a large sauce pan

- cook rice and strain ready

Using another large saucepan

- add coconut oil
- add chili powder, garlic, cumin, coriander
- cook for 1 minute slowly
- add celery, tomato, sweetcorn, oregano,
- stir well
- add black beans
- simmer for 15 minutes
- add rice
- stir well
- season to taste

Corn Cake

Prep time:	20 minutes
Cooking time:	50 minutes
Serves:	12
Method:	easy

Ingredients

- 500 gr sweetcorn 'tinned' or 'frozen'
- 400 gr sweetened condensed milk
- 100 gr butter melted
- 2 tbs vanilla extract
- 4 eggs
- 120 gr plain flour
- 2 tsp baking powder
- ½ tsp salt

Method

Preheat oven to 180*C (Gas Mark 4)

Using a large bowl

- combine sweetcorn, condensed milk, butter, vanilla
- mix well
- add eggs, flour, baking powder, salt
- mix well
- using two 4" x 9" (9cm x 21cm) loaf tins
- butter the inside of the tin
- then coat with flour lightly
- pour the mixture into both tins equally
- cook for an hour

Chef's tip: You can use a blender to achieve smoother dough

You can opt for baking parchment instead of the butter & flour combo.

Index of Recipes